An Eye for the Chance

The Chances
Book 7

Emily E K Murdoch

ARE YOU SIGNED UP FOR DRAGONBLADE'S BLOG?

You'll get the latest news and information on exclusive giveaways, exclusive excerpts, coming releases, sales, free books, cover reveals and more.

Check out our complete list of authors, too!

No spam, no junk. That's a promise!

Sign Up Here

www.dragonbladepublishing.com

Dearest Reader;

Thank you for your support of a small press. At Dragonblade Publishing, we strive to bring you the highest quality Historical Romance from some of the best authors in the business. Without your support, there is no 'us', so we sincerely hope you adore these stories and find some new favorite authors along the way.

Happy Reading!

CEO, Dragonblade Publishing

Additional Dragonblade books by
Author Emily E K Murdoch

The Chances Series
A Fighting Chance (Book 1)
A Second Chance (Book 2)
An Outside Chance (Book 3)
Half a Chance (Book 4)
A Chance in a Million (Book 5)
Not a Chance in Hell (Book 6)
An Eye for the Chance (Book 7)

Dukes in Danger Series
Don't Judge a Duke by His Cover (Book 1)
Strike While the Duke is Hot (Book 2)
The Duke is Mightier than the Sword (Book 3)
A Duke in Time Saves Nine (Book 4)
Every Duke Has His Price (Book 5)
Put Your Best Duke Forward (Book 6)
Where There's a Duke, There's a Way (Book 7)
Curiosity Killed the Duke (Book 8)
Play With Dukes, Get Burned (Book 9)
The Best Things in Life are Dukes (Book 10)
A Duke a Day Keeps the Doctor Away (Book 11)
All Good Dukes Come to an End (Book 12)

Twelve Days of Christmas
Twelve Drummers Drumming
Eleven Pipers Piping
Ten Lords a Leaping
Nine Ladies Dancing
Eight Maids a Milking
Seven Swans a Swimming
Six Geese a Laying

Five Gold Rings
Four Calling Birds
Three French Hens
Two Turtle Doves
A Partridge in a Pear Tree

The De Petras Saga
The Misplaced Husband (Book 1)
The Impoverished Dowry (Book 2)
The Contrary Debutante (Book 3)
The Determined Mistress (Book 4)
The Convenient Engagement (Book 5)

The Governess Bureau Series
A Governess of Great Talents (Book 1)
A Governess of Discretion (Book 2)
A Governess of Many Languages (Book 3)
A Governess of Prodigious Skill (Book 4)
A Governess of Unusual Experience (Book 5)
A Governess of Wise Years (Book 6)
A Governess of No Fear (Novella)

Never The Bride Series
Always the Bridesmaid (Book 1)
Always the Chaperone (Book 2)
Always the Courtesan (Book 3)
Always the Best Friend (Book 4)
Always the Wallflower (Book 5)
Always the Bluestocking (Book 6)
Always the Rival (Book 7)
Always the Matchmaker (Book 8)
Always the Widow (Book 9)
Always the Rebel (Book 10)
Always the Mistress (Book 11)
Always the Second Choice (Book 12)
Always the Mistletoe (Novella)
Always the Reverend (Novella)

The Lyon's Den Series
Always the Lyon Tamer

Pirates of Britannia Series
Always the High Seas

De Wolfe Pack: The Series
Whirlwind with a Wolfe

Noble titles throughout English history have, at times, been more fluid than one might think. Women have inherited, men have been gifted titles by family or gained them through marriage, and royals frequently lavished titles or withdrew them as reward and punishment.

The elder Chance brothers in this series agreed to split the four titles in their family line during the Regency era, rather than the eldest holding all four. It is a decision that defines their brotherhood, and their very different personalities.

Now with the next generation, one Chance father has allowed his son to inherit his title before his own demise, echoing kings and queens who have abdicated their titles throughout history. Perhaps his brothers, the uncles of this next generation, will follow suit...

Get ready to meet a family that is more than happy to scandalize Society...

Chapter One

May 1, 1840

LADY EVELYN CHANCE sighed, rolled her eyes, and pulled a third lace handkerchief from her sleeve as she and the other bridesmaids took their seats.

"If I had known you were going to cry so much at Cousin Lilianna's wedding, I would have brought a whole haberdashery," she muttered, passing the handkerchief to her parent.

George Chance, Earl of Lindow, graying around the edges but still with a sharp jaw and an even sharper mind, sniffed. "It's just—I remember holding your cousin the day after she was born! And here she is, getting married."

"Shhh!"

Evelyn grinned as her mother glared sternly at her father.

"Will you hush!" whispered Lady Lindow sternly. "You're disturbing people!"

"I am not *disturbing* people—I am genteelly dabbing at my eyes," retorted the earl.

Lady Lindow, portlier now than she'd been when she had married but still possessed of that breathtaking beauty that made men stare, snorted. "Pull yourself together, man. She's getting married, not murdered!"

"*Mama!*"

"Well, the odds of a bride being killed on her wedding day must be astronomical... Hold on, I have a piece of paper somewhere in my reticule..."

Evelyn caught her cousin Lilianna's eye and wished to goodness she had shepherded her parents to a less prominent pew.

Thankfully, the bride did not seem to mind. In all honesty, the bride did not seem to notice. The cursory glance she gave her congregation appeared to be mainly to ensure that she was not dreaming. She had that sort of expression on her face, Evelyn thought critically. Focused—but focused on something else.

"...for better, for worse, for richer, for poorer, in sickness and in health..."

It was a beautiful sight. Even Evelyn had to admit her aunt and uncle, her father's brother and his wife, had created a most picturesque setting for the wedding here inside the church. A veritable bower of peonies arched over the altar and the bridesmaids were attired in a most pleasing shade of pink.

No—no, it was not quite a true pink. Perhaps a cherry blossom pink?

Evelyn would have to consider this later, when she was before her paint box. In truth, she rather wished she could send everyone else away, bring her easel out, and attempt to capture the scene. Recalling the exact way the light and shadows fell, the curve of her cousin's cheek, the slightly embarrassed yet delighted face of the groom—

"—I now declare you man and wife," said the vicar magnanimously.

There was a delighted sigh from the congregation, packed with the friends and family of the Earl of Taernsby, as the happy couple became... Well, a happy couple.

Evelyn sighed with them, but primarily at the streak of sunlight that poured across Lilianna's chestnut hair.

She would never truly be able to recreate that on a canvas. Try as she might, there was something truly challenging about hair, especially when it curled like that. She had never quite managed it. In truth, she needed—

"Well, that was a beautiful ceremony," her father said, dabbing delicately at the corners of his eyes as the congregation rose to welcome the Earl and Countess of Taernsby. "Truly beautiful."

"One in fourteen million, four hundred and eleven," said her mother.

Evelyn turned with a slight frown to her mother. "I beg your pardon?"

Lady Lindow grinned, clearly delighted with herself. "The likelihood of little Lilianna dying today!"

Ah. Right. Well, Evelyn was sure she should have been proud of the fact that her mother had a truly remarkable mathematical mind... but it was a tad difficult to feel that when strangers were turning to glare.

It was a little distasteful, to speculate on the death of a bride. Even if it had been for the pure joy in the calculation.

Absolutely certain that she would not be able to explain the eccentricities of her mother, and just as certain that she would not be able to reduce her mother's eccentricities, Evelyn merely smiled. "Well calculated, Mama."

Lady Lindow beamed. "It was easy! Once I realized Lilianna was riding here and back in a carriage, the numbers completed themselves! Then I had to—"

"Very impressive, Mama," Evelyn interrupted. For good-ness's sake, wasn't it supposed to be her parents attempting to keep her in line? "Lucy, why don't you walk out with Mama and Papa and me?"

She gave a meaningful glare to her younger sister, who was dabbing at her own blue eyes. *Help me change the conversation.*

The glare did not do much good.

"I do not call Cousin Lilianna very clever, to wear so few jewels to her own wedding day," Lucy said with a sigh, taking her father's arm as the congregation started to spill into the aisle and follow the happy couple. "I suppose she wished us to focus on herself, not her jewelry."

"She looked lovely," said their father, his eyes misting over again.

"Ah, but additional jewels would have disfavored her odds!" came their mother's voice above the growing hubbub. "The risk of theft, you see! Tempting a criminal with shiny baubles is not very wise."

"Mama, how could you! You cannot assume that seeing jewels is likely to make a man a thief!"

Evelyn groaned. That was the plaintive voice of Lucy, and of course they had managed to find the one topic in the world that would make her absolutely intolerable.

All she needed now was—

"The sooner we return to Uncle John's, the sooner we can enjoy some of that delightful French champagne I've heard he has shipped in especially," said her brother in a clear tone. "Here, Mama, take my arm."

Evelyn glanced gratefully at her brother... only to find that much to her chagrin but not at all to her surprise, her brother—Percy, tall and handsome in a shamefully effortless way—was glancing about in the evident hope that his offer to take his mother's arm had attracted the notice of... say, a rich and beautiful debutante. For example.

Well, at least all the members of her family had played to form. Her father had wept, her mother had calculated, her sister had gotten on her high horse about prison reform, and Percy was attempting to fleece a young lady of a kiss. Evelyn supposed she should not have expected much else; they were Chances, and that meant they had been swiftly set in their ways from a young age.

Still. She had hoped they could all behave like respectable members of Society for the single hour that Cousin Lilianna's wedding required.

Though there was still the wedding reception...

At first, Evelyn had thought she had managed the impossible. Her father had stopped crying, for one, and had only accosted his brother, the father of the bride, with a hearty handshake and a long speech about how it was an honor to see one of his dear nieces married for—oh, about ten minutes.

So far, so good.

Her mother was trickier. After waylaying an elderly, wispy-haired gentleman who was drinking port quite happily, until Lady Lindow informed him dryly that at his age, every sip would decrease his longevity by a factor of several months, Evelyn had managed to steer her toward the card room. That was always a good bet with her mother. If she returned home with less than a tenfold increase on the pennies in her reticule, Evelyn would be very much mistaken.

That was her parents taken care of.

Grasping hold of a cool glass of champagne for a moment and wondering why on earth being the eldest daughter meant she had to take care of everyone all the time, Evelyn cast an eye around the packed wedding reception.

It was most elegant. Uncle John and Aunt Florence had thought of everything. The place was full of the very best and most respectable people—as well as her brother—and Cousin Lilianna appeared to be…

That was interesting. Cousin Lilianna appeared to be missing. But then, so did her husband, so Evelyn was not too worried about that.

Then there was only the matter of her siblings. Evelyn preened as she deposited her sister, Lucy, in a group of ladies interested in social justice, setting them off with a question about prison reform and then slowly backing away, and Percy—well. Percy was the most difficult one.

"I do not need to be dealt with!" her brother protested as Evelyn attempted to march him across the ballroom floor. "I'm not that bad!"

Not that bad. Evelyn swallowed down the retort that his latest betrayal had cut her to the quick and tried to smile. "You are all exhausting at times, and this time is now," she said sternly. "You wander off, Perce—you know you do—and you can't be trusted to be left alone."

He wrinkled his nose. "Hark at you, with your inappropriate

questions, always asking people to be your models!"

"And that is why I have asked Miss Quintrell if she will dance with you," said Evelyn firmly, drawing them to a halt before a simpering, buxom young lady who stared at her brother as though he were a Greek god.

Most unaccountable. Her brother did not have a Grecian profile, for one thing.

Also, he was her brother. Grotesque.

"Miss… Miss Quintrell?" her brother repeated vaguely, his eyes locked on the young lady's—

Evelyn looked away with pink tinged cheeks. Honestly! Were men only interested in one thing?!

Well. Two things.

"It would be my honor, Miss Quintrell, if you would grace me with this next dance," Percy was saying.

At least, he was saying something like that. Evelyn had ceased paying attention, her focus caught by quite another young lady.

Oh, she was fascinating. Not beautiful—not in the traditional sense, anyway, and Evelyn knew most of Society was interested only in symmetry and balance and large eyes and tiny waists.

But she was interested in something quite different: form.

Just looking at her made Evelyn's fingers itch to get out her charcoal. Why, the woman's dark brow and dark eyes were perfect for a charcoal drawing. All she would have to do was place the woman in some impressive light—overhead, yes—and the shadows would be exquisite.

Leaving her brother to charm Miss Whoeverthathadbeen— her exact name had already slipped Evelyn's mind—she wandered across the ballroom without paying much heed to where she was going.

Which was unfortunate.

"Oi!"

"Watch where you're going, woman!"

"Careful—ouch!"

Evelyn ignored them, whoever they were, and found herself

standing right before the woman whose features were so striking.

Now, she had to approach this carefully. Few people, it had turned out over the last year, appreciated being requested to sit as a model for her. It was most disappointing, for Evelyn considered it one of the highest compliments she could give.

So, what was the best way to go about it?

"Yes?" the woman said archly as Evelyn stood before her in mute silence.

Evelyn tried to smile, the words she was thinking spilling out before she could stop them. "I would greatly like to touch your forehead."

The woman blinked. "I… I beg your pardon?"

Blast. It was a word Evelyn was forbidden from saying out loud, her father having tired of it after Evelyn had heard her brother use it and decided it was a most excellent word, but he could not stop her from saying it inside her own head.

Blast, blast, blast—

"I said, I would greatly like to sketch your beautiful face," Evelyn attempted with a smile. "I-I am an artist and—"

"I do not permit strange women to sketch me. I have been painted by the great George Hayter," the woman said proudly. "I do not sit for amateurs."

Evelyn's stomach twisted painfully as her pride was prickled. "I am not an amateur!"

"You are a lady. You cannot be a true artiste," the woman said dismissively. "Go away."

"Go away"?

Evelyn knew the precise shade of pink her cheeks were turning. She had examined herself once in a looking glass; she had roped in her brother and sister to offend her in degrees so she could see the different hues her cheeks became.

This was a level three. Someone had deeply offended my character, nearing vermillion red.

Most unacceptable.

"But I—"

The woman walked away, leaving a small crowd of gawking wedding guests.

Ah. Evelyn tried to smile. Yes, she had not been particularly quiet in that conversation. *Blast.*

Well, in for a penny…

"And what about you, sir?" Evelyn asked brightly, as though the back of her eyes weren't stinging with the sudden awareness that more and more people were staring, and there was nothing she could do to stop them. "Would you ever consider sitting for me, as a model?"

The broad-shouldered gentleman's lip curled. "And who are you?"

Her throat was drying. "Lady Evelyn Chance. And you are?"

"Well-bred enough to know we cannot speak without an introduction." The man's lip curled even more. "I never would have thought a Chance would need telling that, even with the family's well-known… eccentricities."

Evelyn's throat was now a desert, her tongue attempting to tie itself in a knot. The gentleman stalked away, glancing over his shoulder as though he had been mortally offended. The two ladies who had been with him followed him toward the dining room.

Take a deep, calming breath, Evelyn told herself firmly. It was a slight faux pas. No one had noticed. No one would even think to mention it to her—

"I will have to speak to your father about this, young lady," came a stern, genteel voice that Evelyn knew well.

Trying to keep her face bright, Evelyn turned. "Lady Romeril."

Evelyn sank into a low curtsey—far lower than she would offer the Queen of England. Not that she was likely to ever meet Victoria.

"Hmm," said Lady Romeril.

When Evelyn rose, it was to look in the eyes of one of the most important women in Society. Not particularly wealthy, not particularly well-born, or so the rumors said, but a woman with prodigious power.

A stern look from Lady Romeril was sufficient to end one's chances at marriage. An approving look from Lady Romeril was to make a genteel person infinitely more acceptable to be included on invitation lists.

And when Lady Romeril made that particular noise at you... Well. Evelyn knew it could go either way.

"I was merely requesting—" Evelyn began meekly.

"I know precisely what you were doing," interrupted Lady Romeril with an imperious look. "You are starting to get a reputation for asking that particular question, girl. I am not so certain your father would want you getting a reputation of any kind."

He most certainly would not. Not merely because the Chances were among those of the utmost of importance to Society, but because he had expressly forbidden her from doing the one thing her heart most desired: exhibiting her work.

"No daughter of mine is going to debase herself to the judgment of others!"

Evelyn knew it was foolish but could not help herself. The dancing behind her, the joy of the day, the champagne in her veins... "Better that you remember me at all, Lady Romeril. There are so many young ladies in Society these days, I would like to be at least a little memorable."

The older woman, gray hair piled up on her head and a feathered fan fluttering before her, remained silent. Her lip twitched.

Pressing home the very little advantage Evelyn had somehow managed to find, she said, "And if you would ever consider gracing my studio, Lady Romeril, I would be honored to paint you."

"Don't be ridiculous, girl," Lady Romeril said sharply. "If I want to be painted, I will find myself a great name to commission and bestow that honor to him."

Him. Evelyn tried not to let her pique show on her face.

It was always a him. She had tried telling anyone in Society who would listen that a hand of any gender could hold a brush equally well, but no, it had to be a male artist who was respected. God forbid a woman show any scrap of talent.

"Besides," added Lady Romeril, somehow peering down her nose at Evelyn who was a full inch taller, "it is not very ladylike to ask people to sit for you. Model, I mean."

"I quite agree, Lady Romeril," said Evelyn quietly. "But it is very artist-like."

She had said the wrong thing. That was the trouble with Lady Romeril; you never could tell whether your bold words would be approved or loathed. The older woman swelled, her disgruntled expression becoming clearer with every passing second, and Evelyn braced herself for the very public lecture she was about to receive, likely at high volume.

"Well! I have *never*—"

"Ah, there you are, dear—thank you, Lady Romeril, for keeping an eye on her—come on, Evelyn," her father said in a rush as he suddenly appeared at Evelyn's side.

"Have to run, such a shame—hello Lady Romeril goodbye Lady Romeril," said her mother at Evelyn's other side.

Both of her parents had grabbed a hold of an elbow before Evelyn could stop them, pulling her away from Lady Romeril and the rest of the wedding guests who had clustered round them to witness the lecture.

"Honestly!"

That was her mother. Evelyn tried to keep her face entirely rigid, not revealing exactly how mortifying it was to be carefully moved through Uncle John and Aunt Florence's home like a duckling, but it was very difficult.

When her parents finally came to a stop in the cavernous hall, Evelyn wrenched herself free and glared.

"Honestly!" The Earl of Lindow was graying around the temples but that did not take away from the power of his presence. "Evelyn Chance, what have we said about asking people to model for you?"

This is most galling, Evelyn thought as she rubbed at where her father's hands had grasped her. Here she was, spending almost the entirety of Cousin Lilianna's wedding attempting to prevent her family from embarrassing themselves—her father with his handkerchiefs, her sister with her prison abolitionist nonsense, her brother's desperation around anything in the female form that moved, and her mother's inexplicable desire to calculate the likelihood of Cousin Lilianna's death…

And *she* was the one being castigated for being outrageous!

"All I asked," she began, "was—"

"We know what you asked. It's what you always ask," her mother said, cutting across her. "There is a one-hundred percent incidence rate for over two years."

Both Evelyn and her father stared.

Lady Lindow rolled her eyes. "Honestly, have I taught you two nothing? I mean, since January the first of 1838, there has not been a day gone by that Evelyn has not asked someone to be her model. Most of them not family, too."

Evelyn's lips parted in astonishment. "Truly? Every single day?"

It certainly felt that way, but she presumed that her mother was being silly. Perhaps not.

"You must not embarrass us any further," her father was saying. "Asking people right to their faces to model for you—really!"

A hot, sticky, prickling sensation was curling around Evelyn's spine, making her want to curl in on herself and never move again.

She was the embarrassment? *She* was? Her father had made two of her handkerchiefs so soggy, she had abandoned them in the church—and she was the one bringing shame upon the family?

"But—But I am an artist," she said desperately. "It is vital that I continue to challenge myself, continue to try to draw different people."

"You can practice on your brother and sister," the earl said firmly.

"I have drawn them before," Evelyn said before she could stop herself. "I'll never improve if I don't diversify the subjects of my art."

"And what need you to improve?" shot back her father. "It is not as though you will ever exhibit. I have been most clear on that."

She should have stopped herself. She could see the flicker of a pulse in her father's temple, a sure sign he was approaching his limit, but it was just so unfair.

Percy and Lucy—they had hardly wanted to be painted at all, and when they had been a few years younger and none of them had been out in Society, it had been all Evelyn could do to convince them to stay still long enough for her to attempt a painting.

Now she and Lucy were out, as Chances did not believe in waiting for the elder sister to marry before the younger could join her, and Percy was at his club half the time, and besides, she had already drawn them. She needed a new challenge, a new opportunity to test her skills. To ensure she continued to learn, and grow, and develop.

To become a better artist.

Evelyn blinked. Somehow, she had left her parents alone in the conversation for five minutes, and now they were bickering.

"I don't see why I should stop!"

"Because the odds are that—"

"Oh, you and your odds!" Her father threw up his hands.

Evelyn stifled a smile. She could not be sure, not having been born at the time, but her Aunt Alice had once told her that her parents' courting had been a rather argumentative affair. That, she could certainly believe.

"You are most infuriating, you know that?" shot back Lady Lindow, striding up to her husband and halting about an inch from his nose.

"And you," her husband said triumphantly, "are delicious."

"Oh, no," Evelyn said, far too late.

They were doing it again. *Kissing. And in public!*

"Honestly," she said weakly. When this had little to no effect, other than her father's hands now wrapped around her mother's waist and slipping lower, Evelyn averted her eyes and said loudly, "We are at Cousin Lilianna's wedding reception!"

Her parents broke apart. Her mother had a satisfied grin on her face, her lips a dark pink, and her father looked dazed, as though he'd been hit around the head.

Evelyn rolled her eyes. "Remind me again how *I* am the embarrassment of the family?"

"What?" her father asked, swaying slightly.

"Oh, forget it," Evelyn mumbled as she turned away and returned to the wedding reception.

It was reaching that stage of the festivities when those who had drunk far too much champagne were showing it, and those who had not drunk enough champagne were starting to make up for it. Evelyn managed to dodge a confused, elderly gentleman who believed that she was his daughter and avoided the squawks of indignation coming from her sister and her new friends in a corner. Finding herself a nice corner to stand in, Evelyn looked out at the merriment and sighed.

It was most unfair. Here was everyone enjoying themselves, and she felt… distant from them. Set apart, somehow.

Not better than them. Evelyn had seen enough of the world in her three and twenty years to know she had plenty of her own faults—but wishing to paint and draw new people wasn't a fault. She was sure.

"You must not embarrass us any further. Asking people right to their faces to model for you—really!"

And a small smile, nervous at first but growing more confident with every passing second, crept across Evelyn's face.

Well, that is an easy enough order to follow, she thought with a tingling anticipation in her stomach. Asking people to their faces was no longer permitted?

She'd simply stop asking people to their faces.

Chapter Two

May 4, 1840

RICHARD SEMPILL, VISCOUNT and general rake, sighed. "I'm bored."

"My father once said that only boring people get bored," said a far-too-smug voice from the other side of the room. "What does that say about you, eh?"

Richard attempted to throw a cushion at his friend. The trouble was, he did not bother to lift his head from where it was lolling on the back of his armchair, and he barely moved his arm at all.

The soft *flumpf* sound made it clear that the brocade cushion that had been a favorite of his mother's had merely dropped to the carpet, rather than make its way across the study to whack his friend in the face.

"Pathetic."

"I wasn't really trying," muttered Richard in a weak defense of his action.

Walden snorted. "That's what I meant."

Sighing again, Richard forced himself to sit up and glared over at his friend. "What precisely are you visiting me for, other than to insult me?"

"Oh, primarily that," said Walden cheerfully as he turned a page of his book. "You sounded so dour in your last letter, I thought I should hightail it to London as soon as possible and see if I could get you out of this slump you've found yourself in. As it turns out, it is one entirely of your own making, and my sympathy ended almost immediately."

Despite himself, Richard found himself smiling.

Walden really was impossible—but then, that was how they had become friends in the first place. University was a lonely place for an only child who had never been sent away to school and so had never quite learned the easy habit that so many of the nobility had: that of making friends easily.

No, Richard had once been a quiet, studious, awkward young man, and it had been people like Walden who had truly made a point of drawing out the young viscount from his shell.

The trouble was, Richard was now saddled with a cheerful friend for the rest of his life. It was a sort of punishment.

The sound of Walden turning a page of his book seemed to echo around the small room.

"Could you *be* any louder?" snapped Richard.

"Oh, I'm sorry. Does the sound of me bettering myself offend you?" quipped Walden.

Richard's lips twitched. "A tad."

"Well, I will try to do all I can to prevent my superiority from being audible," said his friend with a grin as he mimed turning a page without actually turning one. "The thing is, I arrived here with three intriguing suggestions about what we could do today, and you were the one to turn them all down. So I've taken it upon myself not to waste the day, which has brought me to—"

"You don't even know what you're reading," Richard pointed out amiably.

Walden gave him a look of mock horror, his oval face particularly suited to the dropped jaw and the dark, arched brows. "Not so! I am fully aware that I have been reading this most fascinating work called... erm..."

Richard snorted as his friend not very surreptitiously glanced at the front cover of the leatherbound book.

"...*A Treatise on Practical and Chemical Agriculture, Compiled,*

Principally, From the Scientific Works of Sir H. Davy," said Walden firmly, as though he had memorized it upon entering Richard's study. "And a most fascinating book it is, too."

Snorting again, Richard allowed his head to fall against the back of his chair and sighed. "Oh, hell, man, when did life become so dull?"

"I return you to my original statement," said his friend lightly. "When did *you* become so dull?"

"Perhaps I always have been," shot back Richard, always willing to tease a friend as much as he was being teased. "Perhaps you are the one at fault for befriending me in the first place."

"Now that," said Walden dryly, "I can well believe."

Heaving a sigh, Richard tried to think back to the numerous suggestions his friend had arrived with when he had turned up, most unexpectedly, at Sempill House an hour ago. Now, what had they been?

Oh, yes. The first had been that they go to Hyde Park and walk around staring at the ladies. Not a terrible idea, Richard had to admit, but one without any guaranteed excitement. What if there were no interesting ladies there? What if they saw a beautiful minx—what then? What was the point in speaking to one, particularly under the watchful eye of an insipid chaperone, when he was a mere viscount and Walden had no title at all?

No, that was out. The second idea had been to head on over to the docks, see what ships had come in—but honestly, it was a long walk there and the weather today was most inclement. Richard had been certain it was to rain and had been disappointed and delighted in equal measure when he had been proven right.

So that had been out. Walden's third idea had been to go to White's. Not very inspired at all.

Richard sighed.

"Oh, will you give it a rest?" Walden said, his voice losing that lightness of touch. "Find a pack of cards. Take me to a pianoforte and I'll play for you. Have a nap. Eat an early luncheon. Write a letter to—"

"You are full of good ideas, aren't you?" said Richard archly.

His friend peered over the pages of his book. "At least I'm not sighing away like a princess locked in a tower."

Richard had to laugh. The image was so ridiculous. "I am not sighing like a—"

"Yes, you are, and it's mightily amusing for me only for a limited time," quipped his companion. "You're a viscount, man! You are honestly telling me that the thrills of London are barred to you—or that you have experienced them all to such an extent that you have tired of them? London? One of the greatest cities in the world?"

It was daft, when his friend put it that way. But still, Richard could not pretend he had found much amusement in the place in the last few months since he had returned to England and her capital city.

"Don't you have… I don't know, ledgers to look at? Notes from stewards to review? A housekeeper to dictate menus to? A butler to complain about the state of your cellar to? Petitions from tenants?"

Perhaps another man would have missed the slight envy in Walden's words, but Richard caught it.

"You make me sound very grand and very important," he muttered, glancing over at his friend and seeing his forehead was a mite pink. "Mrs. Anstruther knows her own mind about menus and I wouldn't dare suggest anything about wines to Verwood. I tell you truthfully, being a viscount is not all that exciting."

"You tell me that, a man with neither title nor fortune?" asked Walden jovially.

Only Richard, and perhaps a few other friends, would have caught the tension underneath.

"I'm not saying that—look, my father died when I was six, you know that," Richard pointed out. "I'm not like most of the nobility gadding about this place, newly come into a title and all the excitement that it promises. I've known the responsibilities, the burden, the mind-numbing bureaucracy of being a viscount for years. It's not fun anymore. It's not interesting. It's not exciting."

And it never would be again, Richard knew that. Not after… Not since he had…

"Besides, it's not even much of a title," he said firmly, pushing aside the thoughts that had started to most inconveniently creep into his head. He was never going to think of that place again. "Viscount? I ask you—there's no power in it, no pleasure, no opportunity, yet you're bound by the same inane restrictions that Society places on you!"

"Yes, yes, it all sounds most terrible," murmured Walden, turning another page.

This time, Richard put more effort into throwing the cushion. It hit his friend right in the face. "You know what I mean."

"I know you are bored out of your skull," Walden said conversationally, finally putting the book down and fixing his friend with a serious stare. "I would have thought you would prefer a bit of boredom, after what you've presumably gone through."

Richard's whole body tensed. It took a great effort, to slowly release the stiffness in his arms, his chest, his legs. Finally, there was only his jaw remaining, but try as he might, he could not release the strain there.

"I mean, you were a spy for your country," his friend said, lowering his voice as though the French might have infiltrated Sempill House. "You served your queen. You did things I can only dream of!"

There was a hint of longing in his friend's tone now, a hint Richard did not like.

The man has no idea, he thought viciously. *No idea at all what he's glorifying! The danger, the pain, the heartache, the peril—*

And that is a good thing, Richard reminded himself, managing to pull himself out of the spiral downward with a great effort. *You don't want your friends to suffer what you have suffered. You don't want anyone to endure what you did.*

That is why you did it. To save others.

"—and now you find yourself bored with Society. Well, I suppose most things will be tedious after spending a few years in France," Walden pointed out, as though he had remarked on the very strange coincidence that whenever the sun went down, the place grew a little dark.

Richard shifted uncomfortably in his armchair. "Hmm."

Walden's breath hitched, as if realizing all that he'd said. "I… I suppose you have recovered from the… the difficulties of your time there."

And for a moment, Richard was back there: back in France, in the darkness, bullets flying through the air in all directions, and he had no idea where to turn, where safety could be found. Just as Richard felt as though he were drowning on dry land, there was fire, flames licking up the walls beside him and around him, and there was nowhere out, nowhere to run, nowhere to escape—

"Richard?"

Richard jerked and rose, panting, hands outstretched as though he were once again finding his way from the burning building. His lungs were heaving, tasting smoke through the ragged breaths, and suddenly, someone was holding his hands.

"You haven't recovered, then," said Walden quietly, squeezing Richard's hands and bringing him back to the present. "Not completely, anyway."

Richard blinked. The smoke was gone, the panic slowly draining from his lungs, and he stared into his friend's blue eyes.

He was safe. He was in England. It was over.

Snatching his hands from his friend's and wishing to goodness he did not have to dash tears from his eyes, Richard threw himself back into his armchair. "I have no idea what you're talking about."

His gruff voice was pathetic in its lie, but thankfully, Walden did not say a word. He merely resumed his own seat and looked curiously at his host, as though attempting to study him for an examination later.

Richard swallowed and tried to forget. That was what he had

to do: forget. That was what the government official had told him, when he had finally managed to make his way back to Dover.

"Just forget, man. There's nothing for you back there but painful memories and darkness. Just forget."

Forget. Like he didn't wake up almost every night from dreams so painful and confusing that he thought for a moment he was there still. Fighting for his life…

"You can talk to me about it. If you want."

Richard's head snapped up. "There's nothing to talk about."

"I'm just saying, if you needed to—"

"I *said*, there is nothing to talk about," said Richard firmly, in his best impersonation of the immutable lord Walden seemed to think a viscount ought to have been.

It was largely in the tone of voice, one he had perfected over the years. He had been forced to. Few people listened to a boy of fifteen when it came to obeying their lord and master, but he had been viscount by that age for several years. He had studied the ledgers, he'd known the law. And that had been half a lifetime ago.

"It's not good for you."

Richard's head jerked up. "What do you mean?"

"Wallowing like this. Not talking about it." Walden's face was pinched, his lips a thin line, his expression far more serious than Richard had ever seen on him. "I had a cousin—"

"Don't talk to me about cousins," Richard said darkly. "It's never a true story. People always tell a story about a cousin and instead, it's just something they've made up or overheard at White's."

"My point is, you could be doing yourself a real injury, a true disservice, if you don't let out whatever you've got bottled up in there," persevered his friend with a frown. "Why don't you tell me what happened out there? Why you came back? Why you never talk about it?"

And precisely how would that help? Richard wanted to ask bitterly. Talking about it would only double the trouble. *Then it would not be merely I facing the nightmares, imagery seared into my mind that no amount of drink or sleep or entertainment can burn out, but yourself as well.*

And I won't have you sacrifice your sanity for mine.

Richard swallowed, desperately casting about for another topic of conversation. "Tell me... how is... how is your sister?"

When he met Walden's eyes, he could clearly see that his friend had not been fooled.

And rightly so. Walden was no fool.

But he wouldn't subject his friend to hearing about his time in France. Richard would never do that, not to anyone. If he revealed all, what was the point in him having gone in the first place to prevent others from having to face such terrible things, such terrible places?

No, I am shielding Walden, Richard told himself. And that was a good thing. Perhaps the only good thing still left in his power.

"You know, you could do with some reading yourself, if you ask me," Walden said lightly.

Far too lightly. Richard examined him and saw the slight bob of his throat, the man's pinched expression an echo of the concern that had also been on his mother's face when he had finally returned after two years.

"You look changed, my son."

"Spying will do that to you, Mother."

"No, this is more. Something more. What did you see over there? What happened?"

She had passed shortly thereafter. Richard shook his head, as though that would remove the bad memories from his mind. "Reading? I've read everything."

Walden snorted. "Now that, I do not believe."

"I haven't purchased any new books for the Sempill estate for... Oh, I don't know, a decade?" Richard shrugged. "Save for that one, which my butler insisted on. Everything I own, I have read."

"You must get newspapers, though," his friend said, pointedly looking at a stack of newspapers over on the desk by the window.

Richard rolled his eyes. "Oh, as though there is anything interesting or new in there."

"They are called *news*papers."

"Just because they want to sell a fresh edition every day," Richard said dismissively. "You open up one of those things and all you see is the same, old things day in, day out. The government is corrupt, the queen is with child, France is a terror, the Germanic states are revolting, and there is someone complaining about the state of the roads."

He had ticked them off on his fingers and scowled to see his friend grinning.

"Perhaps you should start your own newspaper," said Walden. "As you seem to know so much about them."

Richard had to laugh at that, and this was a good-natured chuckle. "Even if I had the coin to do such a stupid thing, which I don't, I think there are more than enough papers out there hawking the same, old rubbish."

"Oh, just humor me for once in your life," his companion shot back. "Come on, at least try to read one for five minutes. You might actually find something interesting."

Richard very much doubted it, but as finding a pack of playing cards would mean moving from his seat and playing billiards would mean removing from the room entirely—neither of which Richard wished to do—he supposed there was nothing for it.

The first newspaper wasn't really a newspaper. More a scandal sheet.

Richard sniffed. "As though I care particularly what Lady Romeril said at some toff's wedding."

"Speaking as someone who is not a toff, to someone who is very much a toff... isn't that the whole point of your little Society? Gossiping about others?" Walden teased.

Frowning, Richard threw aside the scandal sheet and picked up a newspaper proper. It did not take him long to find something utterly ridiculous.

"Who cares if Miss Ashbrooke is considering matchmaking again, or if prison reform is needed," he muttered darkly. "I never really entered Society. I became viscount, grew up, went to university, then—"

"Headed off to France most mysteriously, yes," Walden said with a grin. "Did you even meet Lady Romeril? One cannot be said to be in Society if one has not met her."

"To my great relief, I have never met Lady Romeril," Richard snapped. "I haven't met anyone in Society, much to my relief, preventing nonsensical invitations that I would only have to decline, avoiding their banal mutterings about this or that debutante or this or that bachelor."

"You know, for someone who has served his country, you are particularly down on most of the inhabitants of said country," came his friend's helpful reply from behind the book.

Richard sighed.

Perhaps his friend was right. Perhaps he was just dull, himself, as a person. There was a constant in all the activities in which he'd attempted to find relief, and it was himself. Perhaps *he* was the bore, not the things themselves.

It was not a very pleasant thought.

He picked up a fresh newspaper and skipped the first twenty pages or so. Well, they were all full of politics and governmental arguments and economic disasters. The topics would be the same in every newspaper.

No, it was from page twenty-five or so that things became interesting. That was when the personalities of the editors really came to the fore. What they selected to include, or not include, was usually very different.

Richard's attention slowly meandered down the column. A lost dog, a governess seeking employment, several angry letters to the editor pointing out that the world was infinitely worse off now than it had been twenty years ago, and what did the government think it was going to do about it…

And then something odd caught his eye.

Richard blinked. Perhaps he had read that incorrectly. He read it again, more slowly this time, allowing his focus to rest momentarily on every word.

Artist of significant talent but no renown seeks model for practice. No experience necessary. Skills required: sitting down and not moving for hours at a time. Recompense offered. No fools, please.

Richard's eyes narrowed.

Now that was different. He had never seen anything quite like it. Bold, direct, unusually honest—*no fools, eh?*

Significant talent but no renown. Probably some third or fourth son who had been given the choice of the clergy or the easel—and had made his choice.

Skills required: sitting down and not moving for hours at a time.

Almost despite himself, Richard glanced up at the longcase clock just to his right. By his reckoning, he had been sat here almost completely immobile, other than his momentary relapse into French memories, for three hours.

Recompense offered.

He didn't need the money. Oh, he wouldn't say *no* to a fortune dropping into his lap, but he was hardly penniless.

And it was different.

"You're smiling."

Richard immediately wiped the grin from his face. "No, I'm not."

"You're not now, but you were," pointed out Walden. He had evidently been watching him from around the leather corners of the book. "What are you smiling about?"

"Nothing," came the instinctive reply.

Precisely why he did not tell his friend what he had read, Richard did not know. It would surely turn out to be some young idiot who was a dullard himself, and Richard would kick himself for not staying out of it.

Besides, who would want to paint him? He would not go so far as to call himself unsightly, but the few times he'd ventured outdoors, he could hardly say he had turned a lady's head.

No fools, please.

There was something so intriguing about the little advertisement that Richard knew, before he had pulled pen and paper across his desk, precisely what he was going to do.

Answer it.

Why not be a model for an afternoon? It was something different, something new and fresh. His housekeeper, Mrs. Anstruther, was desperate to get him out of the house so she could finish the spring cleaning. It would be something that could blot out the memories that crept around the edges of his mind, threatening to turn any sunny spring day into a cold night in hell.

"Pass me that pen and paper, would you, Walden?" asked Richard, far more calmly than he felt.

Walden grinned. "Finally decided to do something?"

Do something? Certainly, Richard thought with a sigh. *But it won't turn out to be of much interest, I'm sure.*

Chapter Three

May 7, 1840

EVELYN HAD PLASTERED the smile on her face for so long, her cheeks were starting to hurt... and still, she had not managed to find a way to interrupt this imbecile.

"—so you see, that is why some of the greatest painters don't actually decide to use pencil when they are starting to mark out their ideas," the blotchy-faced gentleman said with a simper. "Now, if you were to ask me..."

If he were to ask her, Evelyn could not help but think as she found herself nodding, almost hypnotized, she would have to point out that she had not asked him.

How Mr. Halifax had managed to speak for a full forty minutes without her interrupting, or even speaking, therefore, was quite fantastic.

Not fantastic in a positive way, though.

"—I always find, and I am more than happy to share my expertise with you, a budding new artist. After all, it's only fair that you are given support," declared Mr. Halifax in a patronizing manner that made Evelyn's skin crawl. "I've often thought—and I will give you this little piece of advice, Lady Evelyn, as you are trying to be a painter—"

"I *am* a painter."

"As I said, as you are trying to be a painter," said Mr. Halifax, speaking not so much over her as through her. From the corner of the room, Laurent, her and Lucy's lady's maid from France, cleared her throat to cover a snort. She seemed particularly occupied by the sewing in her hand. Too occupied. Mr. Halifax hardly noticed. "So nice for the ladies like yourself to have a hobby. As I was saying…"

Evelyn slumped back in her chair and wondered idly if Mr. Halifax's throat would eventually give in. That, or she would fall asleep.

Well, it had been a complete disaster. Which was a shame, for the advertisement she had written up had been perfect.

Artist of significant talent but no renown seeks model for practice. No experience necessary. Skills required: sitting down and not moving for hours at a time. Recompense offered. No fools, please.

It had taken her a great deal of time to concoct the precise wording, and Evelyn had been proud of the result. Detailed enough to hopefully entice someone who would not mind her practicing noses—noses really were most awkward—and vague enough that hopefully no one would realize that it was Lady Evelyn Chance, daughter of the Earl of Lindow, who was hoping for volunteers.

Well, not volunteers, precisely. She had put aside as much of her pin money as she could manage. She wasn't going to allow a man to just sit around for nothing. But it had not been a very auspicious morning.

First, there had been Mr. Cooper.

"What, sit around? While *you* paint me?" He had sniffed curiously as the eyes in his wan, pear-shaped face had darted around the drawing room.

Evelyn had attempted to smile. It had taken a great deal of effort to persuade both her parents and both siblings to go out this afternoon. She had wished for the house to herself so that she could interview the applicants who had sent notes through to the newspaper, the editor passing them on to her for a handshake, which had included a half crown. Laurent had been particularly useful in such endeavors and adept at keeping secrets. If all else failed and Evelyn were discovered or the gentlemen who came by talked about their visits to the rest of Society—at least she could plead that she had not been alone.

Despite all the wagging tongues, nothing truly improper would come from her efforts to expand her skills an artist. She'd make sure of that.

For all the interest Mr. Cooper had been showing, though, perhaps *nothing whatsoever* would come from her efforts.

"And can I hold some of your fancy stuff?" Mr. Cooper had asked hopefully. "Some of that china—or the gold stuff?"

When Mr. Cooper had been shown the door, politely, five minutes later, Evelyn had to, all in conscience, have a very awkward conversation with the butler about keeping a watch on the house for the next few nights. Fortunately, the man had a fondness for her, and she could rely on him not to tell the earl and countess about the parade of applicants and the reasons for such vigilance going forward.

Fortunately, she was only *somewhat* certain Mr. Cooper was suffering from kleptomania.

Mr. Sharpe of the lobe-less ears had not been much better.

"I had thought you might be a famous artist," he had said with barely concealed disappointment across his furrowed brow. "Having to use anonymity, you see, because you were so famous."

Evelyn's smile had become tense as she had tried to disregard Laurent's little snort. "Well, as you can see, I am not."

Mr. Sharpe had sniffed. "Disappointing."

"I made no promises," she had pointed out, temper rising.

"Yes, but—"

"Next!"

Mr. Moncrieff had been a Miss Moncrieff. Evelyn had grown excited at that point—perhaps she was an artist herself and understood the challenges of finding a suitable model—until she had opened her pouty-lipped mouth.

"I thought you might be a famous artist," she had said, her

voice dripping in displeasure. "I thought I could take off all my clothes for you and—"

"Next," Evelyn had wearily. There had been no missing the way Laurent had cackled at that one.

By the time Mr. Halifax had arrived, she had started to give up hope. Perhaps the advertisement had not been the cleverest idea in the world. Perhaps her parents were right. Perhaps she would never find someone to sit for her, and her hopes of being a respected artist were for naught.

Which was galling in the extreme. Why, it wasn't as though she could do much else. Daughters of earls had to sit around and drink tea, or find some sort of cause, like Lucy had. The idea that they may wish to improve themselves, do something *themselves*, had apparently never occurred to anyone more noble than a baronet.

"—and that is why you should never wash your paintbrushes in—"

"I am so sorry, Mr. Halifax, our time is at an end," Evelyn said firmly, rising to her feet.

It was perhaps a tad rude, but desperate times called for desperate measures… and Lucy had just entered the drawing room.

Her sister's eyes widened. "What on earth is going on?"

"*Goodbye*, Mr. Halifax," Evelyn said decidedly, actually grabbing the man by his arm now and dragging him toward the door. "Cawthorne will see you out."

"But I haven't finished telling you how to—"

"I am certain I can work it out for myself, thank you." *Honestly!*

There should be a term, Evelyn thought furiously as she practically slammed the door behind Mr. Halifax and left him in the hallway, *for the way a gentleman attempts to tell a lady something as though he were an expert—when it is the lady herself who knows well the topic of conversation!*

"Good afternoon, Lady Lucy." Laurent stood, folding the dress she had spent the last few hours mending—when not making her feelings on the parade of applicants known—over her arm. A lock of raven-black hair escaped her cap, but the lady's maid did not move to fix it. Instead, she sent a wry smile, accenting the dimples in her olive complexion, toward Evelyn before excusing herself, shutting the door behind her far more gently than Evelyn had.

Yes, there would likely be no more potential models to interview today.

"Who was that?" Lucy asked curiously, settling down on the settee and goggling at the now closed door.

"Laurent. Your and my lady's maid both. I would have thought you'd recognize her by now."

"Don't be daft!" Lucy rolled her eyes. "I have never seen such a man here before! You're not allowing him to *court* you?"

"No, I am not being courted by Mr. Halifax, thank goodness," Evelyn said heavily, dropping into the armchair opposite her sister. "Although I am sure he will make someone very happy," she added, feeling slightly guilty.

Well. Perhaps the man could not help being a complete and utter ass. Perhaps there was a lady in search of the sound of a dull, monotonous ceaseless voice to lull her to sleep.

"Oh, no."

Evelyn looked up. "What is it?"

Her sister was shaking her head sadly. "You wanted him to *model* for you, didn't you?"

It was not in Evelyn's nature to lie. It was also not in her nature to always tell the complete truth. It was just easier that way, with a father who cared desperately, perhaps *too much*, for his daughters, and a mother who was quick to calculate the likelihood of your own failure.

Percy had taught her that. His lie, while not large, had been persistent, and when the truth had emerged and the family had discovered he had been not precisely courting their neighbor's daughter, but bedding her with absolutely no intention of marrying her…

Of course there could have been a scandal. But it was the lie that had rankled so deeply within Evelyn's conscience. That someone she trusted, her own brother, could lie to her face—their relationship had never recovered.

Lucy was different. Lucy was her sister, and with just over three years between them, they were close.

But her sister did not always understand.

Evelyn sighed. "It was just… I thought, if I could find someone…"

"You've got to stop asking complete strangers to sit for you," Lucy scolded, as though she were the eldest sibling. "Honestly, it's not proper!"

"Laurent was present for every interview."

"That's not the whole of what I mean, and you know that."

"*Proper* hasn't gotten me very far since my only two sitters decided they were bored of sitting and wouldn't even contemplate standing," retorted Evelyn, a hot prickle of irritation curling in her stomach. "Even Laurent will not hear of sitting for me herself. Too much to do, and she does not like the broadness of her forehead, as she's told me time and again. If you would just consider—"

"Absolutely not," Lucy said firmly. "I have far more important things to be getting on with than standing about for you."

Evelyn sighed. Lucy did, too—*more's the pity*. To her parents' chagrin and her own delight, Lucy had grown up to be a radical.

As though the Chance family did not have enough of those.

"I had not expected so many… well, unpleasant, creepy characters," Evelyn admitted, shifting uncomfortably in her armchair. "I thought finding someone to just sit quietly and doze, even, would be easy enough."

"The world doesn't exist to be your inspiration, Evelyn," her sister said quietly.

More's the pity. Ever since Evelyn could remember, there was beauty and elegance in the world and her fingers had itched to capture it. Somehow, imitating the world and its nature on a canvas was like bottling a moment—precious, and suddenly accessible whenever one wished it. Who would not want to step into a happy memory?

The trouble was, landscapes were all very good. However, if she wanted to be a truly expert artist, then she would have to master the portrait. And that was difficult.

Not that she wanted to admit to as much to her sister, anyway.

"It is scandalous, the way you accost perfect strangers to sit for you as a model," Lucy said firmly. "Mama said so, and I—"

"Quite agree," finished Evelyn with a sigh. It was not as though they hadn't had this conversation before.

"And Papa—"

"I know what our father thinks," said Evelyn, her jaw tight.

He had made himself quite clear. No daughter of his was going to exhibit their paintings in public, so there was no point in worrying herself about improving.

It was galling to the extreme.

"You don't have to sigh like that, Evelyn."

Evelyn sighed again. "But I have painted everyone else I know who will sit for me, and I want a challenge."

Her sister snorted. "A challenge? You try finding yourself at the wrong end of the arm of the law for no good reason other than the fact that you bear a passing resemblance to someone spotted at the end of an alley in the dark, *that's* a challenge."

Evelyn allowed her sister to keep talking for a few moments. It was a good cause, she had to admit, and she had no wish to throw cold water over her sister's passion. Even if Lucy did occasionally throw cold water over hers.

Only when the clock on the mantelpiece chimed the hour, indicating that her sister had been twittering on for at least ten minutes, did Evelyn say, "Yes, and that's all very well, Lu, but it doesn't help me, does it?"

Her sister's eyes flashed dangerously. "Oh, and is everything in this world to be set up to help you, a daughter of an earl?"

Evelyn bit her lip. "You know I didn't mean it like that."

Lucy's expression immediately softened. It was now a gorgeous medley of irritated and sympathetic, one Evelyn would have attempted to capture if she had a sketchbook to hand. "I know that. It's just... Well, can't you make up people in your head? Isn't it enough to have the means to draw and paint?"

It wasn't the worst idea in the world. The trouble was, Evelyn had already tried that, without much success.

Perhaps it was a sign that I am not a true artist, she thought morosely. Surely, the greats could create an image in their mind's eye, then transfer that to the canvas before them.

She couldn't.

Evelyn swallowed down the retort that she simply wasn't good enough. She wasn't good enough *yet*. She was still young. She had plenty of time to learn and grow her craft, did she not?

Even if she did not have a teacher.

And the sense that she was alone, the only one of her family an artist rather than a mathematician or a campaigner, the only one who felt the lure of painting, the only one who understood how frustrating it was to see the world and not be able to replicate its beauty with her hands, washed over Evelyn like a tidal wave.

It was so... so isolating. No one truly understood.

"I want a challenge," Evelyn said aloud, jutting out her chin. "I don't see why I can't have one."

"'A challenge'?"

Both Chance sisters rose from their seats, Evelyn turning on her heels to see what man had dared enter their drawing room without an introduction.

And her lips parted in astonishment.

He... He was the most beautiful man she had ever seen.

Not perfect. There was no perfection, no true perfection, in beauty. There had to be a small flaw, some asymmetry, some dissonance between proportions or something of the like to make something truly beautiful.

And he was. Tall, but not overly so. A lean build, leaner than most, with a dark gaze from brown eyes that challenged and rebelled even as she looked at him. There was a sharp angle to his jaw that suggested he was not one to be easily won over, and a scar flickered over one eyebrow that told a story she was desperate to hear.

The beauty, Evelyn swiftly realized, was not in the body itself, but the way the soul held it. A wary, animalistic readiness to run. A strength, and a confidence in that strength.

He was intoxicating.

"And you are?" asked Lucy, her voice quavering as it often did when she spoke to someone she did not know.

The man raised an eyebrow. "And you are? I came to meet with the artist. The butler directed me here. Where is he?"

Evelyn swallowed, her mouth dry.

Oh, goodness. She had not expected anything like this. Anyone like this. He was in complete contradiction to the other ninnies who had come before.

Still, her sister was right. It was a little scandalous to be drawing strangers, and this man was so potent in his desirability that she would not have been surprised if there were swift rumors spread about the whole of town about the two of them.

Him, and her, alone in a room, for hours on end…

Oh, yes, please…

Of course, that could not be. She was a lady. Her maid, at least, would have to be present.

Though the galling fact that a man in her position would not need a chaperone did not escape her.

"The artist?" Lucy repeated.

Evelyn's head jerked up as her attention focused. It would probably be a very bad idea to even consider this man for the role of model. Laurent was not the type to keep *that* close an eye on her—she'd step out on occasion, citing work to do or perhaps even winking at her as she took note of the way Evelyn would be gaping at this model. No, Evelyn shouldn't be left alone with him, not for a moment. She wasn't sure she could trust herself not to reach out and feel the change of his skin over that scar. Interviewing him on her own to decide whether he was a suitable candidate for sitting for her was absolutely out of the question.

Which was why she had to do it.

"Lucy, I believe our mother wants you," Evelyn said hastily, grabbing her sister's arm and tugging her toward the door—not unlike the way she had swiftly rid herself of Mr. Halifax.

"Evelyn! Ouch, that hurts!"

"Go and see our mother," said Evelyn through gritted teeth, body hot as she passed the man.

Lucy's eyes were wide. "But Mama is out visiting Lady Dalton. Should I not at least send for Laurent? I don't think you should—"

"Don't send anyone. I'll talk to you later," Evelyn hissed as she pushed her sister out into the corridor and slammed the door behind her.

Then she whirled around, leaned against the door, and stared.

He was magnificent. Had he any idea? Perhaps he had already modeled for another artist but was looking for additional work. That would explain it.

Oh, he was splendid. The curve of his fingers, long and strong, would make for an excellent study. Even his nose—so distinct, so full of character—was perfect.

"I came to see the artist," he repeated in a quiet voice, one that resonated with boredom.

Boredom?

"I *am* the artist," Evelyn said.

Her voice had not resonated with boredom. It had quavered, shaking as she'd stepped forward to examine him more closely.

She shouldn't have. She had to.

The man took a step back. "*You?*"

That drew Evelyn up short. Bristling ever so slightly, she glared. "And why not?"

His eyes darted around, as if the man was just realizing he

was alone with a lady. He did not, however, comment on her lack of chaperone. "I just—I thought—"

"I said nothing about who I was in the advertisement," Evelyn said, restraining herself from jabbing the man with a finger. Well, it had been a long day. "Do you think ladies cannot paint?"

"Not in the slightest," said the man levelly. "I just did not think a woman would be so bold as to advertise. I thought a gentleman's son might have been. I had not considered a gentleman's daughter."

Now it was Evelyn who was being examined. She flushed as the man's eyes raked over her, unapologetic in his curiosity.

Well, really! There's no need for that.

"Please, sit," she said, hastily gathering her thoughts for the questions she had to put to him.

She wasn't exactly sure why. She had questioned the other men in an attempt to discern whether they would be suitable, and the queries had been well chosen, swiftly revealing they would not be.

But one look at this man was sufficient to tell her he would be perfect.

All she had to do was convince him of that.

The man inclined his head and seated himself on the sofa. Evelyn mirrored him, then realized she had never formed a question aloud in her life.

Words, Evelyn, words! I know they are not your strong suit, but please—say something! Anything!

"You... You know how to sit, then," she said in a slightly strangled voice.

The man's lips twitched. "For many decades."

"I mean," Evelyn said, her confidence growing now, "you have sat before, for an artist?"

He frowned. "No."

No? It seemed incomprehensible. That a man like this should have been walking about the world for so long without anyone capturing that expression, those taut lines across his forehead that showed he was displeased…

Evelyn swallowed. It would be most pleasant to do so. It would be most pleasant for her heart to calm down and not thunder so loudly that she was certain Mr…. Mr….

Had she even asked his name?

"As far as I can tell, one needs to sit down and not move," Mr. Mysterious said in a lazy tone. "It's something I am accustomed to. In fact, I gather that sitting for you will be so akin to my normal day, I may not be able to tell the difference."

Evelyn could not help but raise an eyebrow.

She would have guessed a gentleman, based on that description. No working man she had ever encountered had ever found leisure time to be as mind-numbing as this man obviously did.

But that did not make sense. She had an eye for the details, something her mother had always applauded, and the details of this particular man did not make sense.

A man with leisure—that would suggest a gentleman. His clothing, too, was of good quality; not fashionable, but then, men's fashions were so tiring sometimes, Evelyn could not blame him if, like her brother, Percy, he had decided not to update his wardrobe every six months.

But his hands… his hands were scarred. Calloused, as though he had done a great deal of manual labor. There was a rangy strength in him that suggested he had, for a time, been short in the dinner department.

And the boldness…

Well, boldness could come from all strata of Society, Evelyn was almost certain. But a gentleman would surely not stare at a lady like—like that.

Evelyn attempted to force down the rising heat, but it was no good. Being alone in a room with a man like this was like being alone in a room with a tiger.

You were almost convinced he would not attack you. You were going to give him no reason to do so. And yet…

"So, will I do?"

Evelyn swallowed. *Would he do?* She could find infinite contours of his body to sketch and practice and would never tire of finding something new. He was a miracle. She had never thought such a man would answer her advertisement—most definitely not after the fools who had traipsed through here earlier.

The man cleared his throat with a raised eyebrow. Evelyn's cheeks burned.

"Yes… Yes, I think you will do," she said slowly.

Well, there was no point in giving him too much confidence. He had more than enough of that already.

The man smirked. "Excellent. And you are?"

Blast. She had completely forgotten to introduce herself. Ah, well, that was what happened when one was faced with inexplicable handsomeness like his.

"My name is Lady Evelyn Chance," she said coolly. "Eldest daughter of the Earl of Lindow. And what is your given name?"

Ah, she had surprised him there. The man's eyes widened, and instead of barely veiled contempt at the world, there was now just a hint of curiosity. "Richard. Richard—"

"No, I don't wish to know any other details about you," Evelyn said firmly.

She had begun this relationship—working relationship—most improperly, ushering her sister out of the room like that. What more harm could the impropriety of addressing the man without his proper title do?

In fact, it only helped matters. She was certain of it. She was not about to lose her innocence to a man she never fully knew.

Richard stared, evidently befuddled. "You don't?"

"Absolutely not," said Evelyn, fingers itching to find a sketchbook this very moment to attempt a replica of that eyebrow and that scowl. "I wish to keep you as a blank canvas—a blank slate, if you will. The less I know about you, the better."

And it will also, she thought ruefully, *keep me from getting too intimate with you. Your full name, your life story, where you live, just what you look like with those breeches off—*

No. Best I don't venture down that particular path.

"Does this mean I have the job?" asked Richard with a wicked grin.

Flutters of heat soared through Evelyn as she hesitated.

Scandalous.

That was what her sister had said. Scandalous, the idea of having a stranger model for her. Evelyn knew their parents would agree—Percy's opinion would firmly not matter to her—and as for the rest of Society…

Well, perhaps Laurent could be persuaded to *claim* she had sat with them for all of the modeling sessions.

It was not as if she intended for the man to be nude. She knew other artists—all men—had access to nude models, but she was not going to be so improper as that.

It hardly seemed fair, really, for ladies to have different expectations of them, but… No, she could not be so improper as that.

Even if no one would know…

The man still wasn't objecting to her lack of chaperone. She did not know what to make of it. He knew she was neither someone of the working class nor married, based on her introduction alone.

He, like Evelyn, would have to know how scandalous simply being alone together in this moment ought to have been.

But he raised no objections.

Evelyn's attention flickered over the man once more. He was a truly excellent specimen. She could not have hoped for better.

"I can pay you six shillings an hour," she said quietly.

It had been difficult, indeed, to consider what to pay the man. What did other artists pay their models? Evelyn, accompanied by Laurent one afternoon, had endeavored to find out and had been accused by one man in his studio of attempting to entice away his models.

The thought of stealing another's model had not occurred to her, though in hindsight, perhaps it should have.

"Six shillings?" Richard repeated.

Evelyn could not tell from his tone or demeanor whether he was flattered or offended. "Too much? Too little?"

His gaze flickered to her hands then back to her eyes. For some reason, it made her unreasonably hot. "Six shillings will do."

There was a quirking smile across his lips that Evelyn did not understand—and would not think about for the rest of the day, she told herself firmly. *Absolutely not. That would be ridiculous. Foolish in the extreme.*

Likely to occur, but foolish.

"Well, you have the job," Evelyn said in as businesslike a manner as she could manage. "Can you start tomorrow?"

There was a flicker of mirth in the man's eyes before he nodded curtly. "What time do you want me?"

Chapter Four

May 8, 1840

T HIS WAS RIDICULOUS. Why on earth was he *nervous?*

Because what he was about to do was ridiculous?

Perhaps. But as Richard walked up the steps to the house he had visited only yesterday, his heart was thumping most unaccountably fast.

It was just sitting in a different chair than normal, he reminded himself. Besides, sitting in front of a beautiful woman had to be better than sitting at home, waiting around for nothing to happen.

Perhaps it was the letters that were doing it. He had not expected to hear from one of the other men with whom he had liaised in France—he had left that life behind, or so he had thought.

Instead, it was lingering, letters full of desperate requests for assistance, of veiled threats if he did not comply, warnings that Richard would be a dead man if he did not once again serve his country.

But he had to put it aside. Today, he was not a spy for Her Majesty's Government. He was a model.

God help him.

He knocked. The door opened, a footman's hand on the handle. The butler appeared and raised an eyebrow.

"Good morning," said Richard brightly.

"I'm sure it is," said the thin-faced man sternly. "Here for Lady Evelyn?"

"I am," said Richard, his chest swelling at being able to say such a thing.

Well, it wasn't as though he were calling on her as an equal—she did not even know he was a viscount. He wasn't courting her, nor was he respected by her in that sort of way... but he was here for her. Bizarre, how even that was something intriguing.

But his whole experience with her yesterday had been intriguing. He'd entered the room and she had not been alone, but then she had practically forced the other young lady—a sister, he'd gathered—out the door.

Then the two of them had sat together. Spoken. As equals. No fretting mama or clucking, old chaperone in sight.

She had an artist's soul, perhaps. One that contravened convention.

He didn't find that disagreeable in the least.

"Side door," grunted the senior servant, and the footman moved to close the front door in Richard's face.

Richard stuck a boot in the door. It hurt. "I'll have you know, I am—"

"Sitting for Lady Evelyn, yes, I know," said the butler with a glower. "Side door."

Richard's mouth fell open. He had never been treated in such a way as long as he could remember! How dare the man...

But of course, if Lady Evelyn did not know that he was not just Richard, but Viscount Sempill, then neither would her servants.

He almost laughed. Well, he had wondered what it would be like to grow up without the tiring burden of being a viscount. Perhaps today he could find out.

"My apologies," he said, bowing to the butler and stepping back. The man seemed to have expected more of a fight, as he blinked quite rapidly. "This way, is it?"

The butler nodded before gesturing at the footman, who shut

the door, this time slamming it.

The side door, then. An experience in and of itself.

Gingerly stepping around the building and discovering, much to his surprise, that the elegance and splendor of the front of the house swiftly melted away as one stepped to the side of the building, where only the servants and the workmen would ever go, Richard found himself standing by a side door. Judging by the delicious smells wafting under it, it was the door to the kitchen.

Well, this couldn't have been right... could it?

"There you are!"

Turning on his heels and suddenly remarkably conscious about where he was putting his hands—had they always just... hung about here, by his sides?—Richard tried to smile.

Instead, his jaw opened.

It was definitely her. Lady Evelyn Chance. The woman who had gone about that song and dance with him, interviewing him as though it were an important job and telling him that she didn't want to know anything about him.

"I wish to keep you as a blank canvas—a blank slate, if you will. The less I know about you, the better."

But she was different. Yesterday, she had been wearing one of those stylish gowns many of the young ladies this spring were wearing, all corsetry and a neckline up to her... well, neck. There had been an imperious look in her green eye, but a softness around her upturned mouth.

Now her attire had changed—and for the better. Richard tried not to stare at the ruffled shirt that dipped low toward her décolletage. Perhaps past it.

Her dark-chestnut hair was different too. Richard swallowed. Not *different*—down. Instead of being pinned up carefully as all women wore it, Lady Evelyn had it down, unrestrained and untamed, gentle waves curling around her shoulders as it fell past her breasts.

Richard swallowed again and discovered much to his surprise that the action made no difference to his rapidly beating heart.

Lady Evelyn was also wearing an apron. In the front pocket were two large paintbrushes. She had her hands on her hips.

"I expected you ten minutes ago," she said firmly. "I am afraid I can only afford to pay you for the time you actually spend sitting for me."

Richard opened his mouth, realized he had no clue what to say to a magnificent woman such as this, and closed it again.

A hesitation. A moment of uncertainty—and one he evidently shared with his hostess.

Lady Evelyn stepped forward across the terrace, a frown puckering her brows. "You... You have not had a change of heart, have you?"

"Change of heart"?

No, not a change of heart. A change of stiffening manhood, perhaps.

Forcing aside the thought of just how attractive the woman was, and how disgraceful it was that he was seeing her in what was essentially a state of undress—*don't think about it, don't think about it*—Richard compelled himself to smile.

"No, not a change of heart," he said brightly. "I was a little turned around by the directions of your butler, that is all."

"'Turned around'?" Lady Evelyn repeated. Then she glanced at the door he was standing beside. "Oh, you mean the kitchen. No, I don't paint in there."

"I thought not," said Richard, trying to keep his voice level.

Did she have any idea how beautiful she was? Perhaps not. Now he examined her more closely, he could see hints of charcoal on her fingers, and on her forehead where she had obviously had an itch while drawing.

He suppressed a smile.

"No, I paint in my studio in the garden," Lady Evelyn said blithely, turning her back on him and presenting him with a delicious view of waist and buttocks that Richard would have to spend a great deal of time not thinking about before bed. "Come on."

There was little else he could do but follow, like a lost lamb.

In truth, it was pleasant to do so—and it meant that she did not see his astonished look as they stepped into 'her studio.' It was…

Well. Some great lords had follies in their gardens, Richard knew, and others had false ruins. A few, mostly dukes, had *actual* ruins. Some followed the trend for temples. He'd run into an earl once who actually had a hermit living in his garden.

But this…

The studio was impressive in both its scale and its design. An octagon, each of its eight sides had a window, large panes of glass welcoming in as much light as possible. The walls were painted different pastel colors, four pairs of them on opposite sides. One rather felt as though one were stepping into a kaleidoscope.

There were easels everywhere. Canvas, notebooks, pots of paint all over the floor and pots of water alongside them, holding paintbrushes. Pencils were scattered underfoot and there were drawings and sketches and paintings pinned up all over the walls with no conception of order. There was a pile of what appeared to be furs or rugs or blankets or something all in one corner and there was paint splattered on all of them.

It was overpowering. It was overwhelming. It was…

Perfect.

"It's just a small space my father had built for me," said Lady Evelyn casually, evidently not realizing just how spectacular and unusual the place was. "There you go."

She was gesturing as she closed the door behind him, again no chaperone in sight, and Richard turned to see what she was pointing at.

Ah. All the splendor of the room, the wild mess, and he had not noticed perhaps the most important part. In the center…

A chair.

"This is where I will be sitting, I take it?" Richard asked, stepping across the space and being careful not to tip over any water pots or, God forbid, paint.

He was not as careful as he should have been.

Granted, he had been momentarily distracted by the way Lady Evelyn had sauntered past him without, it seemed, a care in the world, stepping so close to him that he inhaled the deep, rich scent of her body and a sharpness of what he later realized had to have been turpentine, but still. That did not excuse the way his boot tipped over a small pot of red paint that immediately knocked into two others—green and a light blue—all three of which then poured their delicate treasure across the floor.

"Hell's bells," Richard muttered, lunging forward in an attempt to rescue what little paint there was left.

He gained a sort of purple thumb for his trouble, and little else.

"Oh, I wouldn't worry about that," Lady Evelyn said breezily, settling herself behind a large canvas upon which she had pinned several pieces of paper. "I do that all the time."

And she must do, Richard realized, for now he came to look at the floor—usually the least interesting part of any room—he spotted the patches of color scattered across almost every few feet.

A pink patch there, a small yellow pool there. Near that window was a green line down the wall and more on the floor, as though someone had been balancing a pot on the windowsill then knocked it over.

"Still, your green—"

"Emerald."

Richard blinked. He had seen no jewels. "I beg your pardon?"

"Emerald," repeated the goddess. "It's a green I am working on. I think I've got the tone just right."

He stared. Then he looked down at his boot, which was rather more green than it had been when he had first entered. "Not a sage?"

Lady Evelyn did not look impressed. "I call it 'emerald,' and I say so advisedly."

It definitely looked more like a sage to him, but he was hardly in a position to argue. Not after he had now mixed it with the blue and dark red beside it with his clumsy feet.

The place was, in truth, a mess.

Richard liked it. When was the last time he had seen any place that had been truly lived in, had been enjoyed as it had been designed to be?

"I like this place," he said aloud.

"Good," Lady Evelyn said briskly, "for I intend for you to spend a great deal of time here. Well, go on. Take your clothes off."

Richard knocked over a very expensive-looking white paint. "I beg your pardon!"

He must have misheard her. There was no other explanation possible: young ladies, particularly daughters of earls, did not go around asking men to take their clothes off!

Unless he had been running with entirely the wrong sort of crowd for years... It was true—she *was* here in the room alone with him. That in and of itself was not what he had considered proper behavior for a lady of her class.

Not that he had *minded*, he admitted to himself. But *this*!

Lady Evelyn does not look nearly so flushed as she should, Richard thought as he stared, open mouthed. *Why, she looks positively calm!*

"I said, take your clothes off," she repeated patiently, pointing at the chair in the center of the studio with the end of a pencil. "Come on. I don't have all day. You might, but I don't."

Richard could only gape. "B-But—dash it all, Lady Evelyn, but... but you're a *lady*!"

"Yes, and I have had plenty of practice with the female form," Lady Evelyn replied, with what appeared behind the canvas to be an eye roll. "It is the male form I have had no practice with, as you can imagine. So. Take your clothes off."

"You never told me that would be part of the job!"

She swallowed slightly. "And you never questioned whether it was proper to be in a room alone with me. I imagined you to be more... open-minded."

His pulse was racing uncomfortably now, and Richard was wondering whether or not this had been a fine idea after all.

Sitting in a chair for hours on end—well, that had been easy enough. It would hardly be a departure from his typical afternoon, and the opportunity to walk home with a few extra shillings to buy a pie on the way home... What had there been to lose?

His dignity, as it turned out. And his privacy.

Richard glanced down at his chest—which was completely covered with a shirt, waistcoat, and jacket. The idea of taking them off, bearing his chest to this woman...

No.

No, he couldn't do it. He wouldn't do it. Not for all the shillings in the world.

Lady Evelyn sighed, completely misunderstanding his reticence. "Look, it's very simple. Male artists can paint anyone and everyone in the nude. I deserve my chance to do the same."

"Now, hang on," Richard said weakly.

"Well, perhaps not *everyone*. You cannot exactly walk up to the nearest specimen and demand they strip," mused Lady Evelyn, who evidently considered this a damned shame. "But my point is, why can't I paint any model in the nude? Is artistic genius to be the sole purview of men forever?"

Richard opened his mouth, found that once again, there was very little he could conceive of to say, and closed it.

The woman made an excellent point. It was just a shame that her point wended in the direction of him being forced to take all his clothes off.

"Besides, I have furs and blankets and things," Lady Evelyn added, gesturing to the pile in the corner. "You can drape yourself, I suppose. Artistically. You can do that, can't you?"

What the hell was he supposed to do? There had been no mention of this in the advertisement—he certainly would not have responded if he had known that a prerequisite of the job was stripping off his clothes!

"I... I presumed you knew what modeling for an artist entailed."

Richard's attention jerked up. Lady Evelyn was looking at him curiously, as though he were the most interesting thing she had ever seen.

His spirits perked up a bit there—or perhaps it was his ego. Or something lower down.

"No," he said stiffly. "No, I didn't."

"Ah. In that case, I take it you are offended, perhaps even scandalized, by my continuous request for you to take all your clothes off," Lady Evelyn said vaguely, placing her pencil behind her ear and continuing to examine him.

For the first time perhaps in his life, Richard flushed. "I-I... I will admit, I... I did not expect—"

"Look, you're clearly nervous, and I have no wish to make you feel uncomfortable," Lady Evelyn said, her tone returned to a more businesslike manner. "You are free to go, naturally, but if you would like to stay, why don't we compromise?"

Richard had not moved. The very idea of walking out of here and never seeing Lady Evelyn again was absolutely ludicrous. He could not, would not do it. "'Compromise'?"

Hell, he had only come here for some diversion. Why did Lady Evelyn's opinion of him matter so much? Why did he find it so difficult to say *no* to her? Why had he not once questioned her lack of a chaperone aloud? Could not a potentially doting papa force him to marry her at once should he catch them here, together, merely speaking without the presence of an observer?

Never mind what might happen if the earl caught Richard with his clothes off...

"Yes, a compromise." Lady Evelyn had disappeared behind the canvas again, her voice ambiguous. "If you take your jacket and waistcoat off, maybe roll your sleeves up, I can do an arm and hands study."

"Arm and hands study"?

Richard's jaw tightened. If he only had to roll up his sleeves...

well, then, she wouldn't see. He wouldn't have to reveal what he did not want her to see.

"I think that is a fair bargain," he said quietly. How his voice managed to stay level, he did not know.

"Good," came Lady Evelyn's reply. A pencil jutted out from behind the canvas. It was pointing at the center of the studio. "Agreed. Chair."

Trying not to grin at the way she had evidently become lost in her thoughts, or more likely, her art, Richard stepped forward and sat on the chair. It was a very comfortable one—an armchair that had seen better days, certainly, and had perhaps been ready to be thrown out by the family before it had been claimed by the daughter.

"Off, please."

Richard swiftly lurched to his feet before realizing what she'd probably meant. "Oh, right."

Now he knew he could keep his trousers on, it was a lot easier to remove his jacket and waistcoat. That did not explain, however, the shaking of his fingers as he carefully unbuttoned his cuffs and began to roll up his sleeves.

Not too far up, not near the elbow… there. That would have to be enough. He wouldn't let her see it. No one would need to see that.

"Excellent," said Lady Evelyn, popping her face around the canvas with a furrowed brow. "Now, if you would just sit there with your forearms on the arms of the chair, your hands resting unclenched… I said, *unclenched*."

A nerve jumped in Richard's temple as he tried to release the tension in his arms.

"Better," was the artist's verdict. "Now, just stay there— precisely there. Do not move an inch."

"For how long?"

"Forever, I think," came Lady Evelyn's vague response.

Richard stifled a smile. Well, he had heard about artists entering a highly focused state so that the rest of the world did not appear to be even real, but it was amusing to see it in person.

The minutes ticked by. Every now and again, Lady Evelyn's beautiful face would reappear, her eyes narrowed and her focus absolute. Richard could almost feel the weight of her concentration flickering down his arms, taking in every line, every hair, every curve of his fingers.

It was… Well. He had to admit it.

Sensual.

The rare times he had taken a woman to bed, it had been to fulfill a need. To satisfy a craving. To scratch an itch.

Need fulfilled, craving satisfied, and itch scratched, he would leave.

There had never been any long, pondering gazes or re-splendent *looking* at each other. He had never been looked at before with this sort of intensity.

But then, he'd had nothing to be ashamed of—self-conscious of, if she asked him to push his sleeves back another three inches.

Richard sat up straighter.

"Did I tell you to move?"

"No," Richard said hastily, dropping himself back down in the chair. "My apologies."

"I haven't drawn a man's arms like this in ages," said Lady Evelyn, her voice low, her concentration evidently on the end of her pencil, not the conversation itself.

And a spark of envy, of jealousy, spurted through Richard. "Who was he?"

"'He'?"

Damn it, he had to control himself. "The man you drew."

"'Man'?"

He had to smile at that, even if his mind was still reeling from the idea that he was not the first man who had enjoyed Lady Evelyn's company in this way. "The other man you have drawn."

"Oh, Percy doesn't count as a man," she said imprecisely.

The jealousy was getting worse. *Percy?* She was on such intimate terms with him?

Fine, admittedly she was technically on intimate terms with him as well. She had wanted to know his first name and nothing else—but he had thought that a quirk of their connection, something special.

And now, to find out that she treated all her models this way...

Richard swallowed. Now why the hell did that bother him?

"Yes, I have never thought of my brother as a man," Lady Evelyn mused aloud, the noise of her pencil moving across the paper filling the studio. Her brother. A breath escaped Richard's lips. "He's also an absolute rotter of a liar and currently in my bad books."

"A 'liar'?"

"I cannot abide a liar," Lady Evelyn said fiercely, her eyes flashing. "To deceive is to destroy. No relationship, no connection can withstand the damage. Though I admit, Percy has been making attempts to gain forgiveness for many months now. I may have no choice but to accept him. Eventually."

Richard swallowed. A hatred of liars. Well, he was hardly lying, was he? Omitting the truth, and at her request—that could hardly be considered the same thing.

"And Percy was never a very good sitter. Not like you."

Despite himself, Richard preened.

So, *Percy* was her brother—and a liar, which she evidently was not happy with. Strange. Richard had always approached truth with a loose grip. It had served him well in France. And most importantly, he was a better sitter than her brother. Why the devil that should matter so much was neither here nor there.

Wait a minute. Wait a goddamn minute.

"You said before—"

"If you absolutely must speak, try to do so without moving in any way," Lady Evelyn said curtly, without even looking around her canvas.

Richard opened his mouth, then partially closed it, and wondered what on earth he had gotten himself into. But now that the thought had occurred to him, he simply had to know.

"You said before that you had plenty of experience with painting the female form."

"Hmmmm?"

Blast. He had absolutely no idea how to go about asking this question. One simply did not ask ladies this sort of thing. Why he was about to was anyone's guess. "Did… Did you mean a female nude? I mean, the naked form of a woman?"

Lady Evelyn appeared at the side of her canvas. She was smiling. "You have never heard of a full-length looking glass?"

She disappeared behind the canvas again.

Very slowly, attempting not to move while he did indeed move, Richard crossed his legs to hide the stiffening manhood that was tenting his trousers.

Dear God. So Lady Evelyn had stood in this art studio, completely naked, in front of a looking glass and… and painted a self-portrait.

Where the devil is that painting?

"I thought I told you not to move."

"I thought you were drawing my hands and arms," Richard shot back, his voice strangled as he attempted to gain a hold of himself. "Not my legs."

"You have shifted the weight of your left arm and twisted your right arm inward about a quarter inch," came the swift reply as Lady Evelyn glared around her canvas. "I pay attention to these things, you see."

"If it's just a study, not a formal portrait, I don't see what difference it would make," he said, as firmly as he could.

Cold thoughts, man, cold thoughts!

"And that is why I am the artist, and you are only the model," came the sweet reply. "But I'll let it go this once. This is your first ever time modeling, after all."

Richard tried to remain calm. Well, he was attracted to Lady Evelyn—it was hardly a crime. And they were alone here. And he was technically unsuitably dressed. And they had spoken of her naked body…

Cold thoughts!

"Is there anything you would like to ask about me?" he said aloud. That was it. Change the topic of conversation. *Stop thinking about Lady Evelyn and her naked body—damn it, man!*

"No."

She sounded almost bored. No, not bored. Highly focused.

It was fascinating. *She* was fascinating. Richard had never encountered an artist in this way, in their place of work as it was, and the atmosphere was strangely peaceful while at the same time greatly disconcerting.

Here he was, just… sitting.

Worst of all, Lady Evelyn's total lack of interest in him was a little wrongfooting.

"Are you comfortable?"

No, Richard wanted to say desperately. *No, I cannot understand why I am so damned attracted to you, why I have allowed myself to spend time with you without a chaperone present, and why being here with you, in silence, is far more interesting than anything I have done in the last year.*

"Oh, yes," he said aloud.

"Excellent," said Lady Evelyn with a brief smile around the canvas. "Stay precisely there for two more hours, and I'll give you an additional shilling for each hour."

Richard smiled weakly. And of course, she did not know who he was. That would surely not become a problem in the future.

"'Sit here'?"

"Stop talking," Lady Evelyn said severely from the other side of the canvas.

Richard's smile warmed. Well, he had thought it wouldn't be much different, sitting for an artist compared to sitting at home.

How very wrong he had been.

Chapter Five

May 11, 1840

H E WAS THREE minutes late.

Not that she was counting. Evelyn put aside the pocket watch she had borrowed from Percy—well, not *borrowed*, taken without his knowledge or permission. But no matter, she had expected Percy to keep it properly wound.

So was it showing the correct time? Was Richard truly late?

Evelyn sighed as she sat in the chair in the center of her studio and tapped her pencil against her thigh.

Late. Late!

Precisely why it mattered that he was late, she was trying not to investigate. The need to see him, the aching disappointment that he had not been waiting as usual outside her art studio—apparently, he was too respectful to enter without her permission—was most acute.

Where was Richard?

It was because she wanted to be painting again. That was it, Evelyn tried to convince herself. It had nothing to do with the man in question. She was almost certain she would be this eager, whoever her model was.

No, she could not even lie to herself.

Evelyn sighed, rose from the seat, and peered out of a window once again. Once again, the view to the house did not reveal a waiting Richard.

It was most inconvenient. Here she was, hoping to continue on with the study of his arms, and he was not—

"I do apologize for being late," said Richard hastily, stepping through the hurriedly opened door. "A carriage overturned on the street and it was impossible to get through the crowd of onlookers. I had to double back and go around."

Evelyn smiled broadly—then remembered she should probably not be grinning broadly at a man. Any man. Though should she have been chastising herself for *that* when she knew she ought not to be alone with a man, either?

She most *certainly* should never have asked to see one nude, whatever her justifications.

Evelyn had wrestled most excessively with herself about that. There was no way any of the servants aware of what she was up to imagined she would be *quite* so bold. If anyone in her father's employ had ever discovered such a scene, they'd have been honor-bound to report it to her parents—and she'd have been lucky if the gossip didn't spread to half the town within hours.

She knew the potential consequences, so she'd almost avoided making the request until it had sprung from her lips at last, most unbidden.

Evelyn had been unable to help herself in his presence. That form, teasing her from beneath the layers of clothing. She swallowed.

Swiftly nodding and stepping to her canvas, she busied herself with selecting a pencil to continue on with her drawing.

She did not need to instruct Richard. He knew now to remove his jacket and waistcoat, roll up his sleeves, and adopt the exact same position as last time.

The question was, would she ever attempt to convince him to actually take off his shirt?

Heat blossomed in Evelyn at the mere thought. *It is for my art,* she told herself sternly in the privacy of her own mind. It wasn't because she wanted to see what was beneath that layer of linen!

Well. She did.

But for artistic purposes!

His arms truly were very fine. In fact, Evelyn did not believe she had ever seen forearms quite like them. Strong, and muscular, with a thin scar on one side.

Here was a man, she was quite sure, who had worked with his body for a living. This was not the sort of man who sat as a clerk or used his brain to earn his keep. The question was, what precisely did he do?

No. Evelyn stopped herself before her lips could form the question.

It would be far more suitable if she did not know anything more about the man who sat before her. No entanglements. No pretensions to friendship.

She picked up her pencil and returned to where she had left off two days ago: the particular curve of his right sleeve against his arm as he'd rested his hand on the edge of the chair.

Evelyn swiftly lost herself in the careful movements of pencil across paper. The delicate shadow—it was a very difficult thing to attempt. Her concentration narrowed until the only thing in the world was her pencil and the paper and the arm.

And she reached a point where she needed more. More. *More.*

"Push up your sleeve," she said distractedly, attempting to darken the shading.

"No."

"This isn't actually a debate," Evelyn said vaguely, tilting her head slightly as she moved her gaze from real arm to drawn arm. Had she managed to get that part right?

It was only a few minutes later when she realized her decree had not been obeyed.

Evelyn blinked. The world rushed in on her, reminding her she was standing before an easel, in an art studio, in the world. And there was a man there. And he was not following orders.

"I said—"

"I know what you said, and I know what I said," murmured Richard, not taking his eyes from her. "I am not rolling up my sleeve."

Evelyn bit her lip as she examined him.

Why on earth was the man so reticent? It wasn't as though he wasn't beautiful. Surely, he knew what a fine specimen he was. Surely, he realized there would be no judgment from her even if he were not. She was here to draw, not appraise.

She sighed, placing a hand on her hip as she studied him. "I asked you to take all your clothes off when you first arrived."

"And you suggested a compromise," Richard pointed out.

"I did not make any promises that the compromise would suit forever," Evelyn said sternly. That was what she was supposed to do, wasn't she? She was the artist. He was the model. Wasn't he supposed to succumb to her every whim? "Please. I need to draw the rest of your arm."

He flinched, and Evelyn wondered if it was mere shyness preventing Richard from removing that item of clothing. But shyness… regarding what? Where did this discomfort with his own body come from?

"I will take my shirt off," he said quietly, "if, and only if, you close your eyes while I do so."

Evelyn's aforementioned eyes widened.

Close her eyes? What on earth for?

If it had been any other man, she would have been worried. Why, a man could do a great deal in a few moments if a woman's eyes were shut. What if he… Oh, she didn't know. Stole paint?

Evelyn could not think of anything else dastardly he could do, now she came to consider it. Besides, he had knocked over enough paint to have sufficiently stolen from her, worse luck. It was going to mean she would have to ask her father for an advance on her June and July pin money. He wasn't going to like that.

Richard's gaze was steady, and it was obvious he was not going to budge.

Evelyn sighed and threw up her hands. "Fine! Fine, though I do this in protest. It is most ridiculous."

"It is my only term."

"And I am agreeing, preposterous though I think it is," Evelyn said wryly. "Go on, then."

She closed her eyes.

Only then did she realize just how vulnerable it made her. Her most important sense, gone, just as she heard Richard rise to his feet.

He isn't… He won't come over to me, will he?

Was such a situation not precisely what a chaperone's presence was supposed to prevent?

But a chaperone would have changed her art. A chaperone would have been a barrier, causing both Richard and her to stiffen, to bow to convention, to remain at arm's length and remain polite.

A chaperone's presence would have muted her beating heart.

Her lungs tightened as something spread through her at the thought. It wasn't dread, but desire.

Which is ridiculous, Evelyn told herself silently as she listened to the rustle of linen and the sudden drop of his shirt to the floor and the creak of the chair as Richard settled back into it. She did not desire Richard. She… She admired him. As an object of study. Nothing more.

"You can open your eyes now."

Evelyn opened her eyes—and gasped.

Well, now she knew why Richard had not wished to remove his shirt.

Scars. Scars blossomed over him and along his upper arms, scars that had once been flame. The puckered, taut, shiny skin looked healed enough, but it had clearly not been long since Richard had been in a fire.

Tears prickled the corners of her eyes. Such pain, such agony he must have endured. And here she was, demanding he remove his shirt just to draw his arm.

"I—I…" she breathed.

Richard met her eyes and there was harshness there, and iron, and a determination not to be pitied.

Evelyn swallowed. "You can put your shirt back on, if you wish."

"You asked me to take it off, and I agreed," Richard said in a low, level voice. "Draw."

Almost stumbling as she returned to her canvas, Evelyn blinked back tears. The man had clearly suffered. Perhaps he worked at the docks—there were frequently fires there—or perhaps he had rushed into a burning building to save someone. Someone he loved.

Evelyn's stomach swooped as the thought occurred to her. She had purposefully not asked any questions. Knowing more about the subject before her would distract her hand, make her think about the man instead of the art.

Only now did she regret that decision. Was he married? Had he been married, perhaps, and lost his wife in a fire?

So many possibilities, so many questions, all swirling about in her mind. Only after Richard cleared his throat did Evelyn realize she had not brought pencil to paper in quite some time.

"I have distressed you," he said gruffly.

"No!" Evelyn stepped out from behind her canvas and hastily shook her head. "No, I-I was surprised. I am sorry, that you have suffered so."

Richard's gaze was steady as it met hers. "It is of no matter."

"If you were in pain, then it matters," Evelyn said fiercely, sounding almost like her sister in her vehemence. "I am sorry for that. I am grateful you chose to reveal yourself to me."

"You ask no questions."

"I told you, I want to know as little about you as possible," said Evelyn quietly. "And if you wish to tell me, you will."

He wouldn't. She could sense it in the air. She did not need to catch his eyes to know.

"Besides, it will be a sad tale," she added. "Something like a forgotten candle, or a fallen curtain, or something like that."

There was a silence, and then, "Yes. Something like that."

For a moment, she wondered whether she could… Well. Not *flirt* with him. Not exactly. Show her admiration. Reveal to Richard just what a fine man she thought him.

The trouble was, Evelyn was not sure where to begin.

Her cousin Maude was a tremendous flirt, and Evelyn had always admired the way she spoke to gentlemen without any fear. Not that she herself was nervous around gentlemen in general, not in the slightest.

Around this man in particular? Yes.

Evelyn swallowed. That was the trouble with having led a sheltered life, she supposed. Being the daughter of an earl had its advantages, but it had not given her much instruction on the ways of speaking with admiration to men.

Not that it had ever been a problem until now.

The gentlemen at parties since her coming out had found her eccentricities too much to be borne, it seemed.

"I… I will get back to my drawing," Evelyn said awkwardly into the silence.

It was not so much a retreat as she moved to her canvas, but in a way, it was a welcome screen between them. *It gives Richard the opportunity to collect himself,* she thought as she picked up her pencil, *and me time to remind myself that I am here to draw, not flirt with a man I know almost nothing about!*

Except he was handsome. And brave. And had endured much.

"I had thought you would paint me."

"Perhaps I will, but it was as a study that I chose you. I need to improve my men."

There was a laugh. "I thought you liked your brother."

"Oh, not like that!" Though it wouldn't hurt Percy to endure a few small improvements. "I mean, take landscapes—*landscapes* I excel at. Nature, sunlight, and shadow—those are things I am very good at."

"Indeed."

Oh, that sounded like boasting, did it not? The trouble was,

Evelyn knew she was not exaggerating. Having spent the best part of her life drawing daisies, as well as the little pond here in their London townhouse and the lake in the country, and beetles and birds and mushrooms and mountains…

She was very good.

"And you've… you've drawn yourself. In the nude."

Now was it her imagination, or was Richard a mite short of breath all of a sudden?

Evelyn's own lungs tightened at the remembrance of what she had said to him, the first time he had come for a sitting.

"You have never heard of a full-length looking glass?"

It had been forward, now she came to think of it—but then, she had only been honest. She had painted herself in the nude, several times. It was a lot more challenging than people thought, but finding the looking glass that was almost as tall as she was had helped.

"Yes," Evelyn said aloud, surprised at the hoarseness in her voice. "Yes, I have. But being a woman is only helpful for half of my study on the human form. And being a woman is a hindrance."

"'A hindrance'?"

The poor man, he sounded quite surprised. Evelyn shook her head as she attempted to sketch out the breadth of his chest. It truly was a very broad chest. "Well, there are classes for men, classes where models go and lounge about completely naked—"

"Don't you be thinking, just because I removed my shirt—"

"Yes, yes," Evelyn said, her cheeks pinking. If this was how intoxicated she became around Richard with his shirt off, she could hardly imagine what it would be like, attempting to draw him with no clothes on at all.

Richard, with no clothes on at all…

"So you have always loved art?"

The question jerked Evelyn from a place where, for some reason, it was crucial that both she and Richard were utterly nude. "I beg your pardon?"

There was a gentle laugh from the other side of her canvas. "I don't suppose I am distracting you, am I, Lady Evelyn?"

Distracting? Absolutely not. Almost definitely not. A little.

Evelyn collected herself. "You should call me 'Evelyn,' I suppose. It would put us on a more equal footing."

She did not need to look around her easel to know the smirk that was spreading across Richard's face. She had already memorized it.

"Ah, but we are not equals, are we?"

"I suppose not," Evelyn conceded. "But still. I would like it if you called me 'Evelyn.'"

The words had slipped from her tongue before she could call them back. Even now, she was not certain whether she would have wished to call them back.

"Evelyn," came Richard's low voice.

Evelyn shivered. Perhaps that had been a mistake. It was a small thing, to lose the 'Lady' before her name, but no one outside the family had ever done that before and it was... intoxicating. The thrum of his voice had somehow vibrated through her body, warming it, reminding her that what they were doing was not socially acceptable.

Perhaps that was why she was enjoying it so much.

"Art," she said firmly aloud, mostly to herself. "Yes, I have always loved art. If I had been a man, a younger son, I suppose I might have been an artist. But instead..."

"Instead, you *are* an artist."

Evelyn stepped to the side, looking around the easel. "I beg your pardon?"

Richard spread out his hands, gesturing about her studio. It was most provoking that he had moved from the position she had requested, but it was hardly possible for her to argue. Not with that splendid sight before her.

"You have a studio, you draw, you paint, you pay models," he said with a wry smile. "I am not sure what else you would have to do to be an artist. Do you not think?"

Evelyn stared. *He... He understands. He considers me an artist.* "You truly think so?"

Richard shrugged, and Evelyn could not drag her eyes away from the undulation of the muscles in the movement. "Yes, I think so. You are an artist, Evelyn."

It was so strange; she had heard those words from her family numerous times—usually in the form of complaints, it was true, but still.

Hearing them from Richard's lips meant more, somehow. Precisely why, she did not know, but it did. His approval, his confirmation that she was the thing she so craved to be, made something trickle into her soul.

"You look a tad warm, Evelyn."

Richard's voice forced her to focus.

"And you look a tad out of place, Richard," Evelyn said smartly, as though she could remind him with such a tone that she was the one in charge here. If she were truly an artist, then he should not have been disobeying her. "Here, let me put you back."

Fine, it wasn't strictly necessary for her to step across the studio and place her hands on his shoulder and arm, Evelyn would admit. At least, she would have done, if anyone had accused her of having ulterior motives. Which she absolutely did.

She almost gasped at the initial contact. Where the burns had died away to puckered scars, the flesh was soft, smooth—almost *too* smooth. Where the flames had not licked away at his skin, there was a strength, a roughness of wiry hair.

Richard's head jerked around to face her. "Evelyn."

Evelyn could not move. All she could murmur was, "Richard."

It happened swiftly. How precisely it happened, she did not know. All she knew was that the world suddenly tipped sideways and somehow, she was in his arms, splayed across Richard's lap, and his mouth was on hers.

He was kissing her.

Evelyn squirmed in shock, desperate to get away... until the unbridled passion of Richard's kiss made her melt into his strong arms.

Oh, this was beyond anything she could have ever imagined. His tongue was bold, demanding something from her that she did not know how to give. Tendrils of sparking pleasure were aching across her face, dripping down to her neck, tightening at her breasts and her hands—her hands, which somehow found themselves around his neck and, instead of pushing him away, were pulling him closer.

Closer. Oh, she wanted to be closer—and yet Evelyn was not sure how much closer they could be. His presence was unbearable, his torso and arms enclosing her into a cage of pleasure, and as the kiss deepened…

Evelyn's eyes opened and she gasped.

She was sitting in the lap of a shirtless man kissing him with abandon!

The sudden shock jolted them apart. Richard looked deep into her eyes, his chest heaving as he panted, and Evelyn managed to clamber clumsily out of his lap.

She was panting too. They both were. The giddiness of that kiss, that overwhelming kiss, that perfect—

No.

"I think you should leave," Evelyn said as coldly as she could manage.

After all, this cannot be borne! Sitters are not supposed to go around kissing their artists!

And yes, it had been a delightful kiss. Evelyn raised a hand to her mouth before she could stop herself. A very wonderful kiss. It had been the best kiss she had ever received.

Fine, it was the *only* kiss—but still! If all kisses were like that, she could well understand why so many young ladies in Society risked scandal to get them.

Richard had risen from the chair, which only accentuated his height, the power of him. "Evelyn—"

"I think after all, *Lady* Evelyn is a better idea," she said in a rush, hastily stepping backward. "And I asked—I *told* you to leave."

"Look, I suppose I should not have—"

"No, you should not have," Evelyn said instinctively, going against every cry of her body.

Because ladies should not have been kissing men they barely knew. Because daughters of earls did not kiss gentlemen, let alone common men.

And because if he stayed, if Richard remained here, she would not be able to stop herself from kissing him again.

"Please, give me another chance."

Evelyn could not help but laugh drily at that. "We have more than enough Chances in this family, I assure you! Please, Richard, please leave."

Saying his name had been a mistake. It had softened her tone, made it a plea rather than a command.

Richard took a step toward her. He was still without a shirt. "It won't happen again."

All the more reason for you to leave, Evelyn thought wryly. "I said, please leave."

"Don't you want to finish the study of my arms?"

It was, perhaps, the only thing Richard could have said that would have made Evelyn hesitate.

She glanced at her easel. It would be most infuriating to have a study unfinished. And it would only take another sitting, perhaps two. She was almost certain she could prevent herself from kissing him for that time.

What am I thinking?!

"Please," Richard said, his voice softer now. "I have nowhere else to go."

Despite herself, Evelyn looked over at him and met his eyes. There was honesty there, a truthfulness not even the best actor could pretend.

Nowhere else to go. Who knew whether or not the shillings she paid him for sitting for her was the only coin he was currently earning? The only coin putting a roof over his head and food on his table?

What, was she going to let him starve?

"Fine," Evelyn said warily with a sigh. "But no more kissing."

Richard lowered himself back onto the chair and grinned. "Look, who am I to argue with an artist? But if the muse takes you that way—I'll always keep out an eye for the chance."

Chapter Six

May 16, 1840

"Y OU ARE JESTING," said Walden in what appeared to be horror.

Richard grinned. "It isn't that bad."

"You—You are not serious," his friend repeated, lowering his voice as another gentleman walked past them on the way out of White's. "You're saying this just to torment me."

"Why would I lie?" Richard retorted, enjoying himself.

If he had known that his friend would take the news this badly, he would have told him over a week ago.

Walden's eyes were wide. "Because… Because… Well, because you absolutely cannot do that!"

"And why not?" asked Richard calmly, taking a sip of the afternoon tea they had been served and wishing that it was something stronger. "It's all aboveboard."

Mostly. He had told his friend about the advertisement, how he had answered it, the strange interview he had endured with the beautiful Lady Evelyn Chance, and about how he was going there almost every day now to sit in a chair and be drawn.

The kiss, the way he could not take his eyes off her, that she had invited him to call her 'Evelyn,' how he'd taken his shirt off…

Those details had not seemed quite as important.

Walden's eyes were still wide. "You cannot mean it. You are truly sitting as a model for Lady Evelyn Chance?"

"I am," said Richard, rather proudly.

"Alone."

"Just the two of us in her studio," he said with a grin.

"And you're keeping all of your clothes on, are you?" asked his friend with a knowing look.

Richard hesitated.

"Dear God, man!"

"Just my shirt—look, it sounds sordid when you say it like that!" Richard said hastily, glancing about them to ensure they were not being overheard.

They weren't. There was a large crowd at the other end of the room engaged in an exuberant game of cards, their raucous laughter filling the room.

When he turned back to his friend, Walden was glowering.

"I don't see why you have to get all prim and proper about this." He knew well he should not have been alone with an unmarried lady, any lady, of their class. He most certainly should not have been posing partially in the nude for her. Or kissing her.

Still... No one outside a select few need find out. So was the lady ever truly in any danger?

"She's a Chance," Walden said flatly. "Have you no sense of preservation?"

It was not the response Richard had expected. "What on earth do you mean?"

"She has a brother and a father, three uncles, and goodness knows how many cousins, all of whom will be doing their very best to make sure you marry that woman if anything untoward occurs," his friend said sharply. "You haven't been doing anything untoward, have you? *Have you, Lord* Sempill?"

Using his full title, Richard noticed. His friend truly was worried.

"Look, she's a Chance," repeated Walden.

Richard could not help but grin. "She's very beautiful."

The whack on his arm was not undeserved, but it still hurt.

"You deserved that," his friend said darkly. "Honestly! I knew you wanted excitement, even some danger now that you're back from France, but this is not it!"

"All I am doing is sitting in a chair for a few hours at a time," Richard said with a shrug, once again carefully editing the truth to what would be palatable for his friend to hear. "What's the harm in that? I'd only be doing it here or at home, anyway."

Walden frowned, but said nothing.

That kiss, that stolen moment with Evelyn, returned to Richard's mind and he grinned. It had been bold, and it had certainly gone beyond the expectations of propriety—far more than everything else they had done to ignore convention. But it had been worth it. *Oh, God, the way she squirmed in my arms before leaning in for more...*

"The Chance family is very protective," came the unwelcome intrusion from his friend. "They are known for it, renowned in fact for raising their children to be individuals, but individuals who must always be unimpeachable when it comes down to it."

Good, Richard could not help but think. The last thing he wanted was for Evelyn to be doing that with any of her other models.

"You *are* going to be careful, aren't you?"

Richard focused on his friend, and saw to his very great surprise, Walden was making strong eye contact, his pursed lips conveying the man's genuine concern. "What is the worst that could happen?"

"I don't want to attend your wedding to Lady Evelyn because you have a pistol at your back," Walden said darkly. "Now listen to me, please. I know you never do, but this is important."

"My wedding?" said Richard with a grin, the rest of his friend's tirade lost in the thought of such a thing.

He had never concerned himself with the idea before.

That whack was again, deserved. "I am in earnest! Think before you do anything rash with that woman. They're all impressive, yes, and the Chance family is a prestigious one—but all the more reason to be careful. Men like you, men like us, we don't marry the women we seduce. We don't seduce daughters of great houses."

"*You* don't," said Richard, winking as he rose.

"Richard Sempill—"

"And I won't," Richard said with a sigh, waving the White's footman nearer to bring his things and assist him with shrugging on his jacket and placing his top hat upon his head. "Right. I have an appointment to keep."

Walden groaned. "With Lady Evelyn, I'll be bound."

Richard winked again. "Maybe."

There was certainly a spring in his step as he walked down the street toward the Earl of Lindow's household. Evelyn had not actually engaged his sitting services for this afternoon, but she had said only yesterday that he should pop by the studio whenever he was in the area. Well, he was in the area. Now he had walked to it. Why not pop in?

Richard did not bother knocking at the front door. Instead, he stepped down the side of the house, past the kitchen door, and toward the studio.

"I thought I would drop by," he said in his most charming voice as he reached out and opened the studio door.

As he tried to open the studio door. The thing wouldn't budge.

Ah. It had not occurred to him that when Evelyn said that he should pop by, she may have in fact popped out.

His shoulders slumped. Right. Well, now there was nothing to do but return home and try not to dwell on the nightmares.

"Are you the model?"

Richard whirled around. "I beg your—"

"Yes, you're him," said a gentleman perhaps a few years younger than himself. He had that imperious air so many of the Chances had, but a softness around the eyes and the impressive cut of his suit suggested he was an eldest son. He was seated on the terrace at the back of the house, a book in one hand and an apple in the other. "My sister has given such an exact description of you, there's no mistaking you."

An exact description…

Richard was somehow uncertain whether to be delighted or concerned. "'Description'?"

The man, who had to be Lord Percy Chance, unless Evelyn had several brothers, grinned. "Never fear. It's not nearly so uncouth as all that. She's an artist, my sister, and so she described you as a tall man with a sharp expression at all times."

A sharp—

The man laughed. "There it is."

Shifting on his feet, Richard was unsure whether to be flattered or offended. "Thank you. I think."

"Did you have an appointment with her?" Now Lord Percy's face was more sharp.

Well, he has a right to be, Richard reminded himself. A stranger had just walked around the side of the house and attempted to break into the man's sister's art studio. That was what it could have looked like.

"I didn't exactly have an appointment," Richard said carefully.

Hell, if he had known that he was going to meet Evelyn's brother, he might have put more thought into his attire. He knew he ought to have had a valet, but he had not yet hired one since he had let the last go before his venture to France. Smith had been old, too feeble to accompany his master in the work required of him. Richard's time on the Continent had only accentuated the frivolity of engaging such a servant. As it was, without a valet, this morning, Richard had thrown on the nearest things himself when he had awoken, running late as he had been to see Walden.

Walden's words echoed most uncomfortably in his mind.

"She's a Chance. Have you no sense of preservation? She has a brother and a father, three uncles, and goodness knows how many cousins, all of whom will be doing their very best to make sure you marry that woman if anything untoward occurs…"

So the brother knew about him. Did he know that Richard

posed for the earl's daughter with no chaperone in sight?

Richard straightened up. He hadn't compromised the lady, not really—the kiss did not count, for some reason, and he was not sure why. All he had done was attempt to find Evelyn. *Blast. Lady* Evelyn.

"She's over there, in the garden." Lord Percy gestured.

Glancing in the direction he had pointed, Richard could see a figure through a grove of trees. He had taken the person to be the gardener, nothing more. A figure kneeling over a flowerbed with a trowel generally was a gardener, at least in his experience.

"Ah," he said aloud.

"Yes," said Evelyn's brother, with a hint of suspicion in his voice now. "I say, you are... I mean, this whole thing is aboveboard, isn't it? When my sister said she was paying a man to sit for her... Well."

Yes, well. No more needed to be said.

Tempting as it was for Richard to reveal that he was in fact a viscount, and therefore perhaps 'worthier' of spending time with an earl's daughter, he restrained himself.

He really should have told Evelyn that, the first time they had met. Or the second time. Or the third.

Better she hear the truth from his lips rather than her brother, he was certain.

"I would do nothing to harm your sister's reputation," Richard said aloud.

The tension in Lord Percy's shoulders released. "Good, good. Well, off you go. I shall be here—keeping the two of you within sight, as Laurent usually does." His eyes narrowed just slightly before relaxing again. "Good luck trying to talk to her, though, as she gets in these funny moods sometimes. Concentrating, she calls it. Never experienced the thing myself."

He took a large bite of his apple and returned to his book.

Richard almost grinned. Perhaps if he had met the brother first, they would have been friends. As it was...

The grove of trees had sprung into leaf, and he had to push

past a few heavy branches to reach the kneeling woman. When he approached her, Richard was not surprised to see she did not glance up.

Once again, it appeared, Evelyn had slipped into one of those bouts of intense concentration. During those times, it was almost impossible to get her to hear him.

That was why Richard was able to sit on the grass beside her and just look at her as she peered at the flowers in the bed.

Goodness, she was beautiful. It had been a while since he had been able to be this close to her and it was almost painful, the elegance in her features. Richard had met plenty of pretty women; France was full of them, and there had been times when it had been convenient to cozy up to one or two to gain information.

But Evelyn?

Evelyn was different. It was the difference between the dough for bread and the finished loaf, the acorn and the oak.

She was the finished article.

All thoughts of a proper conversation forgotten, Richard leaned back on his elbows and watched her, transfixed. Was this how she spent her afternoons when they were not together in the art studio? What *was* she doing, now that he thought to wonder? It was most bizarre.

A notebook was in her lap, and a pencil in her hand, as it always seemed to be. Every now and again, Evelyn would lean back and add a few lines to the notebook, then she peered into the flowerbed again.

Richard cleared his throat. "Ahem."

There was absolutely no response.

"Evelyn."

She looked up for a moment, as though she had heard an unusual birdsong or her name being called by someone almost a mile away. Then she shook her head slightly, as though chastising herself silently for daydreaming, and returned to her notebook.

Richard quelled a grin. *Well, she really is leaving me with no choice.*

"Evelyn," he said quietly as he placed a hand on her arm.

Evelyn jerked away as though he'd been stung, her arm lunging out, the pencil her only weapon.

"Good God!"

Richard scrambled back, the thrusted pencil a sharp dagger for the sensation it had given his arm. Thank God he was wearing his thicker jacket. "You stabbed me!"

"Oh, it's you," said Evelyn blithely with a smile. "Hello, Richard."

"You stabbed me with a pencil!" he said in horror.

For some reason, she was giggling. "I do apologize, but you should have gained my attention in a less threatening way."

"'Less threatening'?" Richard stared, transfixed, at the pencil lead mark on his jacket. If that had been his skin… It really did not bear thinking about.

"Yes, if you'd said my name a few times, for example."

He cast her a serious look. "I did."

Evelyn's lips formed an O. "You did?"

The trouble was, being angry at Evelyn was difficult. Staying angry at her was almost impossible. By now, Richard could see the funny side, and though he made a note to always approach the woman from the front in future, he chuckled as he leaned back on his elbows. "You are a dangerous woman, you know that?"

"I was grabbed once by a lout after a ball in the dark," Evelyn said quietly, a shadow passing over her face. "When I was with my cousin Lilianna—the Countess of Taernsby now."

And all of a sudden, guilt swam through Richard's veins thicker than treacle. "You weren't hurt?"

"I was very much startled and did not appreciate the experience," confessed Evelyn, her eyes averted and looking back at the flowerbed. "I admit, I have not been very good at allowing people to grab me ever since."

The guilt turned to stone inside his heart.

Oh, hell. And what had he done? Grabbed her and pulled her into his arms, before bestowing an unwelcome kiss on her lips.

Richard felt like an absolute cad. God in heaven, he hadn't known, he'd had no idea—but perhaps then he should never have done it? What man knew everything about the woman he wished to kiss?

"I… I am so sorry, Evelyn," he said awkwardly.

When she turned to look at him, her eyes had that unfocused quality again. "Why?"

"For…" Hell, he had never had to apologize like this. "For grabbing you, that time in your studio. You know. That time."

When I kissed you, Richard had wanted to say, but he could not bring himself to do so. *When I kissed you passionately and you responded—or at least, I thought you had responded. Now I'm questioning everything and it's all because of you.*

"Oh, that." Evelyn's cheeks pinked. "Yes, well, it was a bit of a shock, but… but I liked it."

She'd liked it.

Richard was ready to stand at the top of the Houses of Parliament and sing into the night—she had liked it!

"Not that that sort of thing can happen again, you understand," she added hastily.

Deflating quickly, Richard said quietly, "Yes. Yes, of course."

Of course he could not kiss her again. Of course he would never know the taste of Evelyn's lips on his again. A moment like that, it was far too good to be true. Far too wonderful to be repeated.

Evelyn blinked, as though astonished to find him there. "But what are you doing here, Richard?"

"I… Well, I was in the area," he said as casually as he could manage, deciding not to tell her that he had come purposefully to see her. "And so I thought I might sit for you."

"I'm afraid I'm working on stamen today," Evelyn said cheerfully before turning away.

Richard blinked. "'Stamen'?"

It didn't sound like a part of the body. Admittedly, he was hardly a doctor—he hadn't paid attention to most of his studies at university, in truth. There hadn't seemed much point. He had been a viscount upon entering, he would be a viscount upon exiting. Nothing he had done there would have much of a consequence.

"Yes, stamen," said Evelyn happily. "See?"

She pointed at a flower with her pencil as though that solved all inquiries, and returned to her close examination.

Richard waited for a moment, then asked, "And what, precisely, is a stamen?"

When Evelyn straightened up to stare, it was with a look of incredulity. "You do not know?"

"It's never come up," he said honestly.

No, when one was a spy in France, the need to know about the anatomy of flowers had not been a vital skill. Perhaps it would have been useful, if he'd been asked to befriend a botanist or some such person. Who knew?

"Oh, it is a most fascinating study, the flower and its component parts," Evelyn said happily, as though nothing could please her more than to explain it. "Look here."

And she handed over her notebook.

Richard took it from her fingers as though it were a precious relic. Never before had Evelyn permitted him to see her artwork; she had told him several times, every time he had requested the honor, in fact, that as she was busy learning, her drawings were not for public consumption.

And now she had given him her notebook to look at?

Reverentially, Richard opened it to the most recently opened page. Upon it was a brilliant drawing of a flower, all the parts labeled in exquisite detail and with impeccable handwriting.

He gasped. He could not help it. It was the only appropriate response to Evelyn moving closer to him, much closer, and leaning over the notebook to point at different parts of her work.

They were so close. So close, Richard could breathe her in.

His gaze darted in the direction of Lord Percy, but the man—a distant figure, really—had his back to them, as if he considered his duty as chaperone fulfilled by merely reading somewhere within sight.

"Here's the stamen, here—and stamen will look slightly different depending on the type of flower, so what you're really looking for is the form, the purpose of it within the plant. That way, you can usually find it."

"'Purpose'?" Richard asked in a croak.

It was not possible for his voice to offer up anything else. Oh, it was powerfully intoxicating, being this close to her. Evidently, Evelyn was unaffected, for she continued to speak about the different parts of the flower.

"Yes, you see here? That's the stamen, covered with pollen as one would hope, and scientists have examined them in their variety across a great number of different plants. They are used for... well, propagation, as it happens—not a topic my mother would wish me to speak of, but there's something truly artistic in the way it moves, isn't there? Can you see? Are you concentrating?"

But Richard could not concentrate. How could he, when every second made him fully aware of just how close they were?

Almost as close as they had been when he had kissed her.

Richard swallowed hard, willing himself to have control over his body. He couldn't just let himself enjoy the proximity. He had to at least *pretend* to pay attention.

"—you see?" Evelyn finished with a wide smile.

His own smile was forced. "I am impressed."

"Oh, don't be. It's just a little sketch," said Evelyn, though her cheeks flushed.

With pleasure at his praise, Richard wondered? Or mere shyness at having shown her work to another?

"You know, you are a true artist," he said impetuously. "A free spirit with... with a brilliant mind."

Evelyn raised an eyebrow as she leaned back. "You almost

sound surprised."

"'Surprised'?"

"As though you thought my art may not be up to scratch," she explained. "What did you think my art was *like*?"

Richard hesitated. *Not like this.*

That was what he wanted to say. Not like this—bold and determined, a confidence visible in the sweep of the lead across the page. Not artistic and scientific, a blend of logic and creativity he would have expected in the hands of an older, more experienced artist.

"I don't know," he said aloud, fully aware it was not a sufficient explanation.

Evelyn's face mirrored his own internal thoughts. "Hmm. Well, I am afraid as you do not have a stamen, I have no use for you today."

Richard repressed a smile. "I don't suppose you could use an audience?"

She blinked at that, evidently thrown. "I—a what?"

"An audience," he said with a shrug, leaning back on his elbows and relishing the way he had confused her. "You sit there, looking at the stamen, and I sit here, looking at you."

Her cheeks had started to pink, but now they were a deep rose. "And why on earth would you want to do that?"

Richard shrugged, amused by the way he had put her on the back foot. "I like to look at beautiful things."

Evelyn looked over her shoulder, spotting Lord Percy off in the distance. "My brother is nearby. I suppose he might act as chaperone—he thinks my lady's maid has been doing so. Or that is, he said as much, and I did not correct him." Her gaze lowered, for a fraction of a second, and Evelyn looked at him boldly. "You're not going to kiss me again, are you?"

"Not today," he said quietly, excitement in the flirtation soaring through him. "Not today."

Evelyn bit her lip and Richard tried not to follow the swelling curves of the flesh, tried not to think about his last contact with them. Perhaps his last contact ever.

"Fine," she said quietly. "I suppose that is not too scandalous."

"Proceed," said Richard with a wide gesture of his hand.

She smiled at that, the color still pink in her cheeks, but a restless smile now creasing her lips. "You are ridiculous, you know that?"

"I have been told, yes," said Richard with a grin. "Go on."

And so she did. Within a few minutes, Evelyn had slipped into that highly concentrating state that he so admired in her, and the bees hummed as they visited different stamen, and a bird sang in a tree, and Richard sat.

Strange. Sitting for hours in his study had bored him. Sitting here, staring at Evelyn for hours… now that was something quite different, indeed.

Chapter Seven

May 18, 1840

"**B**OTHER!"

Evelyn had almost made it safely out of the art supplies shop without dropping anything, which was a small miracle in and of itself—but not quite.

A small cascade occurred in her arms, two of her many brown-paper-wrapped parcels slipping to the floor.

"Here, Lady Evelyn," said the shop assistant with a helpful expression. "Shall I just… ah…"

"Just tuck them on top of the pile," said Evelyn. Laurent's arms were similarly full, the lady's maid barely able to peer over the top of them to peek at her mistress from a few feet behind her. Evelyn grinned.

The trouble was, Evelyn was holding so many parcels, she was not quite sure whether or not the shop assistant could see her smile. Perhaps she should not have attempted to buy that new paint set as well as the box of charcoals. And the new paper was finally in stock, so she'd had to buy a stack of that. And that beautiful sketchbook. And that trio of paintbrushes. And—

"Are you quite sure you and your maid are able to carry all that?" asked the shop assistant, in a tone that clearly declared she did not consider Evelyn able to walk five steps without a small, brown avalanche. "We can easily send them to your address."

"Oh, yes, home is only a few streets away," Evelyn said hurriedly.

The last time she had allowed the art shop to deliver her parcels, they had arrived an entire day later. A whole four and twenty hours, without her purchases?

Perish the thought.

"I see," said the shop assistant slowly. "Well, let me open the door for you, Lady Evelyn."

The door opened—Evelyn could tell because she heard the bell—and she stepped toward the sound. Laurent muttered something in French under her breath that Evelyn had to assume was a complaint. Only when she had stepped into the street and felt the bustle of the busy day, getting nudged and jostled by passersby, did she realize just how difficult this would be.

She could not see where she was going, for a start.

Well, she couldn't just stand here. Evelyn stepped forward, making a turn and heading in the direction of her home. At least, she *thought* it was the direction of her home. Yes, it had to be. She smiled to herself and kept going, one slow step at a time. She brushed past the people on the street, uttering her apologies, and she turned down another street. Then, after many more slow, careful steps, she turned down another.

"My lady?" called the soft, dulcet tones of her lady's maid. She sounded quite some distance away.

Had the maid gotten turned around somewhere?

Evelyn swung around to check and almost tripped over a stone. One of her parcels fell to the ground.

Ah. She had not considered what she would do in such a situation. Right.

Keeping a tight grip on the canvas under her left arm, Evelyn tried to slowly lower herself down, reaching out with her right hand while trying not to—

The avalanche occurred. Scattering across the pavement, a few of the smaller parcels already trodden on by passersby, Evelyn groaned with frustration as her arms emptied and her precious parcels became strewn in all directions.

"Oh, blast it all to—"

"Evelyn?"

Evelyn straightened up, her cheeks flushing. She was not supposed to curse. She had always been so good at keeping it inside. Still, it had been particularly galling to see the box of charcoals crushed.

When she looked up to see who, unlike her merciful maid, would tell of her indiscretion to her mother—or worse, her father—it was to see…

"Richard," she whispered.

There he was, standing just a few feet away. He was staring in astonishment.

Heat burned. It was strange, in a way; she was so accustomed to seeing Richard in her art studio that she had almost forgotten he must exist in the real world whenever he was not with her.

It was a strange thought.

What was even more strange was that he was wearing a shirt, and waistcoat, and coat. The heat twisted into a strange delight. All these people rushing past them, and it was she who had seen him half-naked.

The thought scandalized her, forcing the heat within her upward until it scalded her cheeks. She could *not* be thinking of the man being naked. *Not in public!*

"Having some trouble with our purchases, are we?" Richard asked with a wry smile.

"My lady's maid seems to have gotten lost," she said, her eyes darting around for the diminutive woman also buried behind boxes. No such other person was in sight. In fact, looking around the unfamiliar area, Evelyn was rather unsure if *she* had not gotten lost herself.

"As she often does, I find." He bent down on one knee and started grabbing for the packages.

The flush of embarrassment became one of determination. "I have sourced some art supplies for my next project."

"'Project'?"

"Yes," Evelyn said sweetly, hardly knowing how she was being so daring—and in public, too! "I am about to paint a man in the nude."

Richard had picked up a few of her parcels, but they immediately slipped from his grasp as he stared in horror. "Y-You are?"

"I am," she replied, unable to prevent herself from being delighted at his response.

"But…" Despite the crowds, despite the many people passing them on the pavement, Richard closed the gap between them. When he spoke again, it was in a low mutter. "Who the devil else are you painting, Evelyn?"

Her eyes widened in shock. He was… jealous?

She had intended only to tease about painting *him* in the nude—yet now she thought back, she could see the confusion.

"You do not want me painting anyone else?" she asked quietly before she could stop herself.

There was a crack somewhere to her left. That would have been the paintbrushes, destroyed by a wayward boot.

She did not look around. How could she, when her eyes were caught by Richard's dark ones?

Richard wet his lips before his answer. Evelyn found herself glancing at them before returning to his eyes.

"I… I like our sittings. Our conversations. Our time together."

"So do I," Evelyn breathed.

Somehow, her hand brushed up against his own, and though she wore gloves, the sudden sparking heat shivered through her body.

"Oh, pardon me, miss," said someone who bumped into her, pushing her into Richard.

Evelyn's heart skipped a beat as Richard put out his hands to catch her, but the stranger's words served as an unbidden reminder that intimate though their conversation was… they were in public. Standing in a street, where anyone could see them.

Evidently, Richard had had the same realization. Clearing his throat loudly and stepping swiftly away, he started to gather up her parcels.

She leaned down herself to pick up a few of them and just managed to avoid brushing her fingers up against Richard's. It was a difficult thing not to do, but she'd had enough startled moments today. She was not certain if she could bear another.

"I am glad I was here to be of assistance," said Richard formally, straightening up with half a dozen brown paper parcels in his arms.

Evelyn mirrored him, carrying a great deal of parcels in her turn. Goodness, were they multiplying? She did not recall purchasing so many as all this—and Laurent, wherever she was, carried just as many. "As am I. My mother would not appreciate me speaking to a stranger. At least, not again. I have a reputation in my family for proposing to gentlemen."

Richard dropped all her parcels.

"Proposing that they sit for me as models," Evelyn added, her cheeks burning. *Goodness, there must have been a way to say that properly the first time!* "My family considers me bold enough already."

"I can see that," Richard muttered as he once again picked up her parcels. "I do apologize. There appears to be some mud splattered on this one."

"Oh, that's the box of charcoals, I think, utterly ruined," she replied with a sigh. "I shall just have to see what I can make of them."

"The art shop isn't too far away." His gesture was slight, burdened as he was by a great number of items. "Why not return the charcoals and replace them for new?"

The thought had never occurred to her—would never have occurred to her. Evelyn scrunched up her nose as she started walking toward the direction she was sure led home. The sooner she divested herself of these parcels, and the worryingly powerful presence of Richard, the better. Perhaps it best she hide her face slightly behind the parcels, even if her arms were hardly as full as they had been before.

"Why would I?" she replied as Richard fell in step beside her. "It is hardly the shop's fault that I did not consider my ability to transport my purchases home. Why should they carry the financial burden, merely because I was unprepared?"

Apparently, she had said something most odd. At least, he was staring while squinting, his head slightly tilted.

"What have I said?"

"It's just… Well, you're a lady."

"Well spotted," said Evelyn with a grin as they turned a corner.

Color splattered across Richard's cheeks. "No, I meant—well, a highborn lady. Nobility. Yet you think of the people in that art shop and worry about their livelihoods."

"Oh, not too much," she said breezily, trying to dampen down the jubilation his words had provoked. "I purchase so much from them, I sometimes wonder whether I am the sole customer for that shop. Even so, I believe I still purchase enough pencils from them to send their children to some very good schools."

And he laughed, and all of a sudden, the day was wonderful and joyous, and not a tedious day in which she could not continue her sketching because she did not have sufficient pencils.

"I can see—well, feel, that you have purchased more than pencils," Richard said.

"Yes, I always intend to go there for one thing and return home with a great amount more," said Evelyn ruefully. "Perhaps I should have considered that today before leaving home."

"You mentioned your lady's maid, but you should have also taken a manservant with you on your shopping expedition, Lady Evelyn."

Lady Evelyn. Her smile faltered at the formality—but then, Lady Romeril walked by them, a woman and manservant on her heels, the affluent lady's nose in the air and her eyes quite clearly gawping at the two of them.

Evelyn's breath caught as she tried—likely in vain at this point—to hide further behind the parcels in her arms.

"My lady!"

The tightness in Evelyn's chest loosened at once. Both she and Richard stopped, turning to see the small maid bobbing after them, the rest of Evelyn's parcels tipping in the woman's arms.

Behind the servant, Lady Romeril's widened eyes softened, her head nodding, as if taking note of the presence of a chaperone, before heading back on her way.

Evelyn let out a deep breath. The corner of Richard's mouth quirked upward. *Really. If he wanted to preserve proper boundaries between us, he ought not to have spoken my real name at all. I had been quite adeptly hiding behind parcels before then, if I do say so myself.*

"My lady, this is the longer route home," said Laurent, her dark eye peeking over the parcels at Richard standing beside her mistress. Her eyebrow arched.

Evelyn cleared her throat, speaking softly, though Lady Romeril had turned a corner and was now out of sight. "Richard, this is Laurent, my sister's and my lady's maid. Laurent, Richard."

"Charmed," Laurent said in her thick accent. Richard blinked rapidly, his jaw tensing as he swallowed.

But then the smile was back.

"The errant lady's maid," he said after a moment.

"The mysterious model, I presume?"

Evelyn winced. Laurent knew full well everyone who knew about the modeling supposed Laurent was chaperoning the two of them in the studio. She was *supposed* to know the man already.

Richard turned back in the opposite direction, not answering the question. His gaze fell to the stack of parcels in Laurent's arms. "I was just telling Lady Evelyn that she ought to have brought a manservant with her."

Evelyn thrust her shoulders back as she stepped beside Richard, no longer hiding with her maid in their presence. "Oh, I don't like to bother them. Laurent is usually enough. Usually."

"'Bother' them?" Richard chuckled. "Did it ever occur to you that you are bothering me?"

"You *volunteered!*" Evelyn's flush was most definitely out of control and it did not appear possible for her to prevent even her ears from burning.

Only then did she look over at her walking companion to see the merriment on his face. The delight. The—the teasing.

The flush faded, though her pulse quickened. "You are teasing me."

"I am, I'm afraid, Lady Evelyn," Richard said quietly as they passed a crowd of people around a newspaper seller. "It is quite a liberty, I know, but as you enjoyed the last liberty I took so much..."

His voice trailed away, a full description unnecessary. Evelyn knew precisely what he meant.

Swallowing, she tried to put the memory of the kiss firmly out of her mind, but it was impossible. The giddiness she had felt, not only from the sudden movement, but the sensation of his warmth. The power he'd exuded, and the gentleness with which he had kissed her.

Oh, what a kiss. Evelyn had found it most difficult not to think of that moment ever since it had occurred.

Does he think of it, too?

"I... I hope I am not keeping you from your work," Evelyn said in a firm voice. That was it, a calm, neutral subject. "Where is it you work?"

Richard's eyes glittered. "I thought you did not want to know anything about me? Keep me a blank canvas?"

He was right. That was what she had intended, and it had made perfect sense at the beginning. How else would she be able to treat him as a model? How else would he later sit as Romeo, or Julius Caesar, or Henry VIII, unless she could look past the shell of him and see only the character?

At least, that had been her plan. It was only now that Evelyn was starting to realize, as they turned onto the street of her home, that knowing almost nothing about this man with whom she was spending an inordinate amount of time, was both exciting and... disappointing.

Exciting, because he could have been anyone. Anything. Perhaps he was a duke on the run! Perhaps he was so poor, he could not read or write. Perhaps he was a widower. Perhaps he was an innocent.

Well, probably not the latter. Innocent men did not kiss like that.

"I... I am curious," Evelyn admitted as they reached her home.

Richard's gaze was a curious one in and of itself. It raked over her, as though attempting to decide what to tell her based on how he thought she would react.

Was he a criminal, then? On the run from the law?

Or, Evelyn reminded herself, *is my imagination getting the better of me?*

Those scars, though...

"*Vite, vite*, my lady. Let us go inside. I cannot hold these much longer."

With his free hand, Richard opened the gate, and Laurent was the first one through, heading straight for the back of the house— but not before sending another pointed arch of the brow Evelyn's way.

"I did not have anything in particular to do today," Richard said with a shrug that clearly stated he was not going to reveal anything else to her. "So—the studio?"

She had not left it in a very tidy state. That was what happened when Evelyn found herself exploding in creativity, ideas pouring from her faster than she could get them down. Tidiness was typically left by the wayside.

She nodded and brushed past him. He practically skipped in place before turning to shut the gate.

"Please excuse the mess," Evelyn said awkwardly a few moments later as Richard managed to open the door to the studio with his one free hand and gestured for her to enter. Laurent had haphazardly stacked her parcels beside the door.

He grinned as they went inside. "Why are you apologizing to me? It's your mess, in your studio. Why would you excuse that?"

It was an excellent question. She just always had. "My mother is a very exact person."

Richard's face clouded. "Ah. I see."

No, he didn't. *Blast.* Evelyn always explained her mother poorly. "No, I mean—oh, here, if you do not mind." They placed the plethora of parcels on a small table just to the left of the door, and she stretched her aching arms before continuing as Richard fetched the rest of the things by the door. "I mean, my mother is very exact because she is a mathematician. She likes order, routine—that sort of thing."

He was grinning now as he placed the last of the packages on the table. "I don't suppose that can be very easy. An artistic daughter with a mathematician mother."

"Actually, you might be surprised," said Evelyn, a thrill of boldness soaring through her. "There is a great deal of mathematics within art. Think about perspective, I mean. The order of magnitude that you would wish to diminish an object is in direct proportion to—"

"Hang on, you've lost me here. Not all of us are artists—or mathematicians," said Richard with a laugh, dropping into what Evelyn had long ago considered *his* chair in the center of the room. "Do you not have an example you can show me?"

She had taken three steps over to the cupboard within which she kept her artwork before Evelyn stopped herself.

Goodness, that was close. She had never shown anyone her artwork, not her true creations. Oh, her sketches, her studies, yes. But her paintings?

A lump lodged in her throat as she turned slowly on her feet and saw Richard's expectant eyes, his relaxed and encouraging face.

"I…" *Why are words such a challenge?* "I…"

Richard threw an arm back behind him in a lazy manner that

made him look all the more handsome. Which was most distracting at the best of times. "Why don't you want me to see your artwork, Evelyn?"

Evelyn swallowed. Whatever Richard was, whoever he was out there, they were equals in here. No titles, no surnames, no knowledge of each other beyond the cursory.

But that would all change if she shared her artwork. It was… private.

"I have never shown anyone my artwork before," she said quietly.

Richard's eyebrows rose. "No one? Not even an art tutor, or your parents, your sister?"

Evelyn shook her head. "It's… It's a part of me."

It hurt to admit it, as though admitting to a weakness, or a sin, or a crime. But it was true. To reveal her artwork was akin to stepping out of her gown in the middle of a ball: it was unthinkable.

Once the world had seen her, it could never unsee her. She could never be hidden again.

"I am not here to judge you, Evelyn," Richard said quietly. "I just want to understand this… this perspective, dimensions, mathematical thing."

For some reason, her lungs were tightening. Evelyn did not know why, and a panic, a childlike panic that she had not felt in years was rising through her lungs.

"But if you don't want to show me, don't."

Evelyn blinked. "I… I beg your pardon?"

Richard's smile was far too knowing. "You heard me. I have no wish to force you, Evelyn. God knows I appreciate what it is to be hidden. If you want to show me, that's different. I would rather it were a gift than something demanded."

And she stared.

No one had ever said anything like that to her before. Never. Her brother had wheedled and her father had begged and her mother had once offered to play her at chess for the right to see her artwork. Lucy had asked once, been told *no*, and calmly wandered off.

But this?

Hand slightly shaking and pulse roaring in her ears, Evelyn opened the cupboard.

She knew precisely which piece of art she would choose. There was one particular landscape of Venice that would be perfect for explaining the diminishing size of buildings… There. There it was.

Holding her head high, feet only shaking the smallest amount, knowing that there was no going back from this, Evelyn tried to smile. "Look at this."

Richard had arisen from his chair—when, she did not know—and now strode over to her. There was such power and confidence in his air. How had she never noticed? Like a gentleman. Like a baronet, a man with a title and a place in the world.

He took the proffered painting.

Evelyn stared at it upside down. It was not, perhaps, her best work, but it exemplified the artistic principle well, and she had greatly relished painting it—which, she was starting to realize, was half the challenge in and of itself.

And Venice was a wonderful study. The water, the curving canals, the golden buildings, the way light moved and the people congregated around the edges…

"Was this painted from life?"

"'Life'?"

"Did you go to Venice, paint it there?" was his quiet question, his eyes not leaving the canvas.

Evelyn laughed awkwardly. "No! No, my papa would never consider going to Venice for such a thing. No Grand Tour for us. I have never traveled, despite desperately wishing to do so."

"But you painted this?" Richard asked quietly.

Evelyn's heart twisted. *Ah. It is not very good, then.* That was the trouble with being a lady artist, she wanted to shout from the rooftops. It is so much easier for men! They have more tutoring, more classes, more opportunities to travel, to exhibit.

"I know it is not that impressive," she said hastily, reaching out a hand to take it back. "But as you can see, the perspective shifts along here demonstrate—"

"It's not that impressive," said Richard quietly, holding on to the painting firmly.

Evelyn had not intended for her fingers to brush past his own, she told herself, and that was surely why her stomach had turned over. Not because Richard, of all people, had confirmed what she had hoped never to hear: that her painting was bad.

"Yes, I know," she said dully.

"'It's not that impressive'?" repeated Richard, his voice rising a little. "It's *very* impressive. How did you get the light to look as though it is illuminated within the painting?"

Evelyn stared. "I… I beg your pardon?"

Her studio was spinning. That wasn't right. It was a building. Buildings weren't supposed to spin.

"And the perspective is truly amazing," he continued, his eyes focused not on her, but on the painting. "I feel as though I could step into this painting and walk along here—and here. You are gifted, Evelyn."

"No, I'm not," she said instinctively, her stomach now not so much lurching as tying itself into a knot that would never be undone.

"I have seen a great amount of art in my time," Richard said quietly, finally meeting her eyes. "Good art, too. Yours ranks among that level. Evelyn, you are truly gifted."

It's your ego being stroked. That's why you like standing here, so close to him, Evelyn tried to tell herself. *Your pride is being massaged and that is why such happiness is clouding your judgment.*

Oh, such happiness.

"You flatter me," she whispered.

"I hope so," Richard said with a laugh, "because you richly deserve it. Why have you never exhibited?"

"'Exhibited'?"

It had never been an option for her. Why would it? Evelyn knew her limitations, and they were numerous. The very idea of showing anyone her artwork before she had mastered the human form… It was unthinkable. Besides, her father had been most clear. No daughter of his would ever do something so scandalous as exhibit.

"I would greatly love to have one of these on my walls, at any rate," Richard was saying, his focus flickering to the cupboard behind her. "How many of these have you? Of this quality, I mean?"

Evelyn swallowed. *Lots*, she wanted to say. *Lots, and far better quality, indeed.*

Only then did something he had said nudge the back of her mind. "What do you mean, have one of my paintings on your walls? Do you own much art?"

It was a strange thing for him to have said. Though Evelyn was not intimately acquainted with the working classes, it had always been her impression that it was nobility who could afford to have art on the walls.

For some reason, Richard would not meet her eye. "I meant figuratively, Evelyn. Do… Do you think I am the sort of man who owns Gainsboroughs?"

Her cheeks burned. "N-No. No, of course not."

And that was the real shame, wasn't it? Evelyn liked him—liked him far too much. If they had met at a ball, or a card game, or at one of her family's picnics… Well, perhaps they would not have talked and she would not have felt close to him. But perhaps she would.

As it was, Richard was no doubt untitled, out of her social class, and in a way, her servant. She was paying him, after all.

Paying him.

"Oh, goodness, I have used up your time most selfishly," Evelyn said, hastily returning to the table where her purchases lay. "Where is my reticule? I must pay you for your time."

"Evelyn."

"No, it is unfair of me to—"

"Evelyn," Richard said softly, and he was behind her, taking her hand.

His hand, clasping hers. It was a liberty, most certainly, but one she was reveling in.

"You don't have to pay me for all our time together," he said quietly.

Perhaps that is part of the attraction, Evelyn thought wildly as she looked up at the man with whom she most certainly should not have been falling in love. He was wrong for her—probably entirely out of her social class and with nothing to offer her.

It was intoxicating.

Chapter Eight

May 23, 1840

Try as he might, struggle as he would, Richard could no longer fight it off.

He yawned.

"I saw that."

"No you didn't," he said hastily, trying not to smile. He could still recall the pained look on the young woman's face when he had moved last time. Apparently, he had ruined her finger study. Why shifting his shoulder had done that, he did not know. "You did not see anything because nothing happened."

When he looked up, it was to see Evelyn rolling her eyes. "You do know that I am watching you very carefully, don't you, Richard?"

A shiver of something Richard was not, most definitely not, going to investigate flickered across his shoulder blades. His shirt, along with his waistcoat and coat, lay beside him on a stool. He was nude from the waist up once again. Once again, he had instructed Evelyn to close her eyes as he'd disrobed. It was perhaps the only time she had not been staring.

Yes, he knew Lady Evelyn Chance was often watching him very closely. Part of that was because she was an artist. There was no denying it; the woman somehow had the ability to look around the world and see beauty, even where there was none. The way she captured that inelegance or awfulness on a page was truly transformational. He did not know how she did it.

But it was more than that... wasn't it?

Everything had changed with that kiss. Richard was certain he should not have done it, and perhaps if it had been with a different woman, the memories would not have lingered as they had.

And oh, they had. Every waking moment, and almost all of his unwaking ones, there was the image of Evelyn, shocked and wide-eyed in his arms, lips pink from his kisses, staring up at him.

He could still taste her. Still see the desire in her eyes...

Unconsciously, Richard crossed his legs.

"Blast it all too—"

"Evelyn?"

"I mean, bother."

Richard stifled a laugh even as he hastily rearranged his legs to their previous position. "Now that's something I haven't heard you say before."

"I know." Evelyn's pink face appeared from the other side of the canvas. "I am usually very good at keeping words like that on the inside, but it's difficult when you are being so disobliging."

And that is the trouble with Evelyn, Richard thought as heat crackled through his chest. *She's a complete mess of contradictions.*

An earl's daughter who would rather spend her pin money on charcoal sticks than earbobs.

A beautiful woman who had a smudge of paint across one cheek that she evidently had not noticed.

A refined young lady who said "blast" with the vehemence of a sacrilegious curse. Who seemed to think almost nothing of sitting with him alone, without a chaperone.

An innocent who looked at him sometimes like that...

Richard endeavored to keep his head high, but it was a challenge. Sitting for Evelyn had been something to entertain him, an opportunity to do something a bit different. If he was only going to sit around all day, why not do it with someone else?

That someone else he had presumed would have been a

gentleman…

Oh, no. Here it comes again.

This time, the yawn was so violent, Richard could do nothing to hide it.

"You're yawning!"

"Not on purpose," he said hastily. "Though I challenge you to keep your mouth shut when you're yawning!"

There was silence on the other side of the easel for a moment, then the strange gulp and clatter of a paintbrush being dropped unceremoniously back into its water pot.

Odd. A month ago, he would never have been able to pick out that particular sound.

"I have been most selfish," said Evelyn, stepping out from the easel and looking sheepish. "I have been so absorbed by my work, I have not noticed the time."

"'Time'?"

She pulled out what appeared to be a gentleman's pocket watch from her apron. "Yes, it's past eleven o'clock."

Richard stared. *It can't be.* He had arrived here just past six in the evening for a short session. Evelyn had said the day before that another hour would do it. The study was almost completed and she was eager to get it done…

He could not have sat here for five hours. Where did her parents think she was?

In her studio, perhaps. Though certainly not alone with a man.

Despite Walden's warnings, Richard found the Chances most trusting, indeed.

"Yes, I did not notice the time going, either," said Evelyn conversationally, shaking the pocket watch by her ear carefully as though ensuring that it was still running. "Percy usually winds this up pretty well, so I would hope it is still running to time."

"Your brother winds your watch for you?"

It was a banal thing to say, but Richard could not help it. He was desperate, craving any information about this woman that she would spill. Even the inconsequential was fascinating.

That was perhaps the most challenging thing about this posing business.

Oh, sitting around and doing nothing, that was hardly a hardship.

No, it was being seated opposite a woman he could not fathom. A woman who seemed to have almost no interest in him as a person yet had asked a few leading questions that suggested to Richard's mind that she may have been regretting her decision to leave him as 'a blank slate.'

"My brother winds his own watch for himself, then I borrow it," Evelyn said vaguely, tapping at the glass of the timepiece. "He never usually notices. He's not one for being on time, anyway."

Richard stifled a smile. "So you've stolen it."

"*Borrowed* it," Evelyn corrected, glancing up with a wry smile. "I always put it back. When it needs winding."

He could not help but laugh at that, and she laughed with him. *God, this is intimate.*

Richard had never known anything like it. A month ago, he would have said intimacy was what happened when two people took their clothes off together. Granted, one of them *was* partly naked, but it was not the one of the two of them he would have preferred to have been that way. He could never have imagined something like this: a closeness that was still growing, learning, developing. A need to be together. A heat he only felt when he was with *her*.

Steady on, he told himself sternly, reining back on his internal nonsense. *She knows almost nothing about you. You hardly know her. It's a dream you're attracted to, the idea of her.*

Well. And certain parts of her he could see.

Quick, think of something else. The pocket watch. "My father always—"

Oh, damnation. That is the trouble with trying to make sure your thoughts don't meander off into a foolish direction, Richard thought bitterly. *It leaves one's mouth totally unattended.*

Evelyn had looked up from her stolen—sorry, *borrowed*—pocket watch. "Your father?"

Richard hesitated. He had never... There never had been anyone to talk to about his father. Walden may have listened, but Richard could never have brought himself to speak of the man. He had grown so out of the habit of it, he wasn't sure he knew how to do it.

"You miss him," she said softly.

"How do you know that?"

"Your eyes. They were full of sadness—but a warm sadness, not a cold one," Evelyn said, her voice low and tentative. "Two people who have left on bad terms cannot look like that when remembering the other."

Richard's jaw dropped. "How... How did you...?"

"Artist, remember?" Her smile was wry as she shrugged. "I look at people, really look at them. I notice things. It's the same look my father has about his own father. There was love there, as well as difficulty. But the love is what has remained."

It was astonishing. He had never wanted to speak of his father. His mother had buried herself in her grief and when she had emerged, she had never wished to speak her husband's name again. And Richard... Well. He had been the new viscount. Viscounts were not supposed to dwell on the loss of a father he could not help but mourn.

"Tell me about him," said Evelyn softly. "Unless... Unless you have to leave?"

"No," Richard said quickly.

Too quickly. He shifted in his seat and wondered what on earth this woman was doing to him.

It shouldn't have been possible, should it, to draw such things out of him against his wishes? After all, he hadn't really said anything about his father, yet Evelyn seemed to know so much about him, about the two of them.

She was bewitching. He was bewitched.

"So, tell me about him," came her gentle voice. There was

movement behind the easel.

Was she putting down the study she had been working on and picking up a new piece of paper?

"'Him'?"

"Your father." There was just a hint of mirth in her tone—not merriment at him, but rather, around him. It was most peculiar.

Richard heaved a breath. *Right.* He could do this. *How hard could it be?*

"My father was… I mean, he died a long time ago. I was a child, not even ten years old."

"You were very young."

"I was." Richard tried to think back to that moment, that terrible morning when his mother had sat him down, her eyes red and her voice hoarse, to tell him the news. "I did not believe it in a way because he had been so… so full of life. Do you know what I mean?"

"I think so." Evelyn's face did not appear from the other side of the easel, and in a way, that made it easier.

"He always had something interesting on his mind. A topic of conversation that would never have occurred to me that filled our days with vibrant discourse," said Richard, a smile slipping across his lips, despite himself. "Politics, often, but also religion, or geography, or literature. He encouraged me to read books far advanced for my age."

"And you managed it."

"I look back and wonder whether we should challenge our children more," Richard mused.

Evelyn's flushed cheeks appeared. "'Our children'?"

Oh, hell. "The children of—of this generation," Richard amended hastily.

Her eyes met his gaze, just for a moment, then she disappeared again. "You are like him, I suppose."

"I suppose." In truth, Richard had never thought about it. He had never known his father beyond the impression of a child. Sometimes he could not recall his face, not without the family portraits. "I hope I am. He was a kind man. A good man. He was much mourned and sometimes I wish—"

His voice gave out and he took a moment to collect himself. He would master himself. He would not give in to weakness.

"The pocket watch reminded you of him."

Richard smiled wistfully. She did have a knack of making statements that drew truth out of him. Questions would have felt like an interrogation—and he'd had enough of them to last a lifetime.

"His pocket watch was very precious to him," he said aloud. "It was far too heavy for a child, too bulky, too weighty. It was put away and I only found it again this year. Whenever I look at it, I don't see him. I see the man I think he would have wanted me to be, and I wonder… I wonder if I am that man."

Silence fell between them, but it was a contented one. One Richard had not known since he had returned from France.

"Thank you." Her voice was soft, and genial, and Richard wanted to sink into it. He never wanted the evening to end.

"I suppose the evening has to come to an end," Evelyn said.

Was there a sadness in her voice? Perhaps Richard was only wishing to hear it. The idea of stepping out into the cool, night air, without this woman who had the ability to look not only at his skin, but into his soul and draw it on the page, was most unpleasant.

"I can stay."

What had possessed him to say such a thing?

Clearly, Evelyn had not been expecting such a statement, either. Her brows rose, her lips parting silently.

"If you want me to," Richard added hastily, hating how uncertain he sounded. "If you want to draw me again. One more drawing."

"Are you sure?"

You think I can deny you anything? Those were the words that almost fell from his lips.

Fortunately, he was able to keep most of his dignity and

prevent the words from being spoken. Still. If Richard did not know any better, he would have said Evelyn could hear the unspoken words, anyway.

Her smile was far too knowing. "I would prefer a different view of you. To challenge me, you see."

Richard stiffened. "A different view."

Lord, right at this moment, he could not have taken his trousers off. There was a… Well. An obvious indication of his attraction to the beautiful, young artist.

Try as he might, Richard was not going to solve that in a matter of moments.

"Yes, I think… I think I would like you to turn the chair around by ninety degrees," mused Evelyn, tilting her head to one side as she examined him.

Now it was not discomfort, but panic roaring through his veins. "'Turn'?"

"Yes, to face the window," she said quietly. "Is that suitable?"

Richard swallowed.

Suitable? Perhaps it would have been, for anyone else. But there was a reason that he had required Evelyn to close her eyes each time his shirt had been removed. Even that simple movement would swiftly reveal…

And if he turned like that, his right-hand side to her, she would see…

"You know I will never ask you to do something that you don't want to do," said Evelyn, with a subtle yet fiery look in her eye.

Richard gave a laugh. It was a reminder, as if he had needed one, of the way he had spoken to her mere days ago. God, this woman could tie him in knots without so much as a word—and when she spoke…

Well, it would be foolish to think that he could avoid this forever. He would just have to avoid all her questions, that was all. If worse to the worst, he would simply have to lie.

"Right," he said tautly.

Evelyn had disappeared behind her easel, the light of the single candle behind between them shimmering in the sudden rush of air, and so Richard hoped for a moment that she would coincidentally not be looking at him as he picked up the chair and moved it.

It was not heavy, the movement done within a moment, but of course, that was all it took. When Richard straightened, it was to see Evelyn peering out from behind the canvas, her breath hitching and her eyes wide in horror.

Ah. Yes, it often took people that way.

"Richard," she murmured.

"What?" he snapped before he could stop himself.

This had been a mistake. He should never have—the shirt should always have stayed on. He should have stood his ground, made it clear to her that he wouldn't do it.

"It's nothing," he said stoically, ignoring as best he could the way her attention followed him as he settled back into the chair, this time not looking directly at her.

"It's not nothing. It's… Richard, where on earth did you get all those scars? Not the burns, I mean, the… from a *blade?*"

The odd thing was, Richard himself hardly ever saw them. Oh, Doctor Walsingham had made him take a look at them once or twice, when he had returned to England and finally given in and sought medical attention. The looking glass had made them look garbled, distorted as they were over the top of his burns, and he hadn't liked to look since.

In his memory, the lines in his flesh were still raw.

"I've lived a busy life," he said quietly.

There it was—the scrape of charcoal across canvas. She was drawing him, then. Good. That would hopefully cease all her discussion of it.

"It looks as though you were bound."

Richard swallowed, his mouth now dry. Damn her and her observance. Damn her and the way she could look and truly see. Damn the way his heart was fluttering.

Hearts didn't flutter. They pounded.

Oh, hell, now it is pounding.

"You don't have to tell me about it, if you don't—"

"I don't," Richard said shortly, forcing his mind away from the thin, straight scars, the mottled burns.

Was that smoke? Could he smell smoke?

No, man, get a grip on yourself. That was always the trouble, whenever he started thinking about his time in France again. It was all too easy to get lost in the memories, the fear, the nightmares, lose sight of what had actually happened.

The trouble was, not telling Evelyn the truth now felt far more like lying than anything had before. An omission, that was hardly a lie. No one could be expected to tell everyone everything.

But she was asking now, and she could probably gain an accurate idea of what had happened just by looking at him. Richard sometimes felt the rough edges of the scars when he put on a shirt. He couldn't ignore them, even if he couldn't see them.

And now Evelyn could see them.

"I suppose you once worked at some docks. Fires often happen at docks."

"I've spent time in docks." Well, it wasn't a lie.

"It's a hard life, working with your hands."

And your wits, and your bravery, and nothing else. "I've always managed to make my way through the world."

And she looked at him with such curiosity, as though she had never met a working man in all her life. Perhaps she hadn't, Richard realized with a strange twist in his gut. Other than her own servants and the shopkeepers, the only men she would have interacted with were gentlemen. *To her, you are a strange, exotic butterfly.*

A man who works with his hands.

Though, technically, he was a gentleman, much like the rest of them, he supposed.

"You have traveled, of course."

"My... My work has taken me to new places, yes," said Richard quietly, shifting slightly. It wasn't lying. It wasn't the truth, but it wasn't a lie—everything he was telling her was true.

Evelyn's eyes sparkled. "It's rather intoxicating, isn't it? Not knowing anything about each other."

Quite to the contrary, Richard wanted to say. *I know something about you. I can see you. You've shown yourself to me, and every part of you is precious. It is I who remains unknown, and that always felt safer, until... until now.*

"You were brave."

"You can't possibly know that," Richard muttered, not looking around.

The gentle soar of the charcoal on the canvas. A pause. Another smooth marking made. "You survived. It would take a brave man to do that."

Richard tried his best not to preen. *This is not a chance to gain her pity, man! Or her approbation. Just sit there and wait until all this is over.*

"Was the pain truly great?"

"It was agony," Richard said before he could stop himself. He glanced over, but the easel still hid the artist entirely. Somehow, that made it easier to talk. "I... I thought I was going to die. At times, I wished I had. You're right. I was bound, and thrashed with a—" *Hang fire, man, she doesn't need to know that.* "I was left for dead and there were times, as I waited for the flames, that I wished I had done so."

Had he ever said those words before? Had he ever revealed to anyone what he had seen, what he had experienced?

"But you lived."

Her voice was gentle and encouraging, and Richard found himself unfolding to her as he had done to no other.

"I had too much living left in me," he said with a laugh. "When I managed to leave France—"

"So it was while serving in France, then?"

Richard whipped his head around. Evelyn was peeking out

from around the easel with a knowing smile on her face. "How did you...? What did I say to...?"

"Oh, there are only so many places that a man of England goes to get beaten like that," she said airily, returning to her drawing as if she regularly discussed the maiming of a gentleman. "And I thought I noted your face paling at the sound of Laurent's accent when I introduced the two of you." *Damn.* He hadn't meant for either woman to notice. "Thank you. For serving your country, I mean. Being a soldier. You have paid a very great price."

She met his eyes and Richard felt the weight like a boot kicked into his stomach.

She... She meant it. Evelyn looked at him and saw not a man who had failed, who had been punished by fate for failing, punishment eked out on his very body... but a man who had tried. Sometimes trying was the most important part.

The moment of connection passed. It had been heady, and delicious, and Richard could not permit it to continue.

He could not permit this to continue. He had to tell her—tell her who he was, his name, that he was perhaps not a man on her father's level, but a man worthy of her.

Dear God—'a man worthy of her'? Where had that come from?

"There."

Richard blinked. "There... What?"

"There, I have finished," Evelyn said briskly, wiping her hands on a damp cloth as she surveyed her work. "Do you want to see it?"

Absolutely not, Richard wanted to say. He'd had enough trouble avoiding the real thing, studiously ignoring the edges of his whipping scars as they crept around his side. So it was therefore completely inexplicable that he had risen from the chair and walked toward her.

Evelyn blushed, as he had known she would. Part of him hoped that it was because she felt the intoxication of his male presence, that having a tall and shirtless gentleman walking toward her was having some sort of effect on her.

It was probably only because he was about to see some of her art.

Richard steeled himself for seeing the disgusting evidence of his weakness and saw instead...

"Oh, Evelyn."

Somehow she had transformed all his pain, all that suffering, into something truly beautiful. Clean lines and rugged shading created a picture of... himself. But not himself. A Viscount Sempill who looked proud and yet rightly so. Who held himself with a straight back, despite the scars. Whose marks in fact made him a far more interesting specimen to behold than most.

Richard swallowed hard. *Oh.*

"I shall have to have another go," Evelyn was saying from a long way away. "I haven't quite got the nape of your neck right, and the shading is a mite rudimentary, but—"

"Thank you."

He had not intended to say it. He had not intended to say anything. The scrape of his voice belied the pain and yet it was not the sharp, self-loathing pain of a man who could not bear to face the man he had become.

It was a different sharpness. The breath of new life.

Evelyn was smiling and she touched his arm gently. "You can keep it, if you want."

'Keep it'?

And the logical conclusion of that rushed through Richard's mind and he recoiled. Keep it—keep even more tangible evidence of what had happened? Be forced to look at it, the poor, misshapen, cruelly altered skin he bore?

"No," he said curtly, stepping away from Evelyn and pulling on shirt and waistcoat in quick succession. "I should go."

"Richard, I—"

"I do not wish to speak of it," Richard added as he strode to the door, hating his bluntness, hating that he could not face himself for more than a moment. He stopped, glancing over his shoulder with what he hoped was a smile. "I will see you tomorrow, or the day after."

The expression on Evelyn's face was entirely unreadable—but then, he did not have her skill. "Very well. Until then."

Chapter Nine

May 26, 1840

"**H**IGHER."

"This is as high as I—"

"I *said*, higher," Evelyn instructed as sweetly as she could manage. Which was a challenge, when shouting across Green Park. "Just for a few minutes longer, please, Leopold!"

It wasn't pleading. It wasn't begging. Her tone was somewhere in between, and she hated it, but there it was. When one asked for a favor such as this, one had to prostrate oneself occasionally.

Her cousin, Lord Leopold Chance, grimaced. He was a broad man with the look of a spaniel when confused, which he clearly was in this moment. "When I said that I would assist you, Evelyn, this is not what I had in mind!"

"And yet you look so fetching!" she said with a smile as her gaze darted between the leather pleats of his skirt and the representation she was attempting with watercolors. "Honestly, I don't imagine you'll have any trouble attracting a lady now."

"*Evelyn!*"

"Well, I am sure this will be the latest in gentlemen's fashions in a few years," she said vaguely, her attention meandering from his words to the way the sunlight caused shadows just under his knees. "Don't you think?"

"You think the gentry and nobility will be dressed as ancient

Greeks next Season?"

Evelyn did not reply. She couldn't—not only because she was concentrating very closely on the knees she was now painting, but because she had placed one of her other paintbrushes in her mouth. Her teeth gripped the long handle as she narrowed her eyes.

It had been a wonderful idea of her Aunt Alice, and once the suggestion had been made, Evelyn would brook no arguments. Her cousin Leopold had been volunteered to be her model for the painting, and it had not been too difficult to find a theater who had been willing to let one of their costumes go for an extortionate fee.

That reminded her. She really would have to ask her father for an extension on her allowance for the month after next now. She was in debt to Lucy up to her eyeballs, and Percy would soon wonder why the ten-pound note that he had once had in his wallet had somehow transformed into an I.O.U.

She'd signed it. At least. She wasn't like Percy, lying about a mistress, sneaking about the place, worrying their mother half to death—

"Evelyn, I'm freezing!"

"Nonsense," she said vaguely, tilting her head as she examined the knee she had just completed before glancing up at her real-life model. "I said, keep that bow up!"

"You honestly cannot think I can hold a bow and arrow up like this for hours at a time, do you?" Even as his teeth chattered, Leopold's pinched face took on a sour expression. Evelyn could not think why. "Evelyn, it's agony on my arms!"

"But I've just about finished your knees, and they are almost perfect!" she said excitedly.

For some reason, the narrowed-eyed look on her cousin's face was mutinous. "Do you mean to tell me that for the last hour, I have been burning my arms to hold up my bow and arrow, and you haven't even been painting them? You're painting my *knees*?"

Evelyn smiled weakly. *Well, when he puts it like that...* "You would be amazed at the difference having one's arms up makes in the shadows that fall down one's body, the tension in one's legs..."

Leopold's lips became a thin line. He did not look impressed. "Look, Evelyn—"

She groaned. "I know this speech. Every one of my models has given it to me!"

All but one.

She did not say that latter part aloud. How could she? Richard was not entirely a secret, but he was hers. She had no wish to share him with the rest of her family—not least of which because then Laurent might crumble under the pressure and admit she had not been chaperoning their sessions. Even if she stood firm and gave Evelyn some cover, the Chances were so nosy, they would be ferreting out every single detail of his life, even the ones he did not want to reveal.

Evelyn considered her formidable aunts and adjusted her thought. *Especially* the details that he did not want to reveal.

It was irritating in the extreme that Leopold was being such a bad sport about this, however. After all, he'd always said he liked archery!

"But you practice with a bow and arrow all the time," Evelyn said aloud. "I thought, well, what is the difference?"

"The difference," said Leopold petulantly, coloring as another group of giggling ladies walked past them, "is that when I'm practicing archery, I'm moving my arms so they don't get stiff. And I'm at home, in private, or at the London Archery Club, without people gawping at me. And I'm wearing normal clothes, Evelyn, not this ridiculous getup!"

Evelyn grinned. He *did* look a mite ridiculous, but only because he was standing before the Temple of Peace in Green Park on a casual Tuesday wearing an approximation of what Philoctetes, the Greek mythological hero, wore, while other people in perfectly normal clothing walked past him, staring curiously.

It was going to look totally natural in her painting. After all, it was a scene from Ancient Greece.

"Unless your father has built a ruined temple in your garden, there was only one place I could paint," she called out.

"You couldn't use your imagination?"

Evelyn scowled. He was not to know just how challenging she found it to create these vistas in her mind. It was far easier to create them in reality than immortalize them on the canvas.

That was why they had to be in Green Park, where the Temple of Peace had adorned the place for generations. Much to her cousin's chagrin.

"Ten more minutes," she said firmly, returning to her canvas.

"Five!"

"This isn't a negotiation, actually," Evelyn said brightly, stifling a laugh. "Besides, you know what your mother will do to you if you wander off before I'm finished. You are supposed to be my chaperone as well as model today."

There was a loud snort from the other side of the easel, and Evelyn clamped her lips together. Aunt Alice was formidable. Kind, yes. Gentle, if she wished to be. But not to be crossed.

"You do know it's ridiculous that you're doing this, don't you?" her cousin said conversationally.

"You do know it's ridiculous that you love archery so much that you agreed to be immortalized as Philoctetes, don't you?" she quipped back.

Leopold's laugh was, this time, more good natured. "I suppose so."

Approximately three minutes later, by Evelyn's reckoning, there came a plaintive complaint. "Are you finished yet?"

"I'll tell you when I'm finished," Evelyn muttered.

"What did you say?"

"I *said*, I'll tell you when I'm finished!"

Honestly, I never have this trouble with Richard!

The thought warmed her, burning her cheeks as she attempted-ed to convey the sense of Greek sandals on the painted version of her cousin. Richard was, of course, the perfect model. He never disagreed with her for long, was perfectly happy to sit and not move for hours at a time, and was…

Well. Delicious. Handsome. Brave. Mysterious. Dark and dangerous.

Evelyn shook her head slightly to see whether that would dislodge the ridiculous thoughts. Unfortunately, it did not.

She had been forced to put off Richard today. The light was simply perfect outside and Leopold had said Tuesday would work for him. The note she had sent around had not received a reply.

Evelyn bit her lip. It was still entirely unclear to her whether Richard had to work for a living or not, and she had, rightly or wrongly, stood by her decision from their very first encounter to never ask any personal questions. Had she deprived him, today, of some much-needed income? Was he angry about that?

"You know, we Chance cousins are supposed to be beyond reproach," came Leopold's voice.

"I suppose my brother is no longer a Chance cousin, then?" Evelyn had not meant to say it. She often thought her bitterness toward her brother had finally melted away from her, but then it slipped out.

"I beg your pardon?"

Evelyn grinned brightly as she glanced at him around the corner of her easel. "And your point is?"

"I suppose my point is that we're probably not supposed to stand in Green Park in such a ridiculous getup," Leopold said with a mock sigh. "I suppose I shall have to read about this in the scandal sheets."

The thought had not occurred to her. "Perhaps."

"Beyond reproach will have to be our watchwords tomorrow. I suppose the parents will be expecting us to find potential spouses and marry soon—make up for lost time."

Evelyn snorted a laugh. "What, like Thomas and Lilianna? They weren't beyond reproach." In fact, both had set Society's tongues wagging during their courtships.

"I suppose neither are we, me with my archery and you with your painting," shot back Leopold. "So we'll have to—hullo there. May I help you?"

Evelyn blinked. It was not like Leopold to speak to a stranger, especially when he was dressed as if Hercules had gotten lost on his way back to Olympus. Placing her second paintbrush back in her mouth, she glanced around the easel with a vague sense of curiosity.

The vague sense of curiosity solidified in an instant. Richard was standing right beside her cousin—his face reddening and his lips flattening. He looked furious.

Not Leopold. His eyebrows squished together, his eyes blinking rapidly, evidently bewildered at the fact that a stranger would approach him and apparently be asking some odd questions. But then he was such a good-natured chap, Evelyn thought with a racing heart, it probably had not occurred to him just how unusual it was that his approach to life was so mellow.

But Richard was not, at this moment, a mellow man.

He was saying something to her cousin in an undertone, the words rushing from his lips like water, and when he saw Evelyn looking over at him, he snapped something to Leopold and started marching toward her.

Evelyn took an unconscious step backward. Though there were only about fifteen yards between her model for today and her easel, astonishment rose incredibly swiftly so that she was consumed by it by the time Richard had reached her.

"How dare you?!"

Evelyn blinked. "How… How dare I?"

What on earth had she done? Did he believe it was not appropriate for her to be painting out in public? But no, that could not have been it. Gentlemen did so all the time and even ladies were allowed to practice their vistas; there were some days in the summer when you could not move for easels in this place. Besides, Richard understood the importance of her art.

"I wouldn't have thought it of you," Richard hissed in an

undertone, red blotches in his cheeks. "After all we shared!"

Evelyn's eyes widened, her mind whirling as she attempted to decipher what appeared to be code.

All we shared? Well, there had been that kiss, yes… and their conversations about her art, his father, the way he had bared his back and scars to her…

But what did that all signify when it came to painting *Leopold?*

"I just cannot believe it of you," he spat, clearly furious, although Evelyn could not for the life of him understand why. "I thought we—"

"We what?" she asked. A stray curl escaped a pin and she pushed it back, not letting her eyes leave Richard's. "I don't understand why you're so upset."

He laughed bitterly. "I thought you would say that, but you are no fool, Evelyn!"

"I feel pretty foolish right now," she said helplessly. Why was he so angry? It surely could not have been because she was painting someone else… could it?

"What's going on here?" Leopold had walked over and for some reason, that only appeared to inflame Richard's temper. The man's fists positively shook at his sides.

"*You* keep out of this," Richard snapped.

"*Richard!*" Evelyn gasped.

"Hang on there," said her cousin, raising his hands as though in mock surrender. His eyes darted to Evelyn as if to say he'd caught her intimate use of the man's given name but would not, just now, comment on it. "Look, friend, I am not sure what I have done to elicit your anger—"

"You are no friend of mine," said Richard darkly.

Evelyn looked between the two men, one dressed rather comically as a Greek archer, the other in the plain and simple clothes of last year's fashions.

She had not missed an appointment with Richard, had she? From memory, they had not agreed to meet again at her studio until tomorrow. She had been most clear on that because of today's light. So why did he seem so… so betrayed?

"I cannot believe you and… you and him!" Richard hissed.

Evelyn blinked and put her paintbrush down. "What on earth do you mean?"

"You know *exactly* what I mean!" Richard's voice was low, urgent, as though he had a very important thing to tell her yet could not bring himself to say the words. His eyes kept glancing to Leopold, who was now inexplicably grinning, in a way that denoted a great deal of understanding.

Understanding? But Evelyn had not even been aware that her cousin and Richard knew each other.

Her stomach lurched. The only reason why they would was because Richard moved in the same circles as her family. But that would make him a gentleman at the very least, and perhaps even nobility.

"You like fine, handsome men, then, I see," Richard shot back.

Evelyn gasped as Leopold started to laugh. "Rich—Mr.… Mr. Richard! How can you—what a thing to say! And you can stop laughing, Leopold."

"Oh, why am I not surprised that you speak to him with his first name, too!"

This was all getting entirely ridiculous and Leopold's laughter was not helping.

Evelyn's temper rose. Well, there she had been, having a pleasant day and really working to improve her knees, and now here was Richard shouting about something he did not appear to wish to explain!

And her cousin was still laughing!

"—never thought this of you, Evelyn. I thought you would be different from the other ladies of Society who go for looks alone."

"Richard—sir, I have no idea what you mean," Evelyn said firmly, attempting desperately to get a grip on the situation. "And quit chuckling, Leopold, you know how it annoys me! Aunt Alice shall hear about this, you mark my words!"

"And another thing! I—what did you say?" Apparently, she had said something interesting, for Richard was now staring with wide eyes.

Well, why that had halted his tirade, she did not know. "I said that Leopold's chuckling annoys me. Honestly, it's not that complicated."

"This is going to be good." Leopold smirked inexplicably, rubbing his hands together.

"'Good'?"

"You said something else," Richard said urgently, his cheeks now blazing. "Something about an aunt?"

"Yes, Aunt Alice." *Does he know her? Surely not.* "My aunt, Leopold's mother. He's one of my cousins. And *today*, my chaperone."

For a moment, there was complete and blessed silence—a welcome relief from the barrage of noise to which she had so recently been subjected.

"Ah," said Richard weakly. "Right. I... I see." He looked around. "I suppose you wouldn't be out here in public without a chaperone, would you?"

Evelyn looked between him and Leopold, entirely lost.

"You see, I thought," Richard said slowly, not quite willing to meet her gaze. "A natural assumption, I suppose. When I saw you two together—"

"Quite understandable, old chap," said Leopold calmly, a slow smile on his face.

Evelyn stared. What had he deciphered? Did he suspect the level of intimacy between them? Did he mistake it for something more than it was?

"Easy mistake to make," her cousin was saying.

"It was just... I assumed..." said Richard, his chest hitching.

"I would wish to ensure the respectability of my sister in such a situation," Leopold said solemnly. "Though now that I say that aloud, I'm quite sure Maude wouldn't need a hand. I wouldn't put it past her to defend her own reputation, terrible flirt as she is."

"*Leopold!*" Evelyn said sharply.

Well! This whole situation was most bizarre, but that did not mean he could go about slandering his sister!

"Right," her cousin said hastily. "I suppose this is my cue to exit. It was pleasant meeting you, Mr....?"

"You can call me 'Richard,'" he said gruffly. "I didn't mean— if you need to stay, I would hate to interrupt the artist's flow."

Only then did he meet Evelyn's eyes and there was... embarrassment there as he swallowed noticeably. He *ought* to have been embarrassed for making such a scene.

"Leopold, you cannot leave. I can't be left alone in public with..." She swallowed, glancing at her favorite model.

Leopold took a look around and winked. "It's not so crowded today, I'd say. And any wandering eyes will certainly be drawn to me in this ridiculous getup, not you, upon my exit." He gestured toward his Greek costume and Richard let loose a little chuckle. Leopold's face fell as he looked his cousin in the eye. "Do you need me to stay? I promise I won't tell my mother if I leave early—or yours."

"I suppose... not," Evelyn said weakly. She pulled forward on her bonnet, wondering if the wide brim might shield her identity from any wandering eyes. She was hardly a Lilianna, noted in all the fashionable spots.

"Excellent." Leopold's arched brow vanished as he suppressed a shiver. "Take care of my cousin, Mr. Richard. Now I must away and put on some half-decent clothes."

The two men were shaking hands, Leopold still grinning, Richard not quite meeting the man's eye, and then her cousin was striding through Green Park looking as though he were on the hunt for a hydra.

"Right, well, now he has gone," Evelyn said firmly, dropping her paintbrushes into their water pot and turning to Richard. "Do you intend to tell me just what caused you to behave so abominably?"

At some point, she had put her hands on her hips. When had she done that?

Richard winced then rubbed the back of his neck. It took him a moment to collect his thoughts. When he did so, he was evidently hoping that she would interrupt him at any moment. "It was just... When I saw the two of you, I thought—I mean, I could see his *knees!*"

"It is a period-appropriate costume," Evelyn said, her brow furrowing as she tried to understand his precise objection. "Though I admit I borrowed it from a theater. Did you think it was not historically accurate?"

"Blast it all, Evelyn, you know that's not what I thought," Richard said in a rush, taking a step toward her and lowering his voice. "I thought... I thought he was another one of your models."

"He is!"

"A model to whom you are not related and might have spent long afternoons and evenings with, and may have kissed, Evelyn," Richard said quietly, his eyes fixed on hers.

Evelyn's pulse skipped a beat.

He is jealous.

Now that was something she could not have predicted before today. Richard, jealous? Of Leopold?

He was still speaking. "...tall, young gentleman, and I thought, well, you might want to—I mean, if you found him so damned interesting... You've never taken *me* to Green Park to paint."

Heat was searing Evelyn's décolletage and her corset was suddenly far too tight.

Oh, goodness.

"You don't have any rights over me," Evelyn said quietly.

Her words interrupted Richard's tirade and he looked wretched, giving her a slow headshake, when he met her eyes. "I know."

A moment of silence fell between them and she had no idea

how to break it.

"But I want to," Richard said quietly, and only then did Evelyn notice that his hands had become fists at his sides. As though he wanted to lash out—not at her, but at himself. "I *want* to possess you, Evelyn."

Need poured through her, an aching heat, a desperation to be touched and kissed and held such as Evelyn had never known. It overpowered her.

Oh, the desire in his voice. She had not heard anything like it; and Richard was staring, in public, as though he wanted to devour her. As though possessing her would not be enough. As though there could never be enough of a connection between them.

Fighting down the instinct to ask precisely how he would do such a thing, Evelyn tugged on her bonnet's brim again and managed to say, "Y-You… You do?"

Richard nodded, leaning toward her as though about to kiss her. She did not move, welcoming the closeness, the intimacy, the scandal of it all.

They were in public! Her chaperone had left. They couldn't do this!

"I have wanted to taste you again ever since I kissed you," he whispered, his voice inviting on her throat. "God, haven't you seen it? You, with your artist's eye? Can't you see just how much I need you?"

A whimper escaped Evelyn's throat and for an instant, she wished it hadn't. She should have had better control over herself!

But she had never been more provoked. Had any woman ever withstood such an erotic onslaught?

Seeing the way her whimper made Richard quiver gave her all the more reason to do it again. He shuddered, his hand unclenching and clenching, as though he were resisting pulling her into his arms.

Evelyn swallowed. But this was madness! She couldn't go around permitting herself to be attracted to men like this! She needed to step away, to end this madness.

Such a shame she did not want to.

"A gentleman would… would never say such things to a lady," she managed.

There was a glitter in Richard's eye as he replied darkly, "How would you know what a gentleman and a lady say to each other in the dead of night, when they are all alone?"

Evelyn quivered, that aching need now pooling between her legs, and she did not know how she could stand. She did not know how she could stand it. He was intoxicating, mesmerizing.

"I don't know," she breathed. "But you and I have had conversations, the two of us, at night. What else would you like to tell me?"

Somehow, it was the wrong thing to say. Richard blinked, as though suddenly aware of where he was, as though the last five minutes had been a dream. He stepped back, almost slipping over the grass in his haste, and the ruddiness of his cheeks suggested that he regretted what he had said.

Which was a shame. Evelyn was more than eager to continue.

Only now, however, that Richard had stepped back was she able to take in the wider scene… and she appeared to have created one. There were a great number of people staring, and a few of them were even pointing. Before, she had been alone with a man—her cousin, yes, though passersby would only have guessed as much at a glance. They might have assumed the man with her now to be a relative as well had he not been standing so close and in such a manner.

Oh, dear.

She tugged her bonnet low, hoping no one could identify her. Still, how many lady artists were there in town? She couldn't stay here much longer. She was sure to be recognized.

"You are the artist, and I am only a model," Richard said quietly. "I only do what you want me to do. I only say what you want me to say. I suppose the question therefore is: what would you like me to tell you?"

Evelyn blinked up into his eyes.

Everything, she wanted to say. *This mystery is intoxicating and I am slightly worried that therein lies the attraction; that once I know your full name, your history, who you are, you will cease to become a wonder to me.*

And then I look at you, and I think: never. I will always be intoxicated by you.

Evelyn tried to smile. "I… I had better get home. I ought not to be here without a chaperone. And it's getting late."

It wasn't getting late. But she couldn't just stand here, staring at a man she could not have.

"Let me help you with your things."

"No, it's quite all right." Evelyn was, after all, quite accustomed to this. With a snap of a clasp and the tightening of a buckle, her easel transformed into a small trunk. An even smaller box contained her paints. She tipped out the water she had been using to clean her brushes, highly conscious that he was just standing there, watching her. "Good day, Richard."

Heat quivered within her as he met her eyes, a sad smile gracing his cheeks. "Good day, Evelyn. Remember what I said. I will possess you."

Precisely how Evelyn was able to walk home, she had no idea.

Chapter Ten

May 29, 1840

WELL, RICHARD HAD known it would be awkward, the next time he saw Evelyn. He had just not realized how awkward.

"Ah, you must be the model whom we've heard absolutely nothing about!" declared the woman with cordial eyes and a gracious smile. "Come in, come in!"

There was nothing Richard wanted to do less than enter the Earl and Countess of Lindow's home, but there did not really seem to be much choice.

"Mama, Rich—Mr. Richard cannot—"

"Oh, you'll get far too cold in that studio of yours this afternoon," Lady Lindow was saying to an argumentative Evelyn as they all stood in the hall, Richard drenched to the bone and Evelyn not much dryer. "Besides, I do believe it's a tad wet out."

Richard smiled weakly. This was not how he thought his afternoon would go.

It had started off quite normally. Evelyn had sent him a note saying she had a few hours available this afternoon and, if he would not mind, would he call upon her for some drawing?

He had almost left the house without one of his boots on, much to the chagrin of his butler.

But the heavens had opened as he had walked over London, not bothering to take his own carriage and then unable to find a hackney cab when the rain had come pouring down, and so he had resigned himself to a most uncomfortable wet sitting. Would the chair be quite well, after he had lounged damply in it for most of the afternoon?

As it turned out, the concern was no longer necessary. The butler—Cawthorne, it appeared—had been instructed to keep a look out.

"As soon as Evelyn told me she would be painting this after-noon, I simply insisted she use the old music room," the countess was telling a sopping-wet Richard, to the accompaniment of drips onto the marble floor. "That studio is all very well in the dry weather, but it can be an absolute ice house otherwise. No fire!"

"I don't want fire that close to my paints," Evelyn was mut-tering. "And I got quite wet enough bringing in my equipment, anyway."

It was true—she was a tad sodden. In fact, now Richard came to look at her, she was *very* sodden. Delightfully so. Her gown was clinging to every curve, the edges of her skirts sheer thanks to the heavy rain—

"Ahem," came a rather severe voice.

Richard jumped, expecting to be called out by the Earl of Lindow within a moment. Instead, he accepted the towel the ill-natured butler was offering. "Oh. Thank you."

"You won't be disturbed in there. It's out of the way and now the children are grown, we find little use for that room," Lady Lindow said airily, as though she frequently invited drenched strangers into her home. "I thought Evelyn could use it as a studio, but—"

"There's not enough light."

The last four words were chorused by Evelyn, her mother, the butler, and a young woman who looked remarkably like the artist, though she wearing a man's greatcoat around her shoulders and a scarf around her neck.

"Not so fast!"

Richard jumped. The words had been spoken as a malediction, Lady Lindow's friendly demeanor suddenly disappearing.

The young woman scowled. "You cannot keep me here. I am no prisoner!"

Evelyn rolled her eyes while the butler shook his head despondently. Richard was astonished to see the Countess of Lindow sigh heavily.

"Lucy Chance, you know that wasn't what I was going to do."

"And if you try to keep me here," the woman whom Richard recognized now as the sister who had accompanied Evelyn when they had first met said passionately, "I shall be a prisoner only of conscience!"

"You're making a scene, dear," Lady Lindow said blithely.

Richard smiled weakly as he tried to towel his hair a little dryer. "Oh, don't mind me."

"It's only one of Evelyn's models," Lady Lucy said dismissively. "Besides, as a working man himself, I am certain he would support me! Why, the outrages perpetuated on the working class—"

"No one wants to hear about the working class, dear."

"Aha!"

"Look," said the matriarch of the family, and Richard found himself smiling as he watched the scene play out, "the working classes are a large proportion of the country, yes? Estimates range from seventy to eighty per—"

"And yet they have no power, no privileges of—"

"—their combined income alone is worth—"

"Come on," said a quiet voice by his elbow.

Richard jumped. He had been so taken with the debate as it genially raged between mother and daughter that he had not noticed Evelyn step toward him.

She was smiling. "They'll be at this for... oh, I don't know. Half an hour?"

"And it doesn't worry you? I mean, such an argument?" he asked quietly, rubbing the towel over his face.

When he dropped his arm carrying the towel to his side, it was to see Evelyn grinning. "This, an argument? Oh, you've haven't known us Chances long. No, this will likely as not end in a grand speech about the rights of man, a counter speech about the rights of women, a quick terminology discussion about whether man can mean men only or include women as part of humanity, and then they'll leave the house together."

"'Together'?"

"Oh, yes," Evelyn said cheerfully. "My sister will go along to Newgate Prison, as planned, and my mother, after leaving her in the care of another lady advocate, will visit the lending library in search of a dictionary. We lost our one here. I think our dragon ate it."

Richard blinked. Perhaps there was more water in his ears than he had realized. "'Dragon'? 'Newgate Prison'?"

"We always call our dogs 'dragons.' Don't ask me why. It started so long ago," said Evelyn with a shrug, as though what she was saying was entirely comprehensible. "Percy's dragon right now is called Ermintrude, but she means well. Come on."

There appeared to be nothing else to do but follow her.

Richard had been here once before but had not paid much attention to his surroundings. Now, however, he was highly conscious of where he was dripping. Axminster rugs, the finest Turkish carpet, hardwood floors...

"You're wealthy," he said aloud before he could stop himself.

The embarrassment came swiftly and painfully. Hell, this was why he had never ventured out into polite Society since his return from France. No matter what he tried to do, no matter how hard he worked, he was always going to be nothing but a provincial viscount with no true manners.

Did I just say that to an earl's daughter?

Evelyn did not appear offended. In fact, she laughed. "I suppose I am—or at least, the family is. A few good investments my father made when he married my mother. He called it gambling. She called it a certainty."

Richard was attempting to understand this when Evelyn took a left.

"Lady Evelyn?"

That French accent caused Richard's breath to hitch. He could not explain why. He had met many amiable French people, despite his work in their country.

"Laurent," said Evelyn, her hands clasped. She cleared her throat as she gestured at the open room in front of them. "I suppose Mother told you I'd be practicing my art in old music room today."

"Yes, she sent me to join you." The lady's maid studied Richard from head to foot. "But she is half out the door herself. If I were to make myself scarce and attend to some of the needlework in my room..."

Evelyn tossed her head back and stepped into the room before them. "Yes, yes, thank you. You were with us the entire time." She did not even hesitate as the lady's maid sent a wink Richard's way and kept walking down the hallway. "Here we are."

It was certainly a room that had been out of use for a while. There was—not a *mustiness* in the air, but something that told anyone walking in here that the place had not been disturbed in a long time. Dustsheets covered the pianoforte and harp in one corner. Otherwise, the place was spotless. But it felt... unloved. Uncared for.

"None of the Chances are musical, then?" Richard asked as Evelyn closed the door.

Closed it, and locked it.

He swallowed. Now what the blazes had she done that for?

His concern must have shown on his face, for Evelyn shrugged. "I frequently lock doors when I'm painting. If there's anything more disruptive to my art than being interrupted, I haven't found it yet."

Her words burned into Richard's mind and reminded him sharply of the last time they had met.

"How would you know what a gentleman and a lady say to each other in the dead of night, when they are all alone?"

Oh, hell. Well, he supposed it wasn't possible that they could return to how things had been. Whatever that had been like.

He had been a complete dolt and he knew it. The thing was, Evelyn now knew it, and that was information he simply couldn't get back. It was infuriating. And it had all been of his own doing.

"But no, we're not."

Richard blinked. *Not what?*

"Musical," Evelyn said with a laugh, answering his unspoken question. "I think Lucy can carry a tune best of the three of us, but in all honesty, that particular branch of the arts isn't something any of us are good at. Which is a shame. My mother thought her skills would come through in us. Mathematics and music, after all, are very alike."

He was getting turned around here, and it appeared there was to be no letup in the conversation.

Mathematics? Music?

"I brought my travel easel in and thought we could continue here, if you are amenable," Evelyn said briskly, stepping over to the easel and pulling a set of pencils toward her. "If you are, of course, willing to continue."

Willing to continue.

Oh, he was willing for so much more. That was the trouble, Richard realized with a sinking sensation. He wanted more. And yet at the same time, he couldn't give her more.

He hadn't even told her his full name.

Richard exhaled deeply, hoping it would give him the confidence and conviction to do what was right. Because this couldn't continue, could it? The idea had been an amusing one, to spend time sitting around for an artist. It had been Evelyn, not himself, who had insisted on the lack of information about who he was.

But he had kissed her now. Pulled her into his arms. Whispered such things to her…

"Good day, Evelyn. Remember what I said. I will possess you."

No, he had gone too far now. Worse, he liked her. Cared about her. Telling her the truth of who he was, a viscount with no real prestige but a gentleman nonetheless, was something he had to do.

Would it change the connection they shared?

Hell, if he could act like such a plebian idiot in the middle of Green Park, in front of her own cousin, and she still wanted him here... perhaps their connection, whatever it was, could survive anything.

It was a heady thought. As Richard stepped toward the armchair that had been pulled to the center of the room, he almost swayed with the confidence that rushed through him.

"You must be freezing."

Richard blinked in the act of removing his coat. "'Freezing'?"

"I mean, you look soaked to the skin." Evelyn had let her hair down, as she so frequently did when drawing. It was a small intimacy he greatly enjoyed. "I suppose it will be a relief to get those wet things off."

His eyes bulged at her words. *Off.*

Surely, she did not mean—she could not have meant what that had sounded like, had she?

Apparently, she had. Evelyn glanced over vaguely and said, "Off with it all," and who was he to disobey?

This is madness.

There is that voice of reason, Richard thought ruefully as he pulled off dripping waistcoat and soaking-wet shirt, both dropping to a pile that was surely going to leave a mark. The voice of reason was not a voice he had spent a great amount of time listening to over the last few years. It hadn't gotten him anywhere when he had listened to it, after all.

"I was hoping to work on your calves today," said Evelyn from behind the easel.

Richard almost staggered into the chair. "You were?"

His voice was far too high-pitched, but there was nothing he could do about it. This was complete lunacy! Here he was, locked in a music room alone with a daughter of the house, and he was taking off his clothes!

Oh, he knew the arguments. Models sat nude for their artists all the time.

But not like this. Oh, not like this.

"Are you quite well?" Evelyn asked, her head sticking out around the canvas.

Richard swallowed. Was he? His head was spinning and there was a most irregular patter of his heart disrupting all normal cognition. If he weren't careful, he would do something truly reckless.

Like obey.

"Richard, I am not asking anything of you that another artist would not ask of any other model," Evelyn said softly. "You must be cold in those wet trousers, and I need to work on my calves. But if you don't want to—if you're not ready—I quite under-stand."

Perhaps unbeknownst to the beautiful woman who made Richard want to rip off all his clothes whenever he was in her presence, she had just said the few words that could almost guarantee that he would give into the temptation.

"If you're not ready."

He was ready. Ready for anything. Richard had never met a challenge he had not taken on and he was not going to stop now.

Even if this was so outrageous, it could never be spoken of again.

"Right," he said briskly, as though he frequently took all his clothes off in front of fully clothed ladies. "Right."

Evelyn did not appear from behind her easel. Richard found himself sadly disappointed.

Right.

Boots off first. That wasn't so hard; his feet were perhaps the only dry part of him. Now the trousers…

It was strange. He had never consciously thought about how he took off his trousers. It was not something he'd frequently done before a lady—at least, most of the time, it was quicker and cleaner just to unbutton the front flap, have his way with her, then see her off.

But this was different. This was… sensual.

It should not have been. There was no music, no lace, no velvet. There was no gasping of breath or touching. But as Richard slowly unbuttoned his trousers and slid them down his hips, past his knees, to the floor, he felt vulnerable in a way he had not in a long time.

A *very* long time.

Richard lowered himself onto the chair, luxuriating in the comfort of the cushion behind him, and carefully ensuring that one, he did not think about flames licking around him, and two, he crossed his legs in what he hoped was an artful manner so that it would hide his manhood.

He was naked. Yes. But he was not an animal.

He cleared his throat. "I'm ready for you."

Hell, even that was far more suggestive than he had intended—but to Richard's great disappointment, when Evelyn peered around the canvas, she looked entirely disinterested.

"Good. Don't move."

"Don't move"—was that it?

For the first few minutes, Richard did what he'd been told. He sat there, doing absolutely nothing but staring off into the distance. Most definitely not thinking about Evelyn, and what she would look like naked.

Hell's bells, now he was.

That's the trouble, Richard thought as the sense of being exposed grew in a tangling, twisting net of snakes in his stomach. And it wasn't just the fact that he wasn't wearing any clothes that felt exposing, either. No, somehow it was more than that.

Evelyn had absolutely no idea how seductive this was—how seductive *she* was. It was absolutely intoxicating. It was freeing in a way he had never expected.

He'd have to be careful, or he'd start to get accustomed to

this.

"Thank you."

The words were softly spoken, but with a great deal of strength behind them.

Richard tried to smile. "You asked nicely."

"You could have said *no*."

"You need to practice calves."

Evelyn chuckled, still hidden by her artwork. "I do indeed, but I suppose I could have asked someone else."

Jealousy flared within him. "Another cousin?"

"It's usually a cousin who agrees to model for me, yes," said Evelyn, her voice slightly vague, as though she were not entirely concentrating on their conversation. "I have so many of them, it's often easiest to find one. Less scandalous, too. Though with family, I might have only asked them to roll up their pants."

Richard's eyes widened. Surely, she didn't mean—

"But you are my first model who has... Well." Evelyn's pink cheeks and wide eyes, flyaway curls cascading down past her breasts, appeared to the left of the easel. "Taken all his clothes off."

A strange sort of triumph was sparking around the base of Richard's skull. He was her first—her first naked model, at the very least. It felt glorious, to know that this was something she had never shared with someone else.

Bother. There was that pesky jealousy again...

"I am glad to be of assistance," Richard said in a calm, measured tone that was entirely unlike how he was feeling. "Besides, as you say, it does happen. Artists paint naked models, I mean."

"Yes, but they usually bed them, too."

It was a good thing Richard was already seated, for he would have fallen—not just at the words, but the nonchalance with which Evelyn spoke them.

"Artists bed their models all the time; it appears to be a part of the tradition," Evelyn continued, as though entirely unaware that she was making Richard's brains melt out of his ears. "There is no expectation of commitment, no fanciful dreams of love. They just want something and… and take it."

Calm down, man, Richard tried to warn himself. She wasn't paying attention to her own words; this often happened when she was focused. She didn't mean—she wasn't offering…

Evelyn had disappeared back behind the easel again. The sound of several lines of pencil occurred before she said quietly, "I often wondered, if I had been able to sit with models when I was much younger, whether I would be able to paint so much better now."

Richard swallowed. The conversation had moved on, and he could hardly ask her to return to… to *that*. "But you paint so well."

"You've seen a few of my landscapes, yes," came Evelyn's dismissive voice. "But I do wonder if I shall ever master the human form."

Suppressing the desire to tell her that she could master him any time that she wanted, Richard aimed for a hopeful, encouraging tone. "I am sure you are a fast learner."

"Only when it comes to art. More's the pity," Evelyn said with a laugh. "My mother hoped numbers would be my forte, but sadly not."

"'Numbers'?"

"As I've said before, she is a very talented mathematician," came her reply, each word spoken more slowly this time. Perhaps she was concentrating. "Very talented. A waste of a countess, my father always says."

Richard could not help but smile at that. "Your parents are unusual."

"Oh, the whole family's a debacle, really," said Evelyn cheerfully. "I don't notice it half the time, I think, because I am a part of it. My sister is determined to radically alter the prison system and I would love to travel the world and paint."

"'Travel the world'?"

"I told you, I have had to paint most of my landscapes by

looking at the works of others." There was a true sadness in her tone now. "To actually see mountains, to stand by a lakeside and paint what I see, to revel in the new and the unexpected…"

Richard waited. The pencil scratchings increased in rapidity and he sat there, warmer now the wet clothing had been removed and still finding it utterly bizarre that he was sitting here naked.

Eventually, the pencil sounds slowed. "Art is… It is so much more than the finished result."

"It is?" Richard wondered aloud. He wasn't sure there was anything more to it at all.

"Oh, yes," Evelyn said vehemently, as though they were discussing life and death. Perhaps they were. "The process of creating a piece of art, that is the true challenge. It is the war within oneself, the battle one has with the materials. Desperately attempting to wrangle them into submission, to force the pencil or the charcoal or the paints to give up the right to claim their ownership. To make them create what is in one's head or before you. To know that no matter what you do, no matter how hard you work, you will never entirely win."

Richard's jaw dropped.

This was a woman like no other. He had an eye for them, what gentleman did not—so how his eye could have missed this Chance before the past few weeks, he did not know.

She was spectacular. She was marvelous. She was unlike any other woman he had ever met.

And she was making him feel—

Richard hastily removed the cushion from behind him and placed it over his lap. *Oh, hell…*

"What have I told you about moving?" Evelyn said sternly, stepping out from the easel entirely and glaring.

He smiled weakly and wished to goodness that a riled-up Lady Evelyn Chance was not even more attractive than the sedate version. "I… uh… had a little problem. Well, a *big* problem, actually," he added proudly.

Well, he hardly wanted to sell himself short, did he?

"'A big problem'?" Evelyn repeated.

Only then did her gaze fall upon the cushion. Her cheeks pinked.

"Oh!"

And her surprise entirely disarmed him. How on earth did she do it, Richard wondered. Here he was, having not apologized for the way that he had spoken to her or her cousin, turning up at her home soaking wet, and somehow, he was now seated before her, his manhood so rock solid, he could probably break apart stones, and she was… smiling?

"I shall take that as a compliment," she said lightly.

"You should," Richard said hoarsely.

"But if you don't mind, I'm going to return to my drawing," Evelyn replied with a beaming smile and not a small hint of mischief. "Do you think you can sit still there without moving for another hour?"

"Another *hour*?"

Evelyn did not reply. Her pencil had returned to the canvas again and she was lost.

Richard swallowed. This woman was going to be the death of him.

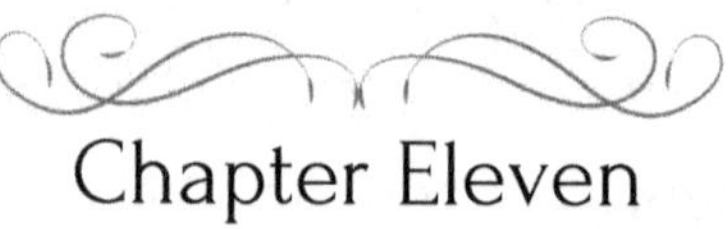

Chapter Eleven

June 5, 1840

T HE AIR WAS sultry. If she had known it would be so stifling, she would have argued with her mother more profusely about whether or not to take her pelisse.

As it was, Evelyn had argued, and her mother had looked at her, and Evelyn had put on her pelisse. And now she was baking.

A gaggle of ladies, all around her age, meandered past her. Evelyn was forced to take a step back, right up against the wall, to prevent herself from being in their path. Their joyful chatter sparked into the late morning air.

"Never seen such a—"

"He didn't!"

"I promise you, he actually said to my face—"

Precisely what the gentleman in question had said, Evelyn was never to know. Their conversation, like their perambulation, rambled on along the pavement, and they disappeared out of sight around a corner before she could overhear any more.

Their absence only served to underline just how alone she was. Which was most strange; had not Richard been most clear about what time they were to meet?

Evelyn pulled her brother's pocket watch out from her reticule. One of these days, someone was going to create a gown that had pockets just like those for gentlemen. One day.

The pocket watch was clear; the hour was almost twenty past

eleven, and he was late.

Evelyn swallowed. And handsome. And charming. And utterly unsuitable.

"What has become of your beau?" Laurent asked, fidgeting in place.

"He's not my beau," said Evelyn softly. "And if you need to excuse yourself for a moment, feel free to do so. I'll be careful not to be spotted." She tugged on her wide bonnet's brim as if to make her point.

Laurent chewed her lip. "Very well. Be *careful*, my lady. Unlike at home, there are eyes here, in such a place."

Evelyn was all too aware. But her thoughts, as ever these days, returned to Richard.

It had taken a good long time to accept, even in the silence and solitude of her mind, that she was attracted to him. It had taken even less time for Evelyn to know, absolutely, that she could not consider a future with Richard... Richard Whateverhisnamewas.

Because was that not precisely the problem? If they had met at a ball, if he'd been introduced as one of her brother's friends, or an earl's third son, or the like, perhaps a courtship could have occurred.

But he was a *model*. He had sat for her naked, and Evelyn was most furious with herself that she had not even taken the slightest peek at... Well. *That*.

She was damned forever to be the man's artist, not his... not anything else.

"Waiting for someone, are you?"

Evelyn blanched. The man was standing unpleasantly close, her hurried thoughts meaning that her mind had not notified her of his increasing presence. He was not a man known to her: tall, leering, with a smile that told her more than enough, and swinging a cane around in his hand as though he were attempting to join a circus.

She repressed a smile. That was not kind. But it was accurate.

And it was in her nature to notice these sorts of things.

"Yes, thank you," she said as politely and yet as curtly as she could manage. "My chaperone." The last thing she wanted to do was invite further conversation.

Apparently, her curtness did not signify. The man grinned. "I've been waiting for someone for a while, and you look like you just fit the bill."

Evelyn attempted to smile. "Is that so?"

Where was Laurent? Or Richard? It would be so much easier to extricate herself from this most unpleasant man, whoever he was, if Richard were to turn up about now.

A hazy smile, a genuine one, slipped across her face. Perhaps on a white charger, dressed as a medieval knight, or a Greek god, or—

"I was certain you would come around to my way of thinking." The man smirked.

Evelyn's smile immediately vanished. *Ah.* Had he thought that smile for him? "Oh, I am afraid you quite misunderstand me, sir."

"Oh, I think we can move directly to first names, don't you?" replied the most irritating, and most incorrect man. "You see, I'm Horace Lister, and—"

"'Lister'?" repeated Evelyn.

Well, that name rang a bell. Had not her mother told her a story about how a Mr. Lister, presumably this man's father or uncle, had been most injudicious as to attempt to steal a kiss from the now Duchess of Axwick?

That did not bode well.

Neither did the way that the man, Mr. Lister, placed a palm against the brick wall right by Evelyn's head and leaned forward with a simper. "You may have heard of me, yes. I am a renowned lover."

"I believe there has been some mistake," Evelyn said weakly. It was most inconvenient that this was the time her heart was to plummet and hide into her chest. She needed bravery! She needed boldness! She needed—

"So sorry I was detained, my dear, I hope you have not been waiting too long?" said a smooth and most welcome voice.

Evelyn sagged with relief against the wall, then attempted to rally. It would not do for this Mr. Lister to believe she could not have defended herself.

She had never punched a man in the jaw before. By all accounts, it was not difficult.

"Richard," Evelyn exhaled happily.

"'Richard'?" Mr. Lister lurched back as though scalded, actually raising his hands clenched into fists before turning and seeing the man who had spoken. "You're not the Duke of Axwick."

Richard blinked. "Should I be? Are you ready, my dear?"

"My dear"? It was a phrase so pedestrian in the mouths of others. Evelyn had heard her father call her mother "my dear" only once, and the look of daggers which the Countess of Lindow had shot him in reply had ensured her father had never used it again.

Yet in Richard's mouth...

Desperately hoping her cheeks did not look as crimson as they felt, and at the same time delighted that Mr. Lister, with his pinched expression, was looking so perturbed, Evelyn accepted Richard's proffered arm. "I have been waiting a while, yes. But Mr. Lister has done his best to entertain me."

Perhaps it was a low blow. Evelyn was never to know just how badly the man took it. Richard was promenading her forward into the building and its cool, welcoming hall.

Only when the door closed behind them did the most startling thing happen.

Richard dropped her arm and just as swiftly grasped hold of her shoulders. He brought her close, far closer than Evelyn thought was probably acceptable in public, forcing her to tilt her head back as she kept hold of his attention.

"He didn't hurt you?" Richard asked urgently, a desperation pouring through his tones that Evelyn had never heard before.

"That man, that Lister, he didn't touch you?"

"No," Evelyn said hastily, the heat in her cheeks now delight that he was so concerned.

As he dropped his grip on her shoulders and blew out heavily, he shook his head. "The blighter is known throughout Society for his rash and impetuous nature, and his convenient lack of hearing when a woman declines his advances. I was worried there, for a moment."

Evelyn was not sure whether to be concerned that she had in fact been in great danger with Mr. Lister, or piqued that it appeared Richard would have worried for any young lady left in the company of such an odious man.

It had been pleasant, if only for a moment, to feel special.

And then something he said rattled at her mind.

"The blighter is known throughout Society…"

But… But that would only make sense if he, Richard, were a part of Society. For all she knew of him, he was no gentleman. Surely, she would have seen him long before now if he had been. How, then, could he know this fact?

Evelyn swallowed. *The attraction is not knowing,* she told herself firmly. He could have read the Society pages. The gossip sheets. Heard the rumors. He presumably could read, couldn't he?

Besides, nothing is ever going to happen. Best to leave it as a delicious mystery.

"You are late. Laurent took off at a most inconvenient time, leaving me alone and a target for that man," she said aloud, hoping to distract herself from the torrid thoughts threatening to trample her mind: thoughts of Mr. Lister leaning forward and Richard rushing forward with a pistol, shooting the man dead, then kissing Evelyn so furious against the wall…

"I… I was momentarily otherwise engaged," Richard said vaguely, not quite meeting her eye.

Evelyn frowned. They were still standing in the entrance hall; if she wished, she could depart at any moment. And he was not being honest with her. There was a lilt in his voice that she had never heard before, one smacking of dishonesty. That, or at least purposeful vagueness.

A vagueness designed to elicit no further questions.

Richard had taken a few steps forward before Evelyn's words halted him.

"'Otherwise engaged'? You… You are modeling for another artist?"

The sudden fear was not one she had expected. After all, had they not already had this misunderstanding but in reverse? Had she not laughed when Richard had presumed Leopold was a strange man modeling for her? Had it not seemed amusing?

It did not seem amusing now. He was hers—her *model*, Evelyn adjusted swiftly in her mind as her pulse throbbed in her ears. It was difficult enough for a lady artist to find a model, but to lose him within months to another artist could not be borne.

"No, I was not modeling for another artist. You are the only person I take my clothes off for," Richard said in a hushed tone, winking.

Blazing heat soared through Evelyn and her footsteps halted. "You are laughing at me."

"I am… I am, yes," he said, his features softening as he saw her genuine fear. "I… As I said, I was otherwise engaged."

"With what?" Evelyn persisted.

It was a foolish thing to do, she knew. That was the whole point of their connection, was it not? That she knew almost nothing about him. Yet there was a delicious panic in that absence of knowledge. She could pretend Richard almost sprung out of the ground on command whenever she needed him and otherwise did not exist… but her mind could not stop reminding her that Richard probably lived a rich and full life in the many hours he was not with her.

Doing what? And with whom?

"I know I said that I wanted you as a blank slate, and in many ways—I mean, it is what the best and greatest artists do," she said wretchedly. A couple entered behind them and, stepping around them, entered the door Richard had been attempting to step through. Evelyn lowered her head to hide her face, her voice a whisper. "But I... Richard, you have to know I feel... I feel..."

Evelyn swallowed, her mouth dry. *Why is this so difficult?*

Perhaps because words were not her forte. Give her colors, give her pastels, give her nothing but a pencil and she could express herself perhaps better than half the people in England.

Depend on her tongue, and Evelyn was a tad worried she would never make herself understood.

"It's just—I mean, you and I... We... At least I thought we..." Evelyn's treacherous, unhelpful words trailed off into the distance.

Oh, this is all so humiliating. Richard was smiling now, but he made no move to speak and save her from this utter foolishness.

Well, she was just going to have to say it.

"You're mine," Evelyn said fiercely. "I don't know how else to describe it, but there it is. You... You do understand, don't you?"

Richard's smile had not disappeared, but a coldness had entered his eyes as he stepped toward her. When he spoke, it was low—so low, she could barely hear him. "I'm not a plaything, Evelyn. I'm a man, a flesh and blood person, with my own needs and desires."

Air caught in her throat. "I-I know that."

"And if you say such things, I will be forced to presume that I can respond in kind," he said quietly, his gaze drifting to her lips before returning to her eyes.

In kind? What on earth did he mean?

"I could say, for example," came Richard's low, thrumming tone, which rippled through her body like thunder, "that *you* were *mine.*"

Evelyn gasped, lips parting, and she could not speak. How could she? The way he'd said such a thing, the possessiveness— but had that not been a facet of their interactions from the very first day they had met?

Evelyn knew she needed to breathe, knew not breathing was only going to lead to trouble, but how could she when faced with such a man saying such things?

"So, do we understand each other?" Richard had leaned back, returning to his normal voice.

"Not in the slightest," Evelyn said helplessly.

He laughed at that and, taking her hand, placed it through the crook of his arm. "Me, neither. Shall we wait for your maid, or are we going to keep up the ruse? *Mrs.* Richard?"

Evelyn gulped. With her rightful title, there was no circumstances under which she'd be reduced to a "Mrs."—most certainly not with a man's given name only. Before she could respond, though, that perhaps for today, she'd just like to pretend, her maid's voice caught her attention from behind.

"My lady. I see he has joined us at last."

"Laurent." Evelyn cleared her throat and nodded slightly over her shoulder at the woman. "Yes... Yes, he has."

She did not need to tell her maid more than that.

After Richard had acknowledged the maid and waited for her to step a few feet behind them, he turned back to Evelyn. "Come on, then—where is it that you have taken me?"

They were walking forward now arm in arm, and as they passed through the double doors, Evelyn felt a rush of comfort.

Here, at least, she could be on home territory.

"This is my favorite art gallery in all of London," she said grandly, lifting her spare hand and gesturing about the place.

It truly was magnificent. Evelyn had hardly been able to believe it when she had first found it. Here was a place that seemed more like a temple than a gallery; its sweeping columns, its high ceilings, the way people automatically hushed as they entered, as though they were entering a place of worship.

And weren't they?

The high ceilings, painted white so as to give greater prominence to the excellent artwork hanging every ten feet or so, soared upward and made one think of the divine.

And that was *before* one started to look at the paintings.

"I had no idea this place was even here," Richard said in wonder as he stared about. "But then I suppose, I have been gone from London for some years."

Evelyn bit down the questions that naturally arose from such a statement. France, that was surely it—but why had he been there for so long? Had he been trying to escape something here in England?

Someone?

"I thought I should begin your artistic education," Evelyn said primly, trying her best to ignore the fact that most people began their artistic education when in short trousers, and this man was both taller and broader than herself. "If you are going to understand what I am aiming for, you need to see the best."

Richard's sardonic brow was wrinkled. "And you believe I have no artistic education whatsoever?"

Evelyn hesitated.

Really, he was most provoking. He knew full well she had absolutely no idea about...

No, that wasn't quite right.

"That—what was that thought?" Richard said swiftly.

Evelyn blinked. "Nothing."

She had spoken instinctively, without thinking, and he appeared to understand.

"Do not just automatically deny it, Evelyn. You may be the artist here, but I have eyes. What did you just think? A seriousness I have never known in you just overcame your face."

Try as she might, there was no way she could deny it. She turned over her shoulder to check on Laurent, who had stayed a respectful few feet behind. Enough to be regarded as her chaperone while allowing them some privacy, her gaze on a painting to the left of her. Keeping her voice low, therefore, so they did not catch the attention of the other ladies and gentlemen who were perusing the art, Evelyn said, more than a mite defensively, "It was just… Well, you are right. I am the artist here. And the more I look at you, the more I see."

Richard's sardonic eyebrow did not lower. "Not the most impressive statement anyone has ever made, you know."

"I just meant… Well." Evelyn inhaled slowly. She could be entirely wrong. But she'd never know. "You are always so closely shaven, Richard."

For a moment, he just stood there and stared. Then he said, "I… I don't understand."

"Well, a man so well shaven is not managing to do that on his own, is he?" Evelyn said softly. She had started to walk toward a most splendid landscape, one that invited one to step into the cool waters of the pool at the base of a waterfall. "So you have a valet."

"Would you believe I can honestly say I do not, that I go to a barber?"

"Every other day?" Evelyn countered with a wry smile. "I doubt it. And your clothes—"

"You don't spend a great deal of time looking at my clothes," Richard said in a quiet voice.

Her burning cheeks did not distract her, and neither did his friendly tone. "Perhaps. But your clothes are of good quality in the main—a little worn, a little old-fashioned… as though you had spent five or six years abroad, perhaps, and were not quite up to date with the fashions here."

Now Richard was not smiling. "You see all that?"

"I see so much more, yet not enough," Evelyn admitted, trying to laugh. "It could almost become a game, couldn't it? Trying to ascertain the truth about you while continually stating that I have no interest in being told. A paradox."

"You are paradoxical yourself."

Evelyn halted by the waterfall painting, surprise jolting her into a stop. "I am?"

Paradoxical? She had never considered herself so. It was perfectly natural, was it not, to wish to be an artist? To see the beauty of the world and wish to capture it?

"You are a lady, a true lady, an earl's daughter, but you fraternize with a man."

"I am not *fraternizing!*" Evelyn protested.

It did not matter. Richard meandered along to a portrait of a very severe-looking couple and she followed him. Laurent remained a careful distance behind.

"Fraternizing with a man you know almost nothing about," he continued. "You spend all your money not on gowns or ribbons—"

"What would I do with more gowns?"

"—but instead on art supplies."

"I would say that is most logical, not paradoxical," Evelyn protested, heat creeping across her torso. "I am an artist!"

She had said the words too loudly. People were staring now, turning to see where the noise was coming from.

Evelyn held her head high and refused to allow herself to be cowed. She had said nothing wrong. In fact, she had spoken most truly. Besides, Laurent was moving closer to lend credence to her status as chaperone.

And Richard was smiling. "That you are. And yet you have never exhibited?"

The suggestion was understandable, perhaps, to someone who had never met her father. "No. No, I will never exhibit."

A flicker of something moved across Richard's face. "Evelyn, your talent is more than sufficient to—"

"But my father's permission is insufficient," she cut across him in a low voice, trying to smile. "And I am not able to change his mind. No one can. Best we do not speak of it."

Because the pain, the knowledge that no matter how hard she worked, it would only be family who saw her efforts, was truly excruciating.

Perhaps Richard could see that. He glanced at Laurent, who stepped back again with the dispersing crowd, her attention caught on a sculpture nearby. "Tell me about this painting."

Painting? How could she think about painting at a time like this?

He mystified her. He befuddled her. He made her want to do things, say things, be things no other person ever had.

And Evelyn knew it could not last.

Oh, it was all very entertaining now. But how long could this go on for? This flirting, for that was surely what it was—Evelyn was no expert, she would have to ask her cousin Lilianna—this flirting would eventually resolve itself in one of two ways.

Either he would take a liberty and attempt to seduce her, with *more* than just a kiss, and Evelyn would be obliged to throw him from her art studio and her acquaintance.

Or… he wouldn't.

It was rather startling for Evelyn to discover that she did not know which fate was worse.

"The painting, Evelyn," Richard prompted quietly.

Evelyn stepped forward hastily. "This painting is—well. It is not much to speak of, really. *This* is the sort of painting you should be looking at."

She had grasped his hand with hers before she had even considered it. Now she had done so, she was not quite sure how to let go.

It did not seem to matter. They stood instead before a painting that had always been one of Evelyn's favorites.

At first glance, it was simple. Just a woman, sitting in a chair, looking out of a window. Sunlight crept in but could not entirely vanquish the darkness within the room.

And that was it.

"This is it?" Richard said, mirroring her thoughts.

Evelyn smiled. "*It*, as you call it, is one of the greatest paintings ever created."

He did not look particularly impressed. "It's a woman sitting in a chair."

"Look at the light," Evelyn said, stepping forward with wide eyes, staring hungrily at the oils. "The shadow, how the firelight in the hearth and the sunlight through the window wage a war over her. To whom does she belong? The home, where she serves and works—or the outside, nature, calling to her? See the folds of her gown, how exquisite the detail."

"There's a tear just on the right. Poorly mended."

Evelyn smiled to hear the interest in Richard's voice—perhaps even despite himself. "And her hair is partly tamed, but only just. Everything in her yearns for something more, to escape what could be described as a prison—see the way the artist has made the lead piping of the windows appear to be bars?"

He was looking at the painting far more closely now, and there was a look of surprise in his eyes. "I am impressed. I had not thought there to be so much to find in one painting. Arguably, there is nothing happening."

"Yet there is everything happening." Evelyn sighed. "I can only *dream* to create something so dynamic in such stillness."

It haunted her, in a way. Paintings like this, they proved it was possible to do something great with such simple structure.

Something she had not managed to master.

"I have heard the Viscount Sempill has another painting by this artist," she said quietly. "I would give a great deal to see it."

It was most strange; there did not appear to be anything on the carpet likely to trip on, and yet Richard stumbled. "What did you say?"

"The artist of this painting, he sold another to Viscount Sempill years ago. An elderly man, I think I read," Evelyn said, her gaze returning to the portrait. "According to the notice of sale, it was even more impressive than this one. Can you imagine? A man who owns a painting like that would have no need to venture out into the world to see beauty."

They stood there for a moment in silence, Evelyn highly conscious of the man beside her but unable to drag her eyes away from the painting before her. And then—

"It's incredible, the passion you have," Richard said quietly. "I do not believe I have ever experienced such a thing for anything."

"But you can see the beauty now, can't you?" Evelyn asked eagerly.

He did not take his eyes away as he spoke. "I can see the beauty now."

Evelyn swallowed. That had not been at all what she had meant, and she had thought for a moment... Well, it was natural to hope Richard had been talking about her, and not the painting.

Who did not want to be beautiful?

Who did not want someone like Richard considering them so?

"Yes, it's a very beautiful painting," she managed.

"That is not what I meant," Richard returned calmly, as though he complimented women every day.

Perhaps he did. Perhaps he had not been late not because he had been modeling for another artist, but because he had been with another woman.

The thought pained her, a physical lurch in her stomach, and Evelyn stepped back. Being close to him was painful as the image of Richard kissing another woman, calling her beautiful, crowded her mind.

"What is it?"

Richard's voice was urgent, but Evelyn did not permit herself to accept the hand he now offered. When had she dropped his hand? She could not recall.

"It does not matter."

"Everything you think matters, Evelyn."

She blinked, startled out of silence by the calm with which he spoke. "I was wondering why you were late."

He examined her closely for a moment. Others moved about the art gallery like a tide, gradually moving down the corridors and around the rooms to inspect and to admire. Even Laurent made her way toward the opposite end of the room, her attention on the painting above her.

Only they stayed still.

"Because," Richard said softly, pink tinging his cheeks, "I was nervous."

Evelyn stared. "Nervous of what?"

"Of you. Or rather, what I become when I am with you."

Evelyn glanced quickly down at the floor, and when she looked back up Richard appeared to have regained control of himself.

"Paintings," Evelyn said firmly, pushing Richard's admission to the back of her mind and promising herself she could examine it more fully when she had returned home. Without him. "Let's look at more paintings."

Chapter Twelve

June 9, 1840

H*AS THERE EVER been anything duller than this?*
Richard almost spoke the words aloud—which would have been most impolitic. It was not his friends' fault, after all, that the delights of a ball no longer gave him any joy.

"—all the way from Brighton!" the Earl of Dalmerlington was saying brightly, his prominent chin in the air. "I always thought it would be a challenge to tempt them here, but eventually, they agreed—and what music!"

The gaggle around the hosts all nodded and murmured positive noises of agreement. The music was, indeed, splendid.

Richard just about remembered to nod at the right time.

The music? What care he about the music?

"I am so delighted that you accepted my invitation," the earl said, turning unexpectedly to Richard. "Why, I thought it would be impossible to get you to agree. You've become almost a recluse lately."

Ah. "Nonsense."

It was perhaps not the most elegant answer, but it was the only one Richard was willing to give. This was, after all, polite Society. Anything he said here would be noted down, he knew, in the mental notebooks of half the ladies within earshot, and the news would spread to the other half before this waltz was up.

He was hardly going to admit to his friend exactly where he

had been so often these last few weeks…

"—fortunate enough that you have returned from your travels," the Earl of Dalmerlington was saying, and Richard forced himself to pay attention. "The place was quite desolate without you!"

Richard tried to smile as the other guests gathered around the earl looked at him curiously. "I am sure London Society has managed to go on quite well without me."

Many things had changed, but nothing of true import. Besides, he did not want any further whispers about where he had been and precisely what he had been doing there. The least said about that, the better.

Not that it had stopped the letters.

—need you here in France. The work is not yet done—

—understand you greatly suffered, but I had hoped you would return—

—even receiving these letters? I have received no word from you in weeks—

Richard's jaw tightened. He had been receiving the letters from his colleagues still in France but had not replied. What could he say? That his nightmares only lessened when he saw a particular woman? That he was starting to see her as a medley of friend and confidante and medicine? That the idea of subjecting himself to the dangers of France again filled him with dread, but not as much dread as the thought that he had turned coward?

"—and the candles you have, most exquisite," someone else was saying.

Richard's friend beamed. "I am so delighted you noticed! I was speaking to my butler only a fortnight ago, and he said there was something very exciting occurring in the candle world. Well, I said, tell all! And he said…"

Whatever was happening in the candle world, Richard would never know. His concentration had meandered as soon as it had become clear that the topic would not involve a particular young woman… which was the only reason Richard had agreed to come to this damned place at all.

It was foolish, perhaps, but Richard had made up his mind. No more secrets. He had fallen into that lifestyle in France and it was time he broke it.

The Dalmerlington ball felt like the appropriate place to be formally introduced to Evelyn. Her family was sure to be on the invitation list, Richard had been certain. How, precisely, she would react to being introduced to a man she knew only as 'Richard,' only to discover he was truly Viscount Sempill…

Well. Richard's imagination veered from delighted, hysterical tears to thumping him hard on the nose. Both were equally likely.

But the evening had dragged on and where were the Chances?

"—and so here we are, with the most splendid candles you can find in the whole of London." The earl beamed.

There were murmurs of approbation and delight in the group, and Richard did his best not to roll his eyes.

Honestly: candles? That is the most riveting conversational topic in London tonight?

No wonder he had left England for adventure.

"You look distracted, Sempill."

Richard jumped. Dalmerlington was smiling blandly and there was no malicious bone in his body, he knew. Still. It was almost too innocent.

"I was merely wondering if all your guests had arrived, my good friend," Richard said aloud. How long had they been friends, exactly? The earl's father and his own father had grown up together. That much, he could remember… "The place is packed. You and your lady wife are clearly a popular invitation."

Dalmerlington thrust out his chest. "Oh, yes, there are few people invited to a Dalmerlington ball who refuse. In fact, I know precisely whom you are waiting for."

Richard almost dropped the glass of wine he had just taken from a footman's silver platter. "You do?"

How was it possible? Had he not been careful, been surreptitious in his dealings with Evelyn? Had he not been circumspect?

But then, you did march up to her in Green Park, stayed with her, even after her chaperone left, Richard thought wildly, wishing to goodness the whole group was not staring at him. *And we went to that art gallery. And the street that one time—*

"Yes, Walden should be here any moment," mused Dalmerlington, his voice breaking into Richard's frantic thoughts. "I expected him to—ah, there he is."

Richard's shoulders sagged with relief. "Oh—oh yes, good. Do excuse me ladies, gentlemen."

It was the perfect excuse to separate himself from that particularly dull crowd. Richard was forced to push through a number of people before eventually reaching Walden, who had just entered.

"You look mightily flushed," his friend said easily, clapping him on the back. "Been putting a few of Society's ladies through their paces?"

Richard's eyes became a stern glare. "What the devil do you think you mean by that?"

Walden stared. "Why, dancing, of course. What else could I mean?"

Ah. Right. Yes. They were at a ball.

"Nothing," said Richard swiftly.

Well, it made a change from being bored out of his skull, he supposed. Now Walden was here, he could inquire on an entirely different matter.

Just as long as he could do it without making a complete ass of himself...

"It's a busy ball," he said nonchalantly. "Don't you think?"

His nonchalance was entirely wasted on his friend. "What is it that you want, Sempill?"

"Nothing," said Richard hastily. *Too* hastily. "Well, something. I just wondered..."

Whether you knew the Chances, he wanted to say. No, not the duke and his family, or the marquess and his—the other ones.

No, not the illegitimate one adopted into legitimacy! The earl. His daughters. One daughter in particular…

It had been impossible to ask around about Evelyn because there simply wasn't anyone to ask. Richard had lost most of his acquaintance after leaving for France. Being entirely incommunicado for several years had that general effect.

Now he only had Walden, and his friend was fixing him with a most unpleasant smile.

"You want to ask about a woman." He chuckled. "I'm going to need a glass of wine for this—wine, or something stronger."

"No, I merely—"

"Because I cannot recall the last time you ever asked about a woman. In fact, I do not think you ever have," said Walden with a crowing laugh. "Have you finally fallen in love then, man?"

Richard swallowed.

No, he wanted to say.

But it would have been a lie. A lie of sorts. Whatever he had fallen into with Evelyn could not be categorized by mere words. *Love* did not do it justice.

Oh, hell, he was in trouble.

"I just thought…" Richard began.

He could not continue. He had become instantly distracted by the couple who had just entered the Dalmerlingtons' ball, looking resplendent in matching green.

The Earl and Countess of Lindow. He had never seen the former that he could recall, but he recognized the latter.

"I'll talk to you later," Richard muttered, pushing past his friend.

"Sempill? Sempill, what on earth are you doing?"

Richard ignored him. It was nothing personal; he would have ignored anyone to whom he had been speaking in that moment.

Because Lady Lindow had glanced about, caught his eye… and smiled.

She remembered him.

Richard did not think. There was no time for thoughts because he had crossed the ten feet between them and was now standing, utterly silent and awkwardly gormless, before the Earl and Countess of Lindow.

The earl frowned. "Do I know you, sir?"

Ah. Right. Society's rules.

Richard had been well drilled in them as a child, particularly when he had inherited his own viscountcy. Strange how they slipped his mind now, all thoughts instead pointing hazily to Evelyn, Evelyn, Evelyn…

"Ah, it's that polite young man who is modeling for Evelyn," Lady Lindow said warmly. "I hope you did not catch a chill after I last saw you."

"No—no, Lady Lindow, thank you." *Get a grip, man!* "I was most grateful for your hospitality, however, and wanted to introduce myself formally to yourself and your family. Is… Is Evelyn with you?"

It had not occurred to Richard for one moment that Evelyn would not be with them. After all, she was out in Society, was she not? Surely, she would be with her parents, available for dancing and for gentlemen to consider her as a match…

Richard's jaw tightened, his temple throbbed, and pain as he had never known before rose inside him.

Why had the thought not occurred to him before? It was possible that Evelyn was being courted by a gentleman from Society. There was plenty of time that he and Evelyn were not together, after all, and they had made no promises to each other.

His stomach lurched. Where had that come from? Did he *want* to make promises to her?

The Earl of Lindow was inspecting him with a great amount of suspicion. Perhaps rightly so, Richard could not help but think. After all, he had called her 'Evelyn' and not 'Lady Evelyn.'

Blast it all to hell, this was all going wrong.

"Look," Richard said hastily.

"I don't know who you are, sir," Lord Lindow began stiffly.

"I told you, he's one of Evelyn's models," his wife said sternly. "Besides, the young man was about to introduce himself, so if you could cease your interruptions for more than five seconds— please, continue."

Richard took a deep breath. This was not precisely how he would have orchestrated it. In an ideal world, Evelyn would have been here. She would have been able to know who he was, finally. Not one of the aliases he'd used in France, the names so familiar to him that sometimes he'd forgotten that under the layers of meaning, there had been a Richard Sempill underneath. His true name.

Concentrate, man!

"My name is Richard Sempill, Viscount Sempill," he said in a rush.

Though his speech was but six words, it had a remarkable effect. Lord Lindow's brow unfurrowed, his expectation that the man before him was nothing but a common gentleman clearly confused.

Lady Lindow's eyes widened. "Viscount?"

"Yes," said Richard, suddenly highly conscious that he was speaking to an earl and a countess. His betters.

No, damn him, he wasn't going to fall into that trap. Why should they be better than himself?

"I believe I knew your father," Lord Lindow said quietly. "At least, I knew of him. A good man. I was sad to hear of his passing, though it was a long time ago."

"A very long time ago, my lord," said Richard, hating how his voice had become stiff.

Silence fell between the three of them, one Richard loathed but could not see how to break. The musicians had struck up again and the dancers behind him appeared to be enjoying something closer to a jig than a waltz. A pair of doors were thrown open to his right, and the scent of delicious food wafted through. Supper was served.

"So, you are Sempill's son," said Lord Lindow slowly. "Haven't heard of you in London."

"I am newly in town, my lord, and—"

"—and you decided to first seek out my daughter and sit for her?"

Richard could not blame the man for his obvious suspicions. Only then did he wonder how Evelyn had been open with her parents about... well, about how open he, Richard, was when she was drawing him. There was no way she could have told them. The earl would have burst into the studio and demanded Richard wed his daughter.

Heat burned through him, tying his stomach into knots. The earl and countess before him had no idea Richard had taken all of his clothes off before their daughter.

"You surprise me." That was Lady Lindow, and Richard turned to her as she continued. "I would not have thought a viscount had much time for sitting about for my daughter to draw him."

There was no censure in her words, but there was no encouragement, either.

Hell's bells, what had he been thinking?

"I admit myself astonished, yet intrigued," said Lord Lindow slowly. "Unless... Unless..."

Richard hesitated. Well, duels were technically still illegal, were they not? It would have taken a brave man to demand a meeting at dawn, but then you never could tell with gentlemen of his father's generation. There were tales of duels fought over a daughter or sister's honor even now, though they were technically illegal.

The earl was frowning. "Unless you have taken on the role of model for my daughter as... a ruse."

Richard swallowed. "I would never—"

"As a ruse to propose matrimony to her!" Lord Lindow said triumphantly.

Richard's mouth fell open. "I... I..."

"Oh, how wonderful!" Lady Lindow looked absolutely delighted.

"Ah," said Richard weakly, his pulse thumping. "Well—"

"That is your intention in all this, isn't it?" Brow drawn, lips pinched, Evelyn's father had never looked so stern, at least in Richard's short acquaintance with him. "Matrimony, with my daughter?"

The man had to be at least five and twenty years older than him, and Richard was certain he could win in a fight with the earl easily.

Wait a moment. Was he truly thinking about fighting Evelyn's father?

Old habits died hard. Richard had always been very careful to ensure that no woman could ever accuse him of offering something so serious, so entirely permanent as matrimony. His instincts to deny, to escape the suggestion, rose within him.

They were met with an equally strong desire to declare that yes, he would marry her.

Richard blinked. *Marry Evelyn?*

It would hardly be a hardship. Marry Evelyn: be with her every day, see her grow in passion and skill with her art, encourage her, be the only one to strip naked for her…

Perhaps she could even paint in the nude. Now *that* would be a most interesting conversation.

Richard cleared his throat heartily and nodded. "Yes—yes. I intend matrimony. I… I wish to marry your daughter."

And it had been said. The panic he had presumed would arise at such a pronouncement did not come.

Instead, he was filled with what could only be described as a golden light. Not that Evelyn would be satisfied with that meager description. A glittering light. A warm, honeyed light.

The Countess of Lindow was beaming. "To think, a viscount for our Evelyn!"

"I know I am not good enough," Richard found himself saying, his tongue entirely overtaken by thoughts he could not marshal.

The earl did not look pleased by his revelation. "Dear me.

Anything terrible I should know about?"

"No!" Richard said, a little too hastily. People were turning now, staring as his word echoed around the ballroom. He lowered his voice. "No, I just meant—"

"You know the sort of nonsense these young people in love say, George," said the countess, and she placed a kiss on her husband's cheek. "You used to say such things to me, once. I distinctly remember—"

"Yes, yes, that's enough of that," muttered Lord Lindow, though Richard thought he saw a smile underneath the grump. "Well, I suppose you want my blessing, man?"

Richard waited a heartbeat. He could be more polite, he supposed; but this was perhaps one of the few occasions in England where he had to stand his ground. "No."

Lady Lindow looked swiftly at her husband, whose grump only increased.

"Because in my view, it is Evelyn's opinion that matters," Richard continued, his shoulders stiff and his sense crying out for him to stop. "Not yours."

There was a most uncomfortable silence, only made more uncomfortable by the musicians finishing off the dance with a triumphant peal and the dancers applauding politely.

Lord Lindow nodded curtly. "Good man. Be off with you, and claim your woman."

"*George!*"

"Oh, he knows what I mean," tutted the earl with a grin. "We won't say a word to her until it's all settled between the two of you. How's that?"

"*How's that*"?

Richard took the proffered hand and shook it in a vague daze, as though the Earl of Dalmerlington's floor was spinning.

So, that was all it took, was it? A conversation with her parents, a handshake, and he was in almost every sense of the word engaged to be married.

Engaged. To Evelyn.

The thought fired through him. "I must find her. Now."

"'Must'? Don't see why there's such a rush."

"Oh, George, you know we weren't much better." The countess grinned, and for a moment, Richard could see the young woman in her, one who looked very much like Evelyn. "Let the young people be. She's not here, my lord. She remained at home. Isn't that right, George?"

Richard did not wait to hear the man's response. His feet were already taking him away from the Dalmerlingtons' ball, out into the cool, London air, and along to a particular house behind which there was a small sort of strange studio.

There was only one place Evelyn could have been.

He found her working. Of course he would.

Evelyn's attention was entirely fixed on the canvas before her. She did not even look up as Richard quietly opened the door and let himself into the freezing studio, a mere candle to the side the only source of light.

Even closing the door behind him with a snap did not rouse Evelyn from her work. There was a paintbrush in her mouth, her lips curled around the handle, and her brow was furrowed. There were a few paint splatters across her cheeks, as though she had leaned too closely to the easel as she'd worked.

And Richard realized he had completely fallen in love with her.

When, he did not know. How, he could not tell.

All he knew was that he had Evelyn's parents' blessing to marry her, and he could easily spend the rest of his life with her like this, watching her grow and succeed and excel, and he would need no other life.

"You're watching me."

Richard almost leapt back. Evelyn had not looked up when she had spoken—her gaze remained on the troublesome canvas— but she had spoken in a direct, soft voice that suggested she had been more than aware of him all this time.

Damn it, he really had to stop underestimating her.

"When you look into the future," he said quietly, "what do you see?"

That gained her attention. Evelyn looked up, both hands clutching her paintbrushes now, her mouth falling open. "What sort of a question is that?"

"One I have been pondering," Richard said quietly, slipping into the seat he now considered his chair. "Recently. Very recently."

"What do you see in *your* future?"

It was most unfair of her to turn the tables on him like that, but Richard supposed she had a right to. It was a bold and personal question.

"I wasn't sure for a long time," he said honestly. "When I was abroad, I lived from one day to the next. I did not think much about the future at all."

"And... And now?"

Evelyn's voice was soft, pliable, like the oils she so rarely worked with.

Richard swallowed. *Now?*

He did not answer. At least, not with words. Perhaps there were a few clues in his eyes, the way his focus meandered down her and back to her face. She was attired in an old day gown covered in an apron, though the item had done little to prevent paint and what appeared to be charcoal from coating her gown.

His warmth, his longing, was clearly evident. Evelyn's cheeks pinked.

"I was not expecting a midnight visitor," she said quietly.

"It's not midnight, is it?"

"A nighttime visitor, then," she corrected. "I suppose you came here for a reason?"

A multitude of reasons erupted in Richard's mind.

Because he wanted to tell her he loved her. Because he wanted to reveal the truth, the truth of who he was. Because he wanted to explain how he had spoken to her parents, gained their permission, their consent to marry her.

Because he wanted to ask her whether she would give her consent, in turn. The only consent that mattered.

And for some reason, Richard said none of this. Instead, he said, "You are so clever. I never learned to paint. No one ever taught me."

He spotted the trap only after he had laid and sprung it.

Evelyn grinned. "Well, there's no time like the present. How about a short lesson now?"

Chapter Thirteen

"**W**ELL, THERE'S NO *time like the present. How about a short lesson now?*"

What had possessed her to say that?

Evelyn heard the words echo in her mind as she tried to understand how and why she had said such a thing.

It was far too forward. It was entirely outrageous.

And the worst of it was, her intentions were even more scandalous than how the words could be interpreted.

Richard was still seated. Evidently, he had not entirely believed her. "What are you working on, Evelyn?"

Evelyn attempted to ignore how just the way he spoke her name made ripples of heat soar through her. "I said, how about a short lesson now?"

A teasing smile appeared on his lips. "You cannot be serious."

"Why not?" she retorted. "You think I cannot teach you?"

How she had known that remark would be taken as a direct challenge, she did not know.

No, that was not entirely true. She knew Richard, knew him well. She could predict how he would respond to certain things and this approach, this method of teasing him into it, was one of the few ways he could be encouraged to be so bold.

Not that he needed to be much bolder.

Richard grinned. "I do not have an artistic bone in my body, and I don't need you attempting to teach me to know that."

Trying very hard not to think of the numerous bones in Richard's body, and how much she had adored seeing that body naked, Evelyn said, "I've always wanted to teach someone else. Are you truly willing to deny me?"

Once again, she spoke words that could have been taken innocently… and once again she saw in Richard's eyes that he wondered precisely whether she was speaking not-so-innocently.

Evelyn's breath was short in her lungs. *This is a mistake. This is a brilliant idea. I'll regret this. I'll always regret not doing it.*

Oh, what on earth am I thinking?

She *wasn't* thinking. She was acting instinctively. Something she had never done before.

"You cannot know, I think, what it is to be entirely different from those around you," Evelyn said quietly, placing her paintbrushes into their pot of water.

Richard snorted. "Don't I just."

"You have no role to play in Society. There are no expectations of you," Evelyn countered. "I am the daughter of an earl."

"A privileged position."

"A cage made of gold is still a cage," Evelyn said quietly. "I have always been different. I'm not like my cousin Lilianna, or Gwendoline, content to parade oneself about Society until one finds a husband. I wanted more."

Richard's throat bobbed. "'More'?"

Well, that was more suggestive than she had intended. "More from life," she said quietly. "I want to be an artist."

"You *are* an artist."

"But I am not respected as one. Not considered anything more than a hobbyist with an expensive taste for paint," Evelyn said with a wry smile. "So why not ignore the expectations of Society entirely? Why not continue to be different? Why not… teach you?"

"I-I can't paint," Richard stammered.

Stammered. Evelyn had never seen him so nervous. So uncertain of himself. Here was a man who was almost always the most confident person in the room… and now he was watching as though she could at any moment do something wild.

Perhaps she would.

"I can't paint." For some reason, Richard's voice was hoarse. "I'm telling you, I can't!"

"Afraid of trying something new? Afraid of failing?"

His breath hitched and a flicker of pain across the man's face, a sting she had not intended to inflict. Evelyn thought back to those scars, the pain he must have felt.

How was that a failure? To bear such torture and continue to live, to defy the odds? Was that not a victory?

Richard had continued to affix her with a stern look. "I am telling you, I cannot paint."

"Nonsense. Everyone can paint," Evelyn said briskly, an idea circling her mind so scandalous, she should not have been considering it. "Here."

He had evidently not been expecting her to step toward him. He had also not been expecting her, based on his lack of resistance, to pull him to his feet.

"Evelyn," he said quietly.

A jolt of desire flickered through her. Evelyn did not attempt to ignore it. This was the perfect opportunity, was it not? Her parents at that dull ball, her brother out gambling, her sister at that rally their parents absolutely refused to permit her to attend and so presumably Lucy was once again disguised in Laurent's clothing...

The house was empty. Everyone but the servants was out this evening. No one was expecting her company to discuss the weather, or chat about gowns or whatever insipid politics had occurred today.

No, she had all the time in the world.

And Richard.

He was still protesting. "It takes years to know how to draw, let alone paint. Evelyn, that's not why I came to see you tonight."

"Oh, stop twittering," Evelyn said, her heart in her mouth as she made the decision to do something so risqué, she could hardly believe it of herself. "Now, stand here."

It was easy enough to remove the paper she had been working on and slip a new, fresh-white piece onto the easel.

Richard was grinning uncertainly. "You cannot be serious."

"Look, here," said Evelyn quietly. "I'll start you off."

She leaned past him to pick up a pencil, highly conscious of the way her shoulder brushed up against him.

It should not have made her breathing quicken. It should not have received an answering hiss from Richard.

It did.

Stay calm, Evelyn attempted to tell herself. *If you truly wish to do this, then… then you are going to have to have a much braver approach than that.*

"See, I'll draw an outline for you," she said quietly.

Trying not to be so conscious of just how closely Richard was standing behind her, Evelyn made short work of the empty page. Within minutes, it was no longer empty and had been filled with the sketched outline of a person. They were standing, arms by their sides.

"There," she said, pleased with her effort.

"See, you have already done it—and far better than I could ever do."

"Just trust me, won't you?"

Evelyn had not intended to turn on the spot and say the words mere inches away from Richard's mouth. She had also not intended to whisper them, to fill her voice with a longing she had barely managed to keep hidden from the moment that he had entered her studio.

Still. For all her lack of intentions, the result she had hoped for was most gratifying.

Richard placed a hand on her shoulder. Then it moved to her arm. "I don't know what you expect me to be able to do with that outline."

"Never fear. I would not expect you to be able to draw without a model," said Evelyn as she stepped from him and toward the chair.

No, she could not sit down—that would hinder her purpose. Besides, she had drawn an outline of a person standing. She couldn't very well then sit and make it even more difficult for him.

As she turned on the spot, it was to see Richard tilting his head. "But I don't know how to start."

"Pick up a pencil," Evelyn said, her mouth dry, "and... and caress me with the tip."

Richard's eyes could not have been wider. "I... I'm sorry, I think I almost passed out for a moment there. Did you say 'caress' you?"

"Look at me and caress my body with the tip of the pencil, but on the paper," Evelyn said, heat stirring in her that she had never felt before.

Oh, this was most improper. This was outrageous. This was more forward than she had ever been in her life!

Richard appeared to be having some difficulties with his trousers. He hastily stepped behind the easel and peered out. "Evelyn, this is too much."

"I know," she said softly. "But don't you want to?"

She held his focus for far longer than she could ever have imagined. In that look, Evelyn attempted to tell Richard so much more than her lips would permit her.

How she wanted him to touch her. How his touch would be most welcome, most delicious... how she would have no regrets if he were to kiss her again.

But how to tell him? How to find the words, when words, unlike watercolors, refused to bow to her wishes?

Richard picked up a pencil and, eyes serious, looked at her. Evelyn reveled in it, finding an unexpected delight and frisson in being looked at so.

Dear Lord, no wonder so many artists had affairs with their models. It was... It was electrifying, to be looked at like this. To be consumed by a man's gaze, to know you were the only thing in the room worth looking at.

"I… I feel I must say again that I cannot draw," Richard protested, his pencil making but a few marks on the paper.

Well, it appeared she would have to do something more drastic to make sure her point came across.

"In that case, don't draw," Evelyn said, cheeks burning but resolve determined. "Just watch."

Richard's brow furrowed. "Watch? I don't under… under… Oh, hell."

Oh, hell, indeed. Or rather, quite the contrary: oh, heaven.

Evelyn had never felt anything like it: this power, this vigor that soared through her as she slowly moved her hands behind her back and untied her apron. It fell to her studio floor with a soft sound. It was the only sound in the building.

The only sound, that was, other than a slightly strangled sound from Richard.

So, the apron was off. What next? Ah, yes.

Evelyn did not remove her gaze from Richard as she slowly lifted her hands to remove her hairpins. One by one, they were dropped to the ground, and little by little, her curls cascaded down her shoulders.

Right. What next?

"Evelyn," Richard croaked as she slowly moved her hands down her side, unbuttoning the top of her gown. "You… You don't have to—"

"I know I don't have to," Evelyn said softly, hardly able to believe she could finally speak. "But I want to."

"But—"

"Don't you want me to?" Her voice was nothing more than a whisper, yet Richard had clearly heard it.

"Yes," he murmured, eyes flashing with desire that Evelyn had known had been lying just below the surface. "Don't stop."

She had no intention of doing such a thing. Now that she had begun, now that she had started to cast off the layers of restriction, Evelyn had no idea how she had ever managed to live like this. It was… *freeing* was not a sufficient enough word to encapsulate the elation that slowly untying and unbuttoning her gown, allowing it to fall to the ground, gave her. The euphoria was akin to that of finishing the perfect painting, yet somehow more so.

What she was doing was wrong—Evelyn knew that. She was a lady. Lady Evelyn Chance. Her family expected more of her, better of her, but nothing had ever felt better than this.

She shivered as the camisole and petticoats fell to the floor beside the pool of cotton that was her day gown. Now there was only her corset, chemise, stockings, and drawers left.

Ah. This part, she had not anticipated.

Evelyn looked up and met Richard's hungry eyes. "Dear me, I appear to need assistance. Would you be a dear, and—"

She did not even manage to finish her sentence. With a groan more animalistic than human, Richard dropped the pencil he had been folding and launched toward her.

Within an impossible amount of time, his body met hers. Evelyn gasped at the sudden contact but gasped again as his lips met hers, possessing her, delving his tongue between her lips to taste her, conquering her as though she were the ocean and he a ship sliding between her wet folds.

"I can't help myself," Richard muttered, raining kisses down her neck as his fingers scrabbled at the corsetry at her back. "God forgive me, I *need* you."

"I need *you*." Evelyn gasped, honesty breaking through the limits of her vocabulary. "You think I would do this for any other reason?"

He laughed at that and she laughed with him, and the studio appeared to be filled with nothing but their laughter and the scent of oils and charcoal.

Evelyn could hardly believe this was happening. Finally, after such longing, after such need, after weeks of not understanding where this had come from or what it was, she could finally succumb to the need that had been building between her legs whenever she saw Richard.

Whenever she was in his thrall.

He was continuing to kiss her neck, his lips brushing along her décolletage and shooting desperation to her core. Evelyn had been clinging to his shoulders, hardly aware how she was managing to stand, but now her right hand hurried to find his left and move it to—

Richard dropped her and stepped back as though burned.

The burning was real, and it was in her cheeks. Evelyn turned away, startled and horrified to discover what she had done in the heat of the moment.

Where had that come from? Why had she—had she made him do that?

"Evelyn?"

"Don't look at me," she whispered, shame rushing through her like a tide. All she had dammed up, all she had tried to ignore, came rushing into her.

Why had she done such a thing?

Footfalls. Evelyn did not need to turn around to know Richard was standing mere inches behind her. She could feel him, sense his warmth. Smell his scent.

"Evelyn, if you want me to touch your breast…"

"I'm sorry," she whispered, hating how swiftly she had been overtaken by her desires.

Slowly, soft hands grasped her shoulders and turned her around. She refused to look into his eyes, preferring to look instead at his chest.

His wide chest. A chest that was familiar to her, even with a shirt on. How strange that was; that she should know Richard's chest far better without clothes than with them?

"Evelyn. Evelyn, there is nothing to be ashamed of."

Perhaps there was not. It had all felt so right, so natural, to move Richard's hand to her breast.

Evelyn slowly raised her eyes to Richard's face. He was smiling. It was not the delighted sneer of a rake, nor the frustrated grimace of a rogue. It was a smile that said what she had done was not only acceptable, but… *preferred.*

"I've never done this before," Evelyn whispered.

Richard nodded, lifting a hand to cup her cheek. "I know. And if we are to continue, you have to be sure."

"I am."

"Because I shouldn't—I mean, you are a lady and—"

"'Shouldn't'? I think we *must,*" Evelyn said quietly, delight now soaring through her as she took note of Richard's hesitation.

He was a good man. A great man. This was the man she wished to spend the rest of her life with, and the sudden realization was enough to shock any final sense from her mind.

Whatever the future held, Richard would be in it. And that was enough.

"Please, Richard," Evelyn said quietly, seeing he would not move forward until she requested it. "Please. Ravish me."

And then he was kissing her—kissing her as he had never kissed her before. Evelyn gasped, surprise jolting her body, and the kiss deepened. She moaned as tendrils of desire became arching need, her body thrumming with the prospect of more, more, more.

She could not have expected this giddiness, this desperation to be closer. In fact, it was only when the kiss ended, Evelyn gasping for air, that she realized her scrabbling fingers had somehow removed Richard's coat and waistcoat. His shirt was somehow only half-buttoned.

And it wasn't enough. "I need—I need—"

"I know." Richard panted, grinning as his fingers made light work of her corset, slipping it over her head and managing to somehow remove her chemise and then her drawers in two fluid movements. "Oh, Evelyn. You are magnificent."

"Magnificent"?

She wasn't sure about that. Magnificent suggested there was much to look at, and from the investigations Evelyn had carried out while painting herself in the nude, there wasn't much to impress.

Though when she caught Richard's eye, she wondered if perhaps she should rethink that assessment. There was a look in his expression that suggested he very much enjoyed what he was looking at.

"You are so beautiful," he said slowly, inexplicably dropping to his knees. "So beautiful, Evelyn."

Evelyn stared, bemused. "I never thought my breasts and… and my secret place would bring anyone to their knees."

Richard swallowed for a moment, gazing up at her, then said softly, "Do you think you can be quiet?"

"Quiet"? What on earth does he mean? "Of course I can be— Richard!"

She could not be quiet. She had cried out his name, half-panic, half-ecstasy, as Richard leaned forward and kissed her secret place.

Evelyn's hands swiftly reached for his shoulders. It was all she could do to find them, her eyelids fluttering shut as the shock of his tongue entering her—her *there*—overcame her.

Oh, this was too much. Too much, and somehow, not at all enough.

"Richard," she whimpered.

His reply was one of lips and tongue, but no words. His mouth possessed her, his hungry tongue slowly licking down the slit of her folds until she opened for him, his hands on her hips, steadying her.

The steadiness was greatly needed. Evelyn's whole mind was reeling from the intimacy, from the cascades of pleasure soaring through her body, the twisting ache in her center needing more as his tongue delved deeper.

"Richard, oh, ohh, yes…"

It was all she could do to breathe as the pleasure pulsed, a tight, aching throbbing between his lips as Richard nibbled her nub and she was gone—nothing more than colors streaming through light, her whole body set alight as the pinnacle of pleasure pulsed through her.

When she finally stopped crying out his name, Evelyn was able to look down with bleary eyes at the man who had brought her to such a climax. "That… That was—"

"I want to make you do that again," Richard said hungrily.

Evelyn almost fell over. "'Again'?"

Was it even possible to feel that sort of ecstasy again? Surely, that had been a once-in-a-lifetime experience; such a thing could not be repeated?

Richard had risen to his feet, frantic hands pulling off his boots and trousers until—

Now *that* was one way to distract her.

There he stood, in all his glory. And it *was* glorious. The planes of his torso and the strength in his arms and legs—those were not surprises. Evelyn had taken her fill of those before, knew them well, had sketched that line and this freckle. She knew his scars, the long, thin ones, the curve across his chest, the painful-looking scars from fire that had flickered across his arms and shoulders and back.

But that…

Evelyn swallowed. She had known what a gentleman's manhood looked like, in theory. The number of art books in the Lindow library was extensive, and her father had been most unusual and permitted her to obtain the ones intended for gentlemen, those with color plates of Roman and Greek statues that did not always feature the delicate fig leaf.

But still. This was… *He* was…

Richard glanced down, looking at what Evelyn was staring at. "Am I suitable?"

Evelyn wet her lips as she stared at the jutting thrust of flesh that bobbed slightly. "Y-Yes. Quite suitable."

He grinned, taking her hand and leading her to the pile of furs and blankets. "I knew these would come in handy."

Evelyn could not help but flush. "That is not why I have them."

"I know," he reassured her, brushing the back of his hand down her cheek, then allowing it to continue as it grazed her collarbone, the peak of her nipple. "I know."

And he *did* know. Somehow, and Evelyn could not explain it, Richard knew everything: precisely how she wanted to be kissed, how she wanted to be lowered down slowly onto the rugs. When he covered his body with hers and she gasped at the sudden intimacy, the sensation of flesh on flesh, the way his wiry chest hair scraped across her breasts and caused an aching flicker of pleasure, he knew to wait, not to move as she settled into the moment.

And all Evelyn could think was that this could not have been happening… and she was so glad that it was.

"Are you certain?"

Evelyn blinked up at him. Until now, there had been a way back. It would have been scandalous if the truth of their activities—unchaperoned—had ever surfaced, but they had not—*she* had not crossed that line which once crossed could never be uncrossed.

She nodded. "More certain about this than anything."

"Are you ready?"

"Ready"? Evelyn flushed to think how damp her secret place was, how it dripped in throbbing need with every kiss that he had bestowed on her.

She nodded again.

And then he was in her, filling her, and Evelyn gasped at the sudden intrusion but felt none of the expected pain. In fact, this was—

"Ohhh," she moaned, wrapping her legs around Richard's buttocks. "Oh, yes."

The rhythm started slowly. With each slow movement of his manhood almost out of her, then deeply back in, Richard stretched her until the tweaks of unexpected stinging had gone and nothing remained but waves of pleasure.

And they were building, the waves of pleasure. Richard was

building them, and he knew precisely how to work her. One hand clasped her cheek, keeping the connection, while the other moved to her breasts, mercilessly worshiping her nipples so that with every twist, tweak, tug, the building need in her center heated up.

And Evelyn looked up into the eyes of the man she knew she loved.

"Evelyn. Evelyn, I have to tell you—"

"I know." She gasped, her hands grasping his shoulders as though doing so would keep her attached to the earth. "I know—oh, Richard!"

The second time she climaxed somehow overcame the first. There was something so intimate, so intoxicating about having the man she loved thrusting inside her, propelling her closer and closer to her peak until she flew off it, that Evelyn almost wept as she clung on to him and the pleasure overwhelmed her.

"Damn—God, yes!" Richard's thrusting had changed. The rapid pace became a frenzy as his face worked and he poured himself into her.

When he fell into her waiting arms, Evelyn could only imagine the picture that they presented. Two happy, sated lovers in a tangle of blankets and furs.

She would have to paint it tomorrow. When she could stand.

Chapter Fourteen

June 10, 1840

T HERE ARE THREE very good ways to wake up.

The first one, Richard knew, was to wake up precisely where you expected to be. That was the most common experience, but you did not realize just how special and important it was until you had woken up quite to the contrary.

The second one, Richard thought hazily as he started to come out of dreamland and into consciousness, was with a woman beside you. Preferably one who was not going to ask too many questions and had been a delight the evening before.

The third way was, he was now discovering, in a pile of blankets and furs with Lady Evelyn Chance wrapped around you, entirely naked save for silk stockings.

Richard had to blink a few times to ensure he was not dreaming.

The memories flooded back.

"Are you certain?"

"More certain about this than anything."

It was all he could do not to jerk himself to a seated position as the remembrances startled parts of him—very specific parts of him—to life. But he did not want to wake her. He needed time to think.

"I never thought my breasts and… and my secret place would bring anyone to their knees."

Well. Right. So that had happened and had not merely been a delicious fantasy he had permitted himself to indulge in.

Carefully, without moving more than an inch, Richard peered down. Evelyn was utterly nude, delightfully soft, and curled into his arms as though there were nowhere else she would rather be.

Richard swallowed. *Right.*

It was an entirely new experience. Oh, not waking up and discovering a woman in his bed. That had happened before, though not for a long time.

No, it was the twin knowledge that he had not only taken the innocence of a woman, but that he had not been very careful about it.

His pulse throbbed in his jaw. Not very careful at all. There in the pocket of his trousers, which he could just make out in a pool of fabric on the floor about five feet from him, was a preservative. A French letter, one he had used once before, carefully washed, and replaced for future use.

Future use like last night, for example.

Hell and all its inhabitants.

Evelyn's movements had changed. Richard held his breath, but it appeared she was still dreaming, for she twisted in his arms as though seeking a more comfortable position. That was, apparently, lying against his chest with her spectacular breasts facing the ceiling.

Richard swallowed. *Do not get ahead of yourself, man,* he thought desperately. *For all you know, the wild, passionate artist you bedded last night will wake up as Lady Evelyn Chance and greatly regret the favor she bestowed upon you.*

And what a wonderful favor it had been.

Lost for a moment in happy memories of thrusting himself into her warm, welcoming folds and just how striking she had felt, tensing around his cock as she had climaxed, Richard only realized his mistake too late.

Oh, hell.

His manhood was erect, standing upright in search of pleasure… and it was jutting right into Evelyn's hip.

Right, this was fine—he could move ever so slowly, and—

"Good morning," mumbled Evelyn sleepily, her eyes still shut.

Richard froze. What was he supposed to do now?

Because the trouble was, he had no regrets about the preceding night. What man would, when he'd spoken to a woman's father, gained his permission in a roundabout way, then discovered to his delight that said woman had wished to be ravished?

Oh, the way she had slowly removed her clothes…

This isn't helping!

But Richard could not pretend he had not done something incredibly serious. Bedding an innocent was something men like him simply did not do. He was supposed to be smarter than that.

But it had been Evelyn.

His Evelyn.

"You are awake, aren't you?"

Richard managed to garble something that sounded a lot like "Yes," even though it was cut a tad short by the flicker of need spilling from the end of his manhood.

Damn it. If he didn't find satisfaction soon, or depart quickly and thrust himself bodily into a cold body of water, he was going to have difficulty.

"Oh," said Evelyn muzzily, opening her eyes and looking down at the flesh prodding into her hip. "Oh, I see."

Richard tried not to sigh. It truly was too bad of his body to utterly betray him. When was the last time he had been so entirely out of control? Ten years ago?

Evelyn turned to press her breasts onto his chest, her head resting on her hands. "I see you desire me just as much now as you did last night."

Richard attempted a "Yes" again but could barely manage the single syllable.

As it turned out, that appeared to be well received. "You

know," Evelyn said, her cheeks pinking, but her eyes defiant, "you kissed me down... down *there* yesterday. I suppose it is possible for a man to be kissed in a similar fashion?"

Richard groaned. "Yes! I mean, you don't have to."

"I know I don't have to. I don't have to do lots of things," Evelyn said quietly, pressing a kiss on his cheek. "But I want to. Will you teach me?"

Just for a moment, Richard closed his eyes. Dear God, had he awoken in a nightmare or a dream? This was too much. How was he supposed to restrain himself?

"Do—Do you not worry that someone will come looking for you?" he said quickly.

Coward!

"Not at all. I frequently stay out here all night then meander in at luncheon. Laurent doesn't even expect to help dress me every morning," Evelyn said softly, a slow smile creeping over her face. "Are you saying you don't want me to?"

Richard's manhood was crying out for attention, for Evelyn's fingers, for her mouth, and unfortunately, that made it difficult to speak. "Christ, yes, but—"

"Right. I'm ready to learn," said Evelyn in a far-too-businesslike manner for Richard's liking. "Where do I start?"

He swallowed. *Where, indeed?*

It was one of the few fantasies he had ever permitted himself to indulge in. Oh, the very idea that there would be a woman willing to obey his every request as she took him into her mouth...

And now here he was, a naked Evelyn kneeling between his parted knees—when had she done that?—looking down at his manhood as though she were examining a new paint color.

Richard groaned and his manhood twitched.

"You really do want me, don't you?" murmured Evelyn with a wry smile. "Well, I'm willing. All you have to do is ask."

Trying desperately to concentrate and giving up almost immediately, Richard said in a low voice, "Wet... wet your lips."

He almost exploded immediately—not at the way she did it, her tongue darting out and leaving a trail of wetness across those perfect lips—but at the way she so swiftly obeyed.

Such a good girl...

"*Really* wet them," Richard said more urgently as he pulled a fur toward him and rolled it up as a pillow. He wanted to see this. "Now... Now kneel lower. Lower, so that your mouth is right—there."

Evelyn did so, her attention seemingly transfixed by the inches of flesh springing up from his curls.

And Richard hesitated. Should he have been doing this? Teaching a lady of Society precisely how to pleasure him?

"If you're not going to teach me," said Evelyn sharply, looking up, "then—"

"Fine, fine," said Richard hastily. *Anything to please her. Anything to be pleased by her.* "You... First, you kiss my tip. L-Lick it. Taste me."

The last few words were a whispered cry, almost begging, and Richard could say no more. Evelyn had obediently lowered her head and pressed her wet lips to his tip, her tongue darting out to taste the trickle of need that had escaped him.

Richard fought off the desire to thrust up into her mouth, but only just. God in His heaven, but she was sweet. Eager to please. Inexpert.

Though not for long.

"Now... Now I want you to use your tongue," Richard managed, fisting the blanket he was lying on as he tried desperately not to reach forward and force her head down over his cock. "You need to get me wet. All of me."

"Like this?"

Evelyn did not waste time. Her tongue darted out, lathering him so completely that Richard had to close his eyes for a moment to focus on not exploding over her lips.

No, he wanted more. So much more.

The pleasure was not subsiding, scalding him as he managed,

"Yes—oh Evelyn, yes. Now… now take me in your mouth, a-as much as you can and… and suck. Suck me. Suck me, please!"

He was begging now, but Richard could not help it. The moment he had first said, "suck," Evelyn had done precisely what he wanted: placed both hands on his hips and slowly parted her lips over his tip and swallowed him down.

Oh, dear God, I am in paradise.

Richard tried to remember to breathe as Evelyn slowly lowered herself over his cock, her wet tongue tasting, exploring every inch of him, the gentle sucking making his head spin.

And then she stopped. "And is that it?"

"'It'?" Richard could barely speak. *'It'?* "Now… Now do all of that while moving up and down my length. Don't—just don't stop, please."

Any thoughts of decorum, that at any point they could be interrupted, that he was ruining one of the most beautiful and precious women in the world—all thoughts disappeared as Evelyn grinned.

"Good," she said quietly. "I don't intend to stop until you climax in my mouth."

It was all Richard could do not to climax immediately, but he was rewarded for his forbearance. Evelyn was as good, or as bad, as her word. Licking, tasting, sucking, she lost herself in servicing him and Richard felt his body stiffen and tauten as he grew closer and closer to ecstasy.

"So close," he panted, watching Evelyn's head bob up and down over his cock and knowing he wanted to give her a taste of what she was working within him. "So—So close. Please, please don't stop, don't—Evelyn!"

He had never lost control like that before. Never realized how liberating it was to give into the pleasure. Never wanted to weep as he did while Evelyn sucked on him at his peak, lapping up his pleasure and swallowing it down as though she could not get enough.

When Evelyn finally leaned back on her heels and looked at

him in awe, lips a dark pink from their ministrations, Richard knew he would never be able to share this with anyone else.

She had ruined him. Ruined him, for all others. And he did not care.

"So," she said lightly. "What happens next?"

Richard did not give her any additional time to speak—to think. He moved swiftly, gripping her wrists and pulling her forward. "Mount me."

Evelyn blinked, as though she had absolutely no idea what he meant. "I—I beg your pardon?"

"I *said*, mount me," said Richard urgently. God, his manhood was thickening again. It was an occupational hazard, it appeared, of being around her. Especially when she was naked.

Evelyn was staring, lips parted. "Do—Do you mean…?"

"Think of it like riding a horse," Richard said, trying desperately to keep the begging tone from his voice. He had *some* pride. Probably. "Trust me. You'll enjoy it."

It could not have been more clear that Evelyn was not sure he would be right, but she shifted forward to straddle him and slowly lowered herself onto his stiffening manhood, her slick folds a surefire demonstration of how aroused she had become as she had ministered to him.

Evelyn's eyes widened. "Oh! Oh, that feels…"

Her voice trailed off, but Richard needed to know, needed to hear her say it. "Tell me, Evelyn. Tell me how it feels."

"I can never explain how I feel right now."

"I need to hear it. I need to hear you," Richard said quietly.

She met his gaze, and something passed between them that was greater than lust, better than desire. It could only have been love.

"I… You fill me, and every time you move, I feel… I feel pleasure," Evelyn whispered.

"Good," said Richard softly. "Now ride me."

"'Ride'?"

"Pretend I'm a horse and you're galloping across a common,"

Richard said with a wry smile. "Your body will know what to do."

Evelyn evidently did not think so, but her devotion to him was complete. Though clearly not sure why she was doing so, she slowly raised herself up until only his tip was nestled within her, and she dropped, faster, onto him.

"Ohhhh…"

"You like that? You like spearing yourself with me?" Richard said, trying to remind himself desperately that he was speaking to a member of the nobility.

One who was naked and whose breasts bounced most deliciously as she moved.

Damn it!

"I like it," murmured Evelyn, her cheeks flushed, but her smile wide. "You know, I might just do it again."

And she did. It was all Richard could do, holding on to the blanket and watching the picture of erotic mystery, to prevent himself from spilling his seed in her within seconds. Evelyn's movements became more fluid as her confidence grew, her breathing becoming panting becoming whimpers as he saw the pleasure build in her.

God, he could do this for the rest of his life.

"Richard I'm going to—"

"Take all the pleasure you can get," he whispered.

Evelyn threw back her head as she rode him to completion, her fluttering moans quieter this morning but still more than loud enough to echo around the studio.

It was too much. Richard had held back, but he could no longer. He allowed himself to revel in the glory of her pleasure and soon his own had arrived.

"Yes—yes, Evelyn, yes!"

Richard lost himself to the thrusting as his climax poured into her. This time, it was she who fell into his arms, and they lay there for goodness knew how long, their lungs ragged, their need to touch each other absolute.

When, eventually, Evelyn pushed herself up and slowly dismounted from him, Richard felt her absence like a thrust of a dagger into his guts. Which he knew well.

"I asked you before what happens next," she said softly, lying to his side and flushing as she spoke. "I suppose I will need to ask it again."

Richard swallowed.

What happens next?

It was an excellent question, and not one he thought he could answer in this moment. There was not enough blood in his brain to make it work. It was still, mostly, south of his waist.

But as his ribcage unclenched and his body started to relax, Richard realized that there was no need to answer that question right now.

He loved Lady Evelyn Chance. He was almost certain she returned his affection—if not, then he had grossly misunderstood the last twelve hours or so. He had her parents' support to ask for her hand. So. All of that was taken care of.

The only thing left was to decide how to propose.

And he couldn't do it here. Richard may have been a rake at times, but he knew enough about the ladies of Society to know there were some expectations when it came to declaring one's love and asking for the lady's hand.

Doing so while lying naked, desire-soaked, and recently bedded was not the way to do it.

So all he had to do was prepare a proposal that was worthy of her in the next day or two, and then Evelyn would know everything.

"I think we enjoy ourselves until luncheon, and you have to disappear off to your family," Richard said quietly.

For a moment, a shadow flickered over Evelyn's face. He had expected it. She had hoped for something more concrete; something more promising for the future for which she clearly wished.

It would all be worth it, he knew, once he had revealed his

identity and asked her to become his viscountess.

"Is that not what some of the greatest artists say?" Richard added. "To enjoy oneself? To be in the moment?"

For a heart-stopping moment, he thought Evelyn was going to disagree with him. That she was going to tell him that she needed more, more than he could give her right now. That he would lose her, merely because he had not prepared a proposal in advance.

She smiled. She kissed him, hard on the mouth. And she giggled. "Well, unless we want a repeat of what just happened, I suppose we had better put our clothes on."

"You drive a hard bargain," Richard said dryly.

It was not much of a hardship, in truth. Evelyn fully dressed was still intensely desirable, and with the knowledge of what they could share, what her mouth could do, it was challenging in the extreme to get his trousers on.

"Blast."

Richard looked up, astonished. "Did you just say, 'blast' again?"

"Well, you have ravished me now," Evelyn said lightly, though her cheeks were pink as she turned to face him by the easel. "I suppose it is only fair that you can start to learn my faults."

'Faults'? The woman had uttered one of the mildest curses known to mankind, and she considered it a fault?

The time for luncheon came and went. Richard felt the hunger of his stomach, but he was far more interested in being here, with Evelyn. She laughed as they talked, him seated in the chair with his shirt off, her by the easel, drawing. He told her about the time that he had been accidentally shipwrecked off the coast of Brittany; she told him of the time she and her sister had been accidentally brought up before the magistrates of Kensington.

"A complete misunderstanding," she said blithely, narrowing her eyes as she attempted something clearly complicated on the paper.

"But—magistrates?"

"My father straightened the whole thing out. It was a misunderstanding, as I said," Evelyn said lightly. "The trouble was of course that Lucy had absolutely done it and I had been apprehended attempting to stop her, but no one would believe an earl's daughter would try to break a prisoner out of Newgate. She was most upset."

Richard was not surprised. "That she was caught?"

"That she wasn't punished!" Evelyn laughed. "She said it was an example of how the rich and powerful continue on with their lives unheeded by… something else. I forget. What was I saying?"

Her cheeks flushed as her attention returned to his eyes—returned after dwelling a while on his bare chest.

Richard grinned. "Weren't you going to teach me to draw?"

And so she did attempt to teach him to draw. It was a complete fiasco.

"What is that, a sheep?"

"It's a horse!" Richard said defensively, trying not to laugh as Evelyn turned his paper upside down as she squinted at it. "Haven't you ever seen a horse before?"

"Not one like that," she retorted with a grin. "Poor thing."

"The horse, or me?"

"Oh, you, most definitely." Evelyn laughed, returning his drawing to him and shaking her head. "I am afraid there is no hope for you. No natural talent whatsoever."

He might have been offended, if he had not been laughing so hard. "That is what I was trying to tell you last night!"

Infuriating woman. Delicious woman. Woman who had completely stolen his affections and could never give them back.

There was a twinkle of mischief in Evelyn's eyes as she returned to her easel and picked up a charcoal. "Aren't you glad that I ignored you and decided to model for you instead?"

Richard swallowed. So grateful. So glad. So unsure of how he had managed to capture the attention of this beautiful, irritating, clever woman that sometimes he was worried that if he breathed wrong, it would all disappear and the dream would be over.

Evelyn had not waited for his reply. Her concentration had left him, focusing instead on the paper before her.

He left her to her art as he remained as still as he could, desperate to please her. Besides, in the comfortable companionable silence in which she worked, he could be thinking—about the perfect proposal.

Chapter Fifteen

June 12, 1840

"...DON'T YOU THINK, Evelyn?"

Evelyn tried to hum her approval. Or disapproval. She could not quite remember what she was supposed to be agreeing to or disagreeing with. How could anyone, when the weather was so lovely?

A honeybee bumbled along somewhere near her. The sun shone down. A bird, a blackbird, sang cheerfully above them.

"I *said*, don't you think, Evelyn?"

"How can anyone think in this weather?" Evelyn said lazily, her eyes still closed. "It's so hot."

Something hit her. It was a book.

"Ouch!" Evelyn sat up, eyes open but narrowed now, and glared at her brother. "I was dozing!"

"We were talking," he said pointedly with a scowl. "I was asking your advice and you fell asleep!"

Ah. Well, when he put it like that, she had been a little rude. But how was she supposed to stay awake when it was this hot? Even sat where they were, in the shade on a few rugs that Cawthorne had permitted them to take outside, it was difficult to keep one's eyes open.

Especially as Evelyn had been kept up all night a few days before...

Flushing at the memory and hoping Percy presumed the

redness was from the heat of the sun rather than any wrongdoing—but how could such wonderful memories be wrong?—Evelyn attempted to make amends.

It was not easy.

"Remind me," she said, lying back down on the blanket and telling herself sternly not to close her eyes. "What were you asking my advice about?"

Percy sighed heavily. "I don't know if I can tell it all again."

"No, go on," Evelyn said, guilt tinging her tone. She really should have been paying attention. It was rare that Percy ever opened up, and it had been months since they had had a civil conversation lasting more than five minutes. His betrayal, his lies, had hardened her heart against him for quite some time. "I really am going to listen."

Her brother shot her a fleeting glance that was most unconvinced, then sighed again. "It's just…"

And whatever it was had to have been important, Evelyn supposed. She couldn't be certain because after those two words, she had sunk down into a warm, comforting embrace and was drifting off over a lake in a curricle, rocking her gently to sleep…

This time, it was not a book. Percy actually shoved her. "You promised you would stay awake!"

"I did not actually promise," Evelyn said hastily, stifling a yawn and wondering how on earth her brother was managing to stay awake in this heat.

"You know what? Forget it."

Evelyn watched in dismay as her brother rose to his feet. "I do apologize, Percy. Look, I'll sit up and everything."

"I've tried, haven't I, to prove myself after lying to you all? Tried to prove that I've changed," he said, cheeks reddening, "and yet you won't even listen to me."

Now there really was guilt twisting in her. "Percy, just sit down and—"

"No, I would much prefer to find someone who actually wants to listen," he said darkly. "If there *is* anyone. You go back to your dozing, Evelyn."

It was not exactly the most encouraging remark, and shame tinged her cheeks as Evelyn watched Percy return to the house.

Blast.

They had been worried about Percy for weeks, the whole family—and she could have gained some knowledge there if it hadn't been so wonderfully warm out. After his misadventures, and his lies, it should have been her priority to listen to him and find out what on earth was going on... if she hadn't been so distracted with far more pleasant thoughts.

Despite her guilt, a smile drifted across Evelyn's face. Well, it was difficult to feel guilty for long when she had so many glorious memories to lose herself in.

Richard.

He was everything she could have imagined and more. So much more. There were times when Evelyn woke up in the night and wondered whether she had merely dreamed him. He was so much more of a man than she had believed could exist: honest and true. Richard was direct, never hiding his feelings or pretending to be anything other than he was.

And he was hers.

Evelyn sat up—she really mustn't fall asleep in the sun, her cheeks would burn and then where would she be—and hugged her knees.

Richard was her secret. That was part of the pleasure of it— that, as well as the fact that though she knew she loved him, there were few other facts she truly knew about him. That would have to end soon; Evelyn had practiced in her mind the speech she would give to her parents, hoping to persuade them to give their consent, and she had managed to find a way to phrase things so that even a beggar man would be suitable.

But she had to wait. For one, both of her parents had been acting oddly around her the past two days, her father going so far as to ask if she had anything to tell him.

He could not have suspected the truth. He would not have

been coy if so.

So no, she did not have anything to tell him. Not yet. Not until Richard made his intentions absolutely clear.

As soon as they were formally introduced to him, her secret, her model whom they thought merely sat for her under her maid's watchful eye, Evelyn was certain that they would approve.

Until then, he was all hers.

Evelyn sighed with happiness. She hadn't done much to deserve this. She would just have to hope that she did nothing to ruin it.

And she had time on her hands now. Why not bring out her current project and see if she could improve the landscape background a little?

It did not take long to bring out her travel easel and set it up. The canvas she was working on was not a large one, and within another ten minutes, her paints were set up on a small table she had brought out of the studio and she had filled a glass bottle with water from the gardeners' tap. She was ready.

Evelyn cast a critical eye over the painting as she lifted the linen sheet she had been using to protect it from the elements. The figure itself was perfect; there was no improvement she could make there, at least, not until her skill itself improved.

But the landscape—there was definitely more she needed to do there. The shadows weren't quite right, and she was not quite happy with the shade of blue she had mixed for the water in the river. Ultramarine. Cobalt. Powder blue. Sky blue. Cornflower.

Evelyn lost herself in the work. That was one of the delights of painting, after all: to cease to exist, to pour oneself onto the canvas and become one with the art. Time stilled, or ceased to be. Sunlight poured down and that was the only sign that she was even here at all. Cerulean here, and a dash of duck-egg white, just to lighten it—there. Her smallest brush, nothing else would do. The curves and ripples of the river's currents was a challenge, yes, but she had practiced so often with the canals of Venice, this would surely be—

"You know, I don't think you can hear me, can you?"

Evelyn jumped. Her gaze disturbed, it took her a moment to look around the travel easel and see Richard standing there, his coat over his shoulder and his face clearly glowing from the heat of the day, beaming.

Hastily covering up the painting carefully with the linen sheet, she said, "You startled me!"

"I have been standing here talking to you for almost a minute," Richard said, only a tad reproachfully. "But then I forget how swiftly you can lose yourself in your craft. What are you working on?"

"Nothing," she said instinctively.

Precisely why she wished to hide this from him, Evelyn did not know. All her mind's certainty focused, however, on these facts.

Firstly, the painting was not complete. Therefore, no one should see it.

Secondly, her skills were not complete. Therefore, no one should see it.

Thirdly, she did not want Richard to see it. Therefore, he should not see it.

Richard was grinning. "What are you hiding under there? I know it's not another model—is it one of those nude self-portraits? I wouldn't mind having one of those on my walls."

Flushing furiously and glancing about to ensure that there were no gardeners or brothers in the vicinity—there were not, thank goodness—Evelyn attempted to wrangle her tongue into gear. "It's not me."

"Then who is it?" Richard asked, throwing down his coat onto the blankets and folding his arms. "You don't have to show me, but...but I would love to see it. I would love you to feel comfortable enough to show me."

Evelyn swallowed.

When he puts it that way...

Evelyn did not quite know what made her do it. Perhaps it

was simply because it was Richard. He was hers, and she was his, and if she could not share this with him, then with whom could she?

She was never going to be more intimate with anyone else.

Still, she could not deny that the shivers rushing down her spine were most strange as she slowly lifted the linen sheet from her painting.

"Th-There."

Richard did not move. He remained staying on the other side of the easel. "Come here."

It was an easy request to fulfill. Evelyn stepped happily into his welcoming arms, accepted the kiss on her forehead with a shiver of pleasure, and knew, completely, that she was making the right decision.

He was the right decision.

"Whatever you are creating on the other side of that canvas, I will love it," Richard murmured, his breath fluttering against her neck. "Just as I love you."

The gasp that escaped Evelyn's throat was short, and sharp, and unexpected.

Love.

The words echoed in her mind like a pealing bell, repeating over and over until all she could hear was Richard's declaration of love.

He loved her.

Giving no thought to whether anyone from the house could be watching, Evelyn flung her arms around Richard and kissed him hard on the mouth.

His response told her everything. His hands clasping her waist, the way his lips parted, welcoming her in…

How long they stood there passionately kissing, Evelyn was not sure. She did know that when they finally broke apart, her face was pink and her heart was full.

"Come and take a look," she said, shyness almost overcoming her tongue.

Together, they stepped around the easel. Richard's arm was around her waist as they stood before it and Evelyn forced herself not to examine his face as he looked at the canvas.

It was still very much a work in progress. The background was incomplete. She had not added any carmine red at all, and the figure… Well, it was the first true portrait she had attempted. There would be better ones in the future, she was certain. Almost certain.

The silence between them elongated until Evelyn could no longer help it. She looked up at him.

Richard's eyes were transfixed on the canvas. Unwavering and unfaltering, there was no hint of emotion in his face. Whether he approved of her work or loathed it, she could not tell.

Evelyn swallowed. He had said nothing. *It was not that bad, was it?*

She looked away from the man and stared instead at the painting. There was another Richard—perhaps not a completely true likeness, but she had done her best. The proportions were right, and so was his manly shape, covered sadly by the fashions of the day. His hair was almost perfect, though she could never capture the vibrancy of the shine when the sun gleamed down on him.

It had been the eyes that had given her the most trouble. The real eyes were filled with teasing and kindness all the time, while mischief and danger darted in at moments.

That was not something easy to capture.

Evelyn looked back at Richard. The man, that was. "Well?"

"Well what?" Richard asked with a grin.

She nudged him hard in the ribs.

"Ouch!"

"You deserved that," she said severely, seeing with relief that he was still smiling. "What do you think? No one else has seen it—no one else even knows I'm working on it. Working on him— you."

"What do I think? I think you are remarkably talented and I am not worthy to be your subject," said Richard with a slow shake of his head. "Do I really look that handsome?"

This time, Evelyn's nudge in his ribs was gentler. Just a tad. "You have to say that because you're in love with me."

"I'm not that in love with myself to think that I really look like that." Richard snorted, leaning forward to take a closer look at the painting. "I am flattered. You have improved all my faults."

Evelyn looked between the man and the portrait. "I don't see any faults."

When he turned back to her, his expression had softened. "You have to say that because you're in love with me."

Her heart stopped.

She *was* in love with him. Evelyn would not deny it, but still—she had not said the words, and it felt exposing, to have Richard point out her affection for him before she had found the courage to say it herself.

Richard's smile had faltered as a light breeze ruffled his hair. "I mean—I presumed that—you do not have to say… If you do not, that is fine. I only—"

"I do love you, Richard," Evelyn said quietly, hating how an unexpected shyness overcame her as the words left her mouth. "I… I love the way that sounds."

It was difficult not to delight in it. Here they were, two people who had found each other—in all the world, he had seen her advertisement and now here he was. Here they were.

"But I still think you are being ridiculous about the painting," Evelyn added, refusing to let the topic drop. "It is not all that impressive. See, the shadows here, they aren't quite working yet and—"

"And because you love me, you should trust that I am telling you the truth," Richard interjected with a serious frown.

Evelyn swallowed down the retort that was on the tip of her tongue and really looked at him. Her Richard. Her model. The only man she wished to look at for the rest of her life.

And she saw the truth there. She smiled.

"Well, it's not perfect, but it is good," she conceded.

Richard snorted again. "That's the trouble with you artists. You are never satisfied."

"And that's the trouble with you models. You always are," Evelyn shot back happily.

Their laughter mingled in the summer air and Evelyn could not recall ever being this happy. The troubles with Percy were forgotten, her frustrations with never being treated like a proper artist were a thing of the past.

And she had a lover. Perhaps she was a true artist, after all.

Chapter Sixteen

June 14, 1840

"HERE," SAID RICHARD with a flourish, pressing his ring into the sealing wax. "Have this sent to Lady Evelyn Chance, will you?"

Verwood raised an unimpressed eyebrow. "I do not believe you wish me to do that, my lord."

It was not the response Richard had expected. After all, the man had served him almost the entirety of his viscountcy. True, his orders had not always been the most logical—giving Smith enough funds for a comfortable retirement and sending all the rest of servants to the country estate then disappearing to France without so much as a message about when he would return sprang to mind.

But still. He was the viscount. Verwood was the butler.

"I think I do want you to do that, actually," Richard said aloud, gesturing with the envelope.

His butler took the letter delicately but made no move to depart the study and enact the order. "I repeat, my lord, I do not believe you actually wish me to do this."

Richard leaned back in his chair and examined his willowy servant closely. What the devil had gotten into the man? Was it not a simple request?

"Look," he said heavily. "I think I have made it perfectly plain what I wish to do. Lady Evelyn Chance and I have an understanding. I wish to make that understanding more permanent. Are you with me so far?"

Verwood inclined his head. "With you every step of the way, my lord."

Damn, but the man was exasperating. "In order to make this betrothal formal, I need to meet with Lady Evelyn. I am sure you can see the logic of that."

"The logic is irrefutable, my lord."

Now the trickle of irritation was starting to seep through Richard. Trying to ignore it, and wondering why on earth he was attempting to negotiate with his butler, he continued. "Lady Evelyn therefore needs to come here. She will need my address. Within that envelope is both my invitation and my address. Do you see the necessity of sending that letter now?"

"No, my lord," said his butler smoothly.

"What the devil do you mean?"

"Am I to understand that the lady still has no idea of your true identity during these… ahem… modeling sessions?"

It had been an awkward conversation to have with his servants, Richard would admit—though it did clear up some confusion about where he had been going all these weeks.

"Yes, you are correct," he said shortly.

"And my understanding is that you do not wish the lady to know of your identity until the moment of proposal. Are you with me so far?"

By Jove, the man was taking liberties. "Verwood, I asked you to deliver that letter, not debate with me about logic!"

"So you wish me to take this letter—"

"Yes!"

"—and have it delivered to Lady Evelyn Chance—"

"Yes!" By God, he would have to take his servants in hand.

"—with the seal of the Viscount Sempill on the envelope," finished Verwood sweetly.

"Yes—oh." Richard stared at the letter in his butler's hand as heat flooded his face. "Oh, damn."

"Do you see the necessity of not delivering this letter now?"

"You think you're very clever, don't you, Verwood?" said Richard with a heavy sigh, holding out his hand for the return of his letter.

His butler did not smile, though Richard imagined it was a challenge. "I wouldn't dare to presume, my lord."

It took but a moment to slit open the envelope, and another minute or so to place the letter into a fresh envelope, which was sealed with a dab of wax but no demarcation of his ring.

There. That hadn't been too difficult.

"And will I frequently be your personal messenger to Lady Evelyn Chance, my lord?" asked his butler none too delicately as he took the refreshed envelope. "It is usually a footman's task."

Richard had to smile at that. "I trust *you*, Verwood. And I hope your messenger service will not be necessary much longer. I hope she will be Lady Sempill before long."

Lady Sempill. It was a strange thought. There had been times in the past when he had been almost certain that the viscountcy would die out. There were no other heirs, no convenient cousins, not even—as far as he could tell—an illegitimate brother somewhere about. His father had been loyal, and he himself had not considered matrimony.

Not until now.

Richard glanced about his study. This would make a wonderful studio. It faced full south, gaining the benefits of sunshine and brightness almost all year round. In fact, if he cleared out that card room on the west side of the house, he could make that his study and this could be Evelyn's.

Her, here, in his house. *Their* house, by then. It was a strange feeling, one of warmth and uncertainty.

It would be a new era. There would be a viscountess again. It was in a small way a step down for Evelyn; she was the daughter of an earl, after all, but still—they would have plenty of opportunity to see her family, she would hardly be taken out of her circle.

He may even have to find room in the garden for another studio…

"Will there be anything else, my lord?"

Richard snapped back to the present. The proposal had not happened yet. Until Evelyn knew who he was, knew truly how much he could offer her, there was no point in daydreaming. At least, not too much.

"No, no, just the delivery of that letter," he said aloud. "Oh, and ask Mrs. Anstruther to come up here, will you?"

What followed was a very awkward conversation with his housekeeper.

"A woman!" Her nostrils flared.

"A new mistress of this house," Richard amended. He had foreseen the difficulty, naturally, but had not imagined it would be considered this unsurpassable. "You were kindness and efficiency itself when my mother was alive."

"But that was the dowager viscountess, m'lord!" The stocky Mrs. Anstruther appeared to be having some difficulties arranging her thoughts in a fresh direction.

Richard tried not to look impatient. "Any woman that I marry will become the new viscountess, Mrs. Anstruther."

Mrs. Anstruther's eyes widened. "A new viscountess?"

It took a further five minutes for his housekeeper to concede that yes, she supposed her master could marry if he wanted to, and yes, technically that would make the woman a viscountess— no, *the* viscountess, Richard suggested—and that would make her the woman in charge of the property.

The new viscountess, that was. Not Mrs. Anstruther.

She did not look convinced as she departed from his study, but Richard did not have any more time to pacify servants.

He needed to prepare the house.

Only now that he was attempting to see it through Evelyn's eyes did Richard realize just how passive he had become with his property. Why, there was chaos everywhere. The library had never been tidied before this century, it appeared, the garden looked as though wolves had attacked the east border, and his bedchamber...

Well. Richard was not a tidy man by nature.

It took the combined efforts of Richard, Mrs. Anstruther, Verwood—when he had returned from Evelyn with a short note agreeing to his suggested outing tomorrow, her lady's maid in tow—two maids, an undermaid, a footman, and a gardener to get the place in order. *Spick and span*, Richard thought with an exhausted back as he surveyed the progress made. Almost habitable. How had he lived like this for so long?

The very last task on his list was to go through his study. The desk was almost lost to a pile of correspondence he had not responded to; his spying days firmly over, he had not seen fit to reply to the many letters from his colleagues in France. He was not going to return to that life—he could not. He had a new life to think of. A life with Evelyn.

A restless night followed. Evelyns cascaded around him in his dreams, some laughing at him for offering matrimony, others running from him because his proposal speech had been uninspiring. One Evelyn asked him to paint his love for her and had wept when Richard had been unable to capture his affection through paint.

When Richard finally awoke, it was with relief that the day was finally here.

Today, he would propose matrimony to Lady Evelyn Chance.

His letter had suggested ten o'clock—not too early, but early enough that they would have the rest of the day to luxuriate in being a betrothed couple. He had been, however, after further reflection that providing his address might prove too direct, rather circumspect about the place to meet.

"I've never arranged to meet a man on the corner of two streets before," Evelyn said cheerfully from under her blue parasol. Laurent the lady's maid stood a few feet to her mistress's side, offering Richard a wink. "It all feels mightily scandalous, do you not think?"

Richard tried to smile. Now she put it like that, he could see how his request had been outrageous.

That was the trouble with spending the last few years in France as a spy. One did not have to concern oneself with the petty trivia of Society's expectations.

"I hope you do not mind," he said, his nerves fraying and his tone suggesting far more panic than he wished.

"'Mind'? Not at all, it's an adventure, as promised," Evelyn said, slipping her arm into his without a second thought. "So, where to?"

Richard swallowed. He had considered this most carefully, he had thought, but now he had to enact the plan, it seemed… Well. Foolish.

"I have managed to secure permission to visit a private house," he said carefully. "The… the owner has a stunning art collection. It has never been shown in public."

As he had predicted, Evelyn's eyes widened. "What—truly, never before?"

"Not in my lifetime," Richard said truthfully. "I thought you might wish to see them."

"In a private house?" Evelyn asked eagerly.

He nodded. It had seemed easiest this way; slowly revealing himself would be a far more entertaining and enjoyable experience, for the both of them.

"Well, I admit myself curious," she said, glancing around. "Which way?"

Richard did not speak much as he guided her along the street, Laurent keeping graciously a few steps behind them. Precisely what he was going to say, he did not know. Living on the edge, taking each day as it came, never bothering to plan because who knew what was going to happen… that was more his style.

It had kept him alive. Only now did he wonder whether it would help him truly live.

When he stopped outside his home, he glanced nervously at

the woman beside him. "Here we are."

Evelyn peered up at the redbrick townhouse, closing her parasol and narrowing her eyes against the bright sunlight. "It's a pleasant building. A private home, you said?"

Richard's throat was remarkably dry. "Yes."

"It is so rare to be permitted to see private art collections," she said curiously. "You are completely certain that the owner does not mind?"

It was all he could do not to grin. "I am certain. The owner… The owner understands your love of art. He thought that you would appreciate seeing his collection."

Evelyn pursed her lips. "Indeed. How intriguing! Shall we go in?"

Richard had to admit, Verwood did an admirable job of keeping his face straight as he welcomed the two of them in, a footman ready to collect their things beside him.

"Sir, miss."

"'Miss'?" repeated Evelyn with a raised eyebrow.

"Oh—I, I thought it would be more pleasant if we did not give our full names," Richard added hastily. *Blast, he should have thought of a better explanation than that.* "It's… It's more private."

"Oh." Clearly, she had never been referred to as 'miss' before, and from what Richard could see, Evelyn appeared to like it. "Incognito."

He could not be further from incognito if he tried. "Something like that."

As the footman hung up Evelyn's bonnet and parasol and Richard's top hat, but before he could step away, Laurent cleared her throat.

"My lad—*miss*," she said. "I will follow this man to the servants' quarters for some tea. My throat is parched."

Verwood raised a brow at Richard, and Richard shrugged. The butler gave the order.

It was not as if his own servants would gossip about the two of them left alone without a chaperone. Especially since Evelyn was soon—he was certain—to be his viscountess.

"Very well," said Evelyn cheerily. The footman and Laurent walked away.

Richard watched her as she slowly turned on the spot and took in his hallway.

"What do you think?" he asked finally, unable to help himself.

Evelyn did not answer immediately. She continued to turn and look around her, while Richard attempted to guess what she was marveling at.

It was just his hallway. Nothing spectacular—nothing compared to his country estate, at least. These red bricks did not permit much of an entranceway, but there was sufficient room for an umbrella stand, a coatrack, two landscapes, a small console table by the front door, and a longcase clock.

And that was it. As far as Richard was concerned, there was not much here to entertain.

"What is it?" he asked again eventually, unable to help himself. "What do you see?"

Evelyn started, as though she had entirely forgotten that he was there. "Oh, hello."

"Hello," said Richard, stifling a smile. "What are you looking at?"

"Just trying to imagine the person who lives here," she said softly. "I think I have a good impression of him."

That did not sound particularly as though it boded well. Richard attempted to hold his head high and not catch his butler's eye as he asked, "Oh?"

"Yes," mused Evelyn, a thoughtful look on her face. "He is a wealthy man, I think. Not extravagant—the ceiling has needed to be painted for perhaps a summer or two, but it would last another and he has evidently decided not to part with the funds until it is desperate. And yet these paintings—a Rembrandt and a Sir Godfrey Kneller. Not cheap painters to have in your home. And look at the frames."

Richard did so. He remembered ordering them from Sotheby's.

"Impressive. Gold gilt, and in a style that fits the paintings," pondered Evelyn quietly. "Here is a man who thinks about these things. But he's not vain."

Richard's chest puffed out. "He's not?"

She shook her head. "Look at the coat stand."

For a moment his heart lurched almost out of his ribcage. Hell, had he accidentally left something there that would betray him?

"Those scarves of many different colors," Evelyn said, pointing. "A red one, a blue, a yellow—no one's complexion could suit all those colors. He does not care, even if he must look ridiculous in at least one of them."

Richard's shoulders slumped and he deflated. *Ah.*

"How very well put, Miss," said Verwood gravely. "I quite agree."

Richard shot him a look, but his butler only inclined his head dutifully.

"Let us look around the rest of the house," Evelyn said lightly. "I suppose the Viscount Sempill will wish to return to his home eventually."

It was fortunate, indeed, that Richard had not been attempting to walk at that moment. He would surely have tangled his feet in a knot and slipped over, making a most disagreeable mark on the carpet, and undoubtedly his own face.

How the devil did she discern that?

"You do not need to look so startled," said Evelyn, laughing at his surely astonished expression. "I do not suppose it matters overly if I know to whom we are indebted."

No, Richard supposed not—though he would have to alter part of his speech now. "I just... How did you...?"

"The man is not very observant," said Evelyn with a grin. "Much like you. You haven't noticed that his post has been left here, on the table, and not brought through at breakfast?"

Richard stared down in horror. He had not had breakfast, his attention entirely affixed upon getting the house ready for her visit. The post, most unfortunately, he had entirely not noticed during their wild clean and tidy of the place.

> *Viscount Sempill*
> *14 Bourdon Street*
> *Mayfair*

Evelyn was peering through the doorway into the drawing room. "Shall we continue? I have heard Viscount Sempill is a truly renowned art collector—why did you not say you knew him?"

Richard tried hard not to wince as he followed her into the drawing room, but it was a challenge. "It... It was actually the current viscount's father who was the art collector. I believe."

"Oh, yes, I remember now. I wish he had continued collecting," Evelyn said vaguely as she glanced about. "Dear Lord, is that a Mercier?"

That was the common refrain as they moved throughout the house. Every room revealed another artist Evelyn raved about for several minutes before they moved a few feet to the left and she discovered another artist she could not believe was here.

"A Reynolds right beside a Ramsay!"

Each one of her comments cast the paintings in a fresh light. Richard had never paid much attention to them, yet as Evelyn chattered about this one's use of red or this artist's love of symbolism, he realized he lived within a treasure trove.

Soon, they both would.

"Well, I must say, this has been delightful." Evelyn beamed as they reached the second floor. "I did not believe one building could hold so many treasures!"

"And there are just two more to go," Richard said quietly. "I... I hoped this would be a memorable day for you."

Unbidden, Evelyn slipped her hand into his. "Every day with you is memorable. Whenever I wish to return to one, I can close my eyes and step into the moment. It's crystal clear."

His heart lurched. This was it. This was the moment.

"I thought you would like to see a portrait of the man who collected such striking artworks," he said aloud.

Evelyn nodded and they progressed along the top corridor, drawing to a halt by the almost full-sized portrait of his father.

Richard watched her carefully.

"He was truly a striking man," she said quietly. "Look at his bearing. You can tell he was a kind man."

"He was," Richard whispered.

It was the wrong thing to say. Evelyn turned to him with a look of curiosity. "You knew him?"

"Not nearly so well as I would have liked," he replied honestly. *Are fingers supposed to tingle like this?*

Evelyn's attention, however, had returned to the painting. "I know almost nothing about him, save his art. I suppose he had a son, the current viscount?"

Surely, she could hear the thunder of his pulse. Surely, she could see that anticipation was painting his cheeks pink? "Yes. Yes, he had a son."

"He has looked after the collection remarkably well," said Evelyn, peering closely at the oils. "Though this one will need a little cleaning."

That jolted him from his stupor. "It will?"

"Oh, yes," said Evelyn, gesturing with her little finger. "Along here, see? I would have hoped the viscount would have noticed. Perhaps he is not so attentive to art as his father."

"I think he has grown a recent appreciation," said Richard, his mouth dry. "There… There is a painting of him farther down the corridor, if… if you would like to see it. Finish off our tour."

Evelyn sighed, and for a heart-stopping moment, Richard thought she would decline. But then…

"It is hard to accept that the tour is almost over, but I suppose the man must be permitted to return home. We'll end with the current Viscount Sempill, then."

So we will, thought Richard, his pulse throbbing at his temple.

So we will.

Their footsteps seemed to echo painfully loudly as they stepped along the corridor. Richard could not recall the distance between the two portraits being so long, but eventually, they turned a corner and—

"There," Richard said quietly, turning to face Evelyn with his own portrait behind him.

Evelyn stared at the portrait. Then she stared at him. Then her gaze returned to the portrait, her face expressionless.

Precisely what Richard had hoped for, he was not sure. More than this, certainly. He had not expected there to be such silence, or such a lack of response from the woman he loved.

Dear God, had he aged so greatly over the last five years that it was impossible to recognize him in the painting?

Richard cleared his throat. "I… I am Viscount Sempill."

"Yes," said Evelyn quietly. "Yes, I see that."

There were no further words. Richard waited for a moment, wondering whether she was stunned from the delight of discovering his true identity, and decided he had to say something. "I am Richard Sempill, Viscount Sempill."

"As I said. I see that."

"You do not look happy." The words had spilled from Richard's mouth before he could stop them.

Only then did Evelyn's eyes snap back to him, and he was horrified to see that instead of delight, or shock, or surprise, or laughter that she had been caught out… she looked furious. Her lips positively trembled as her eyes narrowed.

His Evelyn, furious? At him?

"So, you are a liar," she said conversationally.

Richard's head throbbed. "No, not a liar, I—"

"You kept this a secret from me—you were probably laughing at me all the way through this tour," Evelyn said quietly.

"No!" Richard could not understand it. How was this going so wrong?

"And you were undoubtedly laughing at me at the art gallery—oh, I spoke of Viscount Sempill then. You could have told me!" Evelyn had taken a step back as though remaining close to him were untenable.

Richard took a step forward, maintaining the gap between them. This was all going wrong—but he hadn't done the speech. Yes, that would solve everything. The speech.

Rapidly dropping to his knees on the carpet, he said in a rush, "Evelyn, the last few weeks with you have been so wonderful that I want to make them last the rest of my life. Will you do me the honor of—"

"You have had plenty of opportunities to tell me the truth," Evelyn said, speaking over him and breaking Richard's flow. "Why did you not tell me?"

Richard stared, aghast. "You said you didn't want to know anything about me!"

Two pink dots had appeared on Evelyn's cheeks now. Mrs. Anstruther was peering at them from the other end of the corridor. Richard attempted not to notice her.

"I said I wanted a blank slate, not a liar!" Evelyn's cheeks were brilliant red now. "You know how I feel about liars, Richard! Or should I call you 'my lord'?"

The words sounded stilted from her mouth, wrong, utterly unpleasant.

This was supposed to be the day they became engaged.

"You can call me whatever you want," he said, rising from his knees. "Look, your father did not mind that I—"

"'My father'? When have you spoken to my father?"

Ah. That was a mistake. Richard was not sure why, or how, but it was. "It was… just a few words exchanged at the Dalmerlingtons' ball."

"That was the night that we—that you bedded me," Evelyn whispered. "What did he say to you?"

But now, a prickle of anger was forming in Richard. "That was the night *you* decided to take your clothes off—Mrs. Anstruther, go away!"

There was a gasp and a scurrying sound at the end of the corridor, but Richard did not look around. "You gave yourself to me. I made no demands," he said in a low voice.

"Because my father had already offered me to you on a platter, hadn't he?" Evelyn hissed, her eyes full of pain. "I should have known. My God, he hinted at such—that he thought I had something to tell him. How could I not have guessed? He expected you to ask me for my hand days ago! Of course little Evelyn can *play* at being an artist because the men in her life will just marry her off, anyway."

"You asked me to keep the truth from you," Richard pointed out, trying to find logic in the argument, knowing he was partly in the wrong—but not entirely.

Evelyn's eyes were flashing. "You told me that you had worked at the docks! How many viscounts do that!"

"You guessed that and I—I mean, I have *spent time* at docks. It wasn't a lie." God, his words were getting twisted in his mouth. "You asked if I'd traveled and I have. You never asked—"

"Did you not think I would wish to know if you were conniving with my father, tricking me into feeling—into thinking I felt—"

"I love you!" Richard said desperately.

He had expected that to work—or if it did not work, at least shock Evelyn into agreeing that they were in love and could muddle through this misunderstanding together.

A shadow flickered over Evelyn's face as it became stony. "A man who loved me would not lie to me—a man who loved me would not barter for me with my father behind my back."

"It wasn't like that."

"I am a free spirit, an artist!" Evelyn said fiercely. "And I won't be lied to. I won't be passed from one man to another. I won't do it, Richard."

"Evelyn, wait!"

She did not heed him. Without waiting for him to say another word, Evelyn had flown down the stairs, skirts whipping back in her haste. Desperate though he was to catch up with her,

Richard could not do it. She left even her bonnet and parasol behind. She left even her *maid* behind, unless the woman was waiting outside for her. By the time Richard reached the hallway, the door had slammed, leaving him alone.

Alone. Alone? How could he be alone, when Evelyn was in the world?

Richard slumped onto the floor. *Oh, hell. How had this gone so wrong?*

Chapter Seventeen

June 16, 1840

EVELYN DID NOT know what everyone was getting so upset about. She wasn't hurting anyone, was she? She wasn't in the way—not now that she had moved three inches to the left. She wasn't making any great demands on anyone, she had been quiet... What more did they want?

"Evelyn, get up," Lucy said with a sigh.

"Absolutely not," Evelyn replied calmly. There was no point in getting upset. Getting upset hurt, and she didn't want to hurt anymore. Besides, why should she get up?

"You need to get up. You can't just lie there."

"Until you offer me a reasonable statement as to why I should move," Evelyn said, eyes fixed upward, "I don't see why I should."

Lucy sighed. Then she suddenly appeared in Evelyn's view, glaring down at her older sister with a most malevolent look. "Because ladies do not lie on the drawing room floor and refuse to get up."

"Nonsense," retorted Evelyn. "I am, and I'm a lady."

It was, apparently, a problem for everyone, despite the fact that everyone save her sister and herself and the servants were out of the house. Laurent had appeared there yesterday not too long after Evelyn, and when she had asked what had transpired to make Evelyn leave without her—without, even, her bonnet and parasol—Evelyn had refused to explain. What had she cared if she had been spotted without a chaperone on the streets of London?

Who cared about anything?

Their parents had taken Percy to a dinner, poor thing, and Lucy and Evelyn had been told to entertain themselves.

And so she was. She didn't know why Lucy had to care so much.

"I'm not in your way," Evelyn said from the drawing room floor. Really, the ceiling was most impressive from this angle. "You can easily step around me, or spend the evening in any other part of the house."

"Evelyn—"

"In truth, I presumed you would spend the evening in the library. I chose the drawing room purposefully to remain out of your way," Evelyn continued doggedly.

All she had to do was keep talking, explaining herself, and she would not have to think about the agony. The weight of it. The way that her world had come crashing down because of a stupid man.

Oh, she was such a fool.

"If anything, I think I should be congratulated for dealing with this so well," Evelyn said aloud.

Lucy tapped her foot as she glared down at her sister. "So I see."

Evelyn sighed. It really was very simple, as she had explained to her family over the breakfast table that very morning.

"Firstly, I am not speaking to you, Father," she said severely.

Her father's mouth had fallen open. "What have I done to deserve that?"

"Secondly, I am not speaking to you, Mother," Evelyn continued.

The Countess of Lindow thrust out her chin. "Now, your father, I can understand, as he wasn't able to stop himself from hinting we knew you might be hiding some news the other day, but as for myself, I was waiting patiently for you to speak up."

"You didn't stop him from offering me out like a plate of canapes," said Evelyn sharply. "Percy—"

"I have no idea what everyone is so upset about, and I would rather keep it that way," said her brother, raising his hands in a sort of surrender and rising from the table. "I have an early morning appointment, anyway."

"So that leaves Lucy as the only person to whom I am speaking at the moment," Evelyn said heavily.

There was a delicate cough behind her.

"And you, Cawthorne," she added. "Obviously."

"Evelyn," said her mother firmly. "I cannot claim to understand precisely what has happened, but—"

"The end of my life as we know it, I'm afraid," said Evelyn.

She knew she was being dramatic, but there was nothing she appeared to be able to do about it; the pain etched into her ribcage was painful, pouring through her, infecting every inch of her.

"And are you going to be like this all day?" asked Lucy calmly, pouring herself a cup of tea.

"Yes," said Evelyn.

"Right," said her sister.

That had been that morning. Evelyn had spent the rest of the day mostly lying on the drawing room floor, staring at the ceiling, and crying.

They were not the most entertaining amusements, but they were all she could manage for now.

Lucy was still staring down at her. "This is a tad much, even for you."

"I have an artist's temperament," Evelyn said with mock hysteria.

It sounded far more impressive in her head than out loud. She did not blame her sister for frowning, although it did look amusing from this angle.

"Hmm," said Lucy slowly. "Did you not once say that 'an artist's temperament' is just a man's excuse not to do anything properly?"

Evelyn opened her mouth. Then she closed it again. Then she frowned. "How very disobliging of you to remember that I said that."

"Hmm," repeated her sister, her frown not disappearing. "Are you going to get up now?"

"No." Try as she might, Evelyn could not prevent tears from prickling in the corners of her eyes.

Damned tears. *Blast them!* Her eyes were sore, the skin around them itching, thanks to the copious tears she had shed after she had run from Richard's house.

From the house of the Viscount Sempill, that was.

"I love you!"

"A man who loved me would not lie to me—a man who loved me would not barter for me with my father behind my back."

It was a betrayal, that was what it was. One of the worst kind. After all the nonsense Percy had put them through, she would have thought Richard would understand. Would realize that her desire for mystery and excitement could not trump her need for honesty.

"You do look awful, you know."

Evelyn sighed and sat up, her head spinning slightly at the sudden movement. "You are not much of a comforter."

"I don't actually know what has happened," Lucy pointed out blithely as she stepped away from her sister and settled herself in an armchair. "It makes sympathy rather a challenge. Besides, I've used up quite a bit for a man wrongly accused of murder who is about to be hanged by the neck until dead."

That's the trouble with my sister, Evelyn thought darkly as she clambered up and dropped onto the nearest sofa. *She always manages to make you feel ridiculous.*

"It's very simple," she said aloud.

Lucy raised an eyebrow. "It's never simple with us Chances, is it?"

Evelyn sighed. "No, not really."

The fireplace was empty, the hot days making it senseless to light fires, but she could not help but feel cold.

Everything that she knew—or that was, the delightful ignorance she had enjoyed—was over. In the center of it all was a man who had seemed so exciting... only to discover that he was nothing like what he'd seemed.

"Are you going to tell me?" Lucy asked quietly.

Evelyn looked up. That was the thing with her sister; she appeared to have unlimited compassion. She had never known anyone quite like Lucy for always seeing the best in people, always making it absolutely clear that there was something to be admired in someone.

"It's very simple," she said shortly. "I hired a man to be my model."

"Oh, yes, I met him." Lucy nodded. "He seemed pleasant enough."

"Oh, he was. Very pleasant." *Perhaps too pleasant.* "But he lied, Lucy. He lied."

Her sister's eyebrows were raised now. "Goodness. What did he say that was untrue?"

And that was the problem, wasn't it? For try as she might, Evelyn found it a challenge to pinpoint precisely the point where he had lied.

That Richard *had* been untruthful was obvious. He had not told her that he was Viscount Sempill, information she would have liked to know. He had misled her, made her think he was nothing but a common man, no gentleman at all. He had almost certainly been laughing at her when she'd attempted to talk to him about art, and paintings.

The man had a Rembrandt!

But when one attempted to explain that, it all felt... foolish.

"He did not tell me who he was," was all that she could manage aloud.

Lucy nodded. "That must have been painful, you having asked him outright."

Evelyn bit her lip. This was the problem; it sounded foolish now. *She* sounded foolish. "Actually I... I never asked him outright."

"Oh." Her sister cocked her head. "But it must have come up in conversation, surely. One's name generally does."

Squirming in her seat did not appear to make any difference to her internal discomfort. "Actually, I... Oh, Lucy. I told him not to tell me."

Her sister hesitated. "Ah."

Ah, indeed. Evelyn could not square the circle. She knew that she had been betrayed, been lied to—she could feel it in her gut. All the hackles that Percy had raised with his ridiculous lying were heightened. She knew what it felt like to be lied to, and it felt like this.

And yet... and yet...

"I wish to keep you as a blank canvas—a blank slate, if you will. The less I know about you, the better."

"It sounds to me as though you have created your own problem," said her sister helpfully.

Evelyn scowled. "That's very helpful, thank you."

"Well, let me try something that I think *will* be helpful."

Lucy rose and stepped over to the wall paneling by the window. Precisely what she was doing there, Evelyn did not know.

Her sister pressed at a seemingly inconsequential part of the paneling. It most definitely was not inconsequential, however, because a small door sprang open and revealed—

"How on earth did you know that was there?" Evelyn stared as Lucy pulled a bottle of brandy from the secret cupboard along with two glasses.

Lucy shrugged. "It turns out that when you're the middle child, you can sit very quietly and think about prison reform for so long that your brother, who thinks he is very clever, barely notices you."

Evelyn stifled a grin. It was the first smile since the revelation of Richard's true identity, and it was something she was in sore need of.

But brandy? Perhaps her sister was even more of a dark horse than she let on.

Evelyn felt the need to confess. Perhaps if Lucy understood the severity of what the man had been hiding, she'd stop making such sense. "He's a viscount. Viscount Sempill."

"I see. So," said Lucy, pouring a healthy dollop of the golden liquid into each glass and handing one to her, "let me get this straight. You asked the man to model for you. You asked him to tell you nothing about himself, not even his full name. Now you have found out his full name, and that he owns what is apparently one of the most delightful art collections in the country—"

"How do you know that?" She had not intended to snap, but intentions were hardly attuned to actions these days.

Lucy frowned. "It's all anyone talked about when the last viscount died—or rather, it was all *you* talked about last year. Remember? You said it was an art collection to die for."

Evelyn took a large swig of the brandy. It burned all the way down her throat, but it made her feel more alive, her mind sharpening. "Such a pretty art collection."

"—and now you are upset with him for having done precisely what you asked him to do," finished off her sister.

It is most unfair of Lucy to be so… so blasted reasonable.

Evelyn did not say that aloud. "It's more complicated than that."

Lucy raised an eyebrow as she took a large gulp of her brandy—without, Evelyn noticed with a wry smile, wincing a bit. Just how long had her sister known about that secret cupboard?

"It doesn't sound complicated to me," said Lucy quietly. "It sounds like you are angry at him and you're not sure why."

It did. Not that Evelyn was about to admit that.

Taking another large gulp of her drink and wondering how she would stand upright after this, she tried to see if there was a way she could explain it better.

She'd asked him to keep a secret, and he had, and now she

was upset. No, that wasn't it.

She'd asked him to keep his name a secret, and he had, and…
Blast.

She'd wanted to keep an air of mystery about him, and now that air was gone. Yes, that was it!

But that was hardly a crime, was it? Certainly not deserving of some of the things she had shouted at their last meeting.

"I said I wanted a blank slate, not a liar! You know how I feel about liars, Richard! Or should I call you 'my lord'?"

Evelyn sighed. "I don't seem to be able to explain it in any rational manner—not a huge surprise, given my—"

"Artist's temperament, yes," Lucy cut in. "I know Percy's deception, his lies, upset us all, and I know you have had an aversion to liars ever since. But what has your model done?"

What has my model done?

So much. Evelyn could hardly believe she had lived without him. Whenever she attempted to look back and remember her life before Richard had stepped into this very drawing room and offered to be her model, there was just a gap there. A strange, empty gap. Her life had had less color, less vibrancy. As though her life had gone from charcoal to oils.

But no, she couldn't think like that, could she? He was gone from her life now, and she would not return to charcoal.

"He modeled for me, that is all," Evelyn said curtly.

Lucy just smiled.

"That is all," she repeated defensively. "And he—he took off all his clothes."

Oh, blast. She had not intended to say that out loud.

For the first time in their conversation, Lucy's cheeks were pink. "I beg your pardon?"

"For art," Evelyn added hastily.

It appeared that did not matter. "I'm sorry. Did you say he took off all his *clothes*? And Laurent allowed this?"

Evelyn didn't mention their lady's maid. "And he agreed with Father that he would marry me, before even talking about it with me first, either of them," Evelyn added, certain that her sister would agree with her on this.

She clearly did. Lucy's brow furrowed and she finished the last of her brandy. "Now *that* is most unacceptable."

"You see!" Evelyn spoke with triumph, but it melted away the instant her sister started to shake her head.

"Not really. Oh, it was foolhardy indeed for the viscount and Father to discuss your marriage, I agree… but is it possible that they spoke only of theoretical? That he was sounding out Father, rather than making an agreement?"

Evelyn opened her mouth to immediately refute the ridiculous idea. Then she closed her mouth again.

She did not actually know, did she?

"And as far as I can see, it's all perfect," continued Lucy blithely, tucking her legs under her in the armchair and grinning. "I mean, what lady hasn't wished to have an eye on the goods before matrimony?"

"*Lucy!*"

"You think that because I care about prison reforms that I have no other thoughts in my head?" she challenged.

Evelyn bit her lip. *Well, yes. In a way.* Lucy was always so passionate about the transportation laws, about how unfair it was that some crimes could be done away with thanks only to a little coin. It was all she spoke of.

No, that wasn't quite right. It was all Evelyn had listened to.

"He sounds like the perfect match for you, if you ask me," her sister was saying. "He doesn't mind sitting around all day for you to draw or paint him, which is something I find most tedious. He is a good-looking man, I suppose, in his way. What do *you* think of him?"

Unbidden and most welcome images of Richard, naked beneath her as she rode them both to pleasure, rose in Evelyn's mind.

Heat burned her cheeks. "He… He… He is amiable."

"And you have the benefit of knowing that you fell in love

with him before you even knew whether he had a title or not," finished Lucy as she placed her brandy glass down on the floor beside her. "You *are* in love with him, aren't you?"

Yes.

Evelyn wished to deny it. She wanted to rip out her heart and rid it of this contamination, this sickness. This pain that it was causing. This knowledge that she would never be the same again because she loved Richard Sempill.

She looked helplessly at her sister. "I love him."

"You fell in love with him as he was, then. No name, no title, no rank, no fortune," Lucy said, ticking off her fingers. "You fell in love with him. And now you can't love him despite discovering he is respectable?"

And the kernel of truth that had buried its way into the center of Evelyn finally revealed herself, surprising even her. "Part of the charm was that he *wasn't* respectable. At least, I did not presume so—it was… oh, forbidden. Not a titled man, not like one of the primping popinjays who so often attempt to gain our attention at a ball or a concert or the theater. He was just… Richard."

It was almost shameful to admit it. That was it, wasn't it? Some of the attraction lay in the danger of not knowing, of the mystery. Now that that attraction was gone, was there enough love left?

Evelyn looked up at her sister, and there was no judgment in her eyes. She was a fine sister, a wonderful sister. "What am I going to do?"

Lucy grinned. "Who am I to advise the great *artiste*?"

She took it back—her sister was the most irritating, most infuriating—

"Fine, fine, I'll give you my opinion, though with the caveat that I should not consider it advice. I am hardly an expert in these matters, after all," said Lucy with a shake of her head. "Just answer me this. When you look at him—when you affixed his visage with your artistic eye—"

"*Lucy!*"

"—what do you see when you look at him?"

Evelyn blinked. It was a most odd question, indeed. What did she see when she looked at him? "Richard. Obviously. The Viscount Sempill now. What are you talking about?"

"I mean, when you truly look at him, when you look past the planes of his face and the contours of his clothes, what do you see?" Lucy asked quietly.

Evelyn was in half a mind to clamber back down onto the drawing room floor and gaze up at the ceiling. She would gain just as much comfort from that as the nonsense her sister was spouting.

But then she allowed her mind to wander. *When I look at Richard.*

And she remembered laughter, and delight, and silliness. How he teased her, that sparkle of mischief in his eyes telling her that she was about to see him being wicked. She thought of the vulnerability he shared in removing his clothes, the way he held himself proudly because of what he had done, who he was. And she thought of that moment, Richard smiling on his knees declaring his love for her, and how she had reacted in panic. In pain.

When she looked at him, she saw all the possibility. The bravery and the joy and the inability to admit when he was wrong. She saw a man who challenged himself and could be a challenge to her. Who had seen her for what she was: an artist, despite Society telling her she could not be.

He was everything.

Evelyn groaned and dropped her head into her hands. "I... I see the future. Blast it all to hell."

When she looked up, Lucy was grinning. "Well, then. What are you going to do about it?"

Chapter Eighteen

"Y OU DO KNOW that you are an absolute imbecile," said Walden cheerfully. "Don't you?"

If Richard had not been riding a horse, he would have thrown something heavy at his friend's head. As it was, he scowled.

"Yes, that will help you get the woman of your dreams back," said Walden with a snort. "You really are an ass, you know."

"Yes, I think we have that portion of the conversation covered," Richard said darkly.

Apparently, they had not.

He had not invited Walden out for a ride in Green Park for a dressing down, but it appeared that was what he was to receive. Irritating though it was, what Richard found far more irritating was that he did not seem able to dispute a single one of his friend's points.

It was infuriating.

"I mean, you must have known," said Walden fairly, as though Richard was supposed to be an expert in the ways of love in general, and artistic daughters of earls specifically. "Could you not predict that she was going to explode?"

"No," Richard said curtly as they guided their steeds around a corner of the path.

No, he had not. And perhaps that had been his own fault. The plan had seemed so clever at the time, so wonderful. Perfect.

It had never occurred to him that Evelyn would not have been impressed and then overawed—in the best possible way, of course—with his plan.

His proposal.

To see her vanish down the stairs and not even be able to catch her as she'd fled out of the door had been a bit of a shock to the system.

"It explains where you've been, I suppose." Walden's words jolted Richard back into the moment.

"'Where I've been'?"

His friend rolled his eyes. "You know they asked me at White's whether you wished to give up your membership?"

Richard winced. They had in fact rescinded his membership, despite Verwood paying his annual dues promptly, while he had been in France. It was galling. It was nonsensical. And it had been a hell of a headache with the paperwork to reinstate him.

"I haven't been *that* absent," he said aloud.

Walden scoffed, his mare nickering at the sudden noise. "Man, I have seen neither hide nor hair of you for almost a month! You haven't come to the theater, you entirely ignored my invitation to that Mozart concert—"

"In my defense," Richard said, a half-smile creasing his lips, "I did not want to go."

"And though some said you had attended the Dalmerling-tons' ball—"

"I did!" protested Richard. "You and I spoke there! I mean, I did not stay for long…"

"Not long enough to have a proper conversation, and I was only half an hour late. If you asked Lady Romeril, she would say that I was on time," said Walden, his lips quirking.

Richard sighed. She would, too; the doyenne of Society had very clear rules and expectations on when a gentleman should arrive at a ball. It was most provoking. It was apparently very gauche, indeed, to be the first at a ball—but someone had to be, did they not?

"And you lied to her."

His stomach twisted, nausea most unpleasant rising as bile

clenched around his throat. "I did not lie."

"An omission of the truth, then," said Walden, and Richard was surprised to see a serious look on his friend's face. "An error."

An error.

That was putting it mildly. Richard could not recall making such a disaster of his decisions. He had always relied on his gut and it had never failed him—well. Other than the fire. And this.

At the moment, he could not tell which was worse.

"I did not lie," he repeated.

"Look, I am hardly one to berate you. The truth is a beautiful thing and therefore, it doesn't do to take it out into the sunlight too often."

Richard looked over at his friend with a scowl. "You are laughing at me."

"I am pointing out that truth is a delicate thing and even when someone feels like they are telling the truth, they could be lying," said Walden, staring unflinchingly. "For example. What were you doing in France all those years?"

Oh, hell.

Though he endeavored not to drop his friend's gaze, Richard was not able to think of a clever lie in this moment. The truth would not do; telling the truth, all of it, could only bring danger to those he cared about. Was there still not danger? Wasn't that why he was constantly being asked to return to France?

So, a version of the truth, then.

But was that enough? Were there gradations of the truth? If so, when was there too much falsehood mixed in with a story to call it the truth?

Richard sighed. "Don't make me lie to you, Walden."

"You take my point."

"It is poorly made, but I take it all the same," Richard said, shaking his head dolefully. "There is a difference, I know, between telling the truth and telling a lie. But the gray area in between, the vagueness, the omission of details…"

His voice trailed away as he looked around them.

They had come out near the top of the park. Luscious trees in full leaf fluttered slightly in the lazy, summer wind. There was hardly a cloud in the sky, drawing out the inhabitants of London with parasols over the ladies and top hats on the gentlemen. There was a buzz of heady warmth in the air. This was the sort of weather in which scandal was born.

"You truly think you've lost her, then?"

Richard turned. Walden was beholding him with a compassionate, almost pitying look. In any other situation, he would feel hard done by, examined like that. At the moment, Richard would take all the pity he could get.

"Yes, I think so," he said quietly. "I knew how she felt about liars. I did not consider myself one, but… there it is."

There it is. The end of a love story that had only just begun. God, he was an idiot.

It was, in its own way, mortifying. Here he was, a viscount from almost the cradle, a man who had served his country and lived on his wit and ingenuity… and he had completely underestimated her. Underestimated what she needed.

Evelyn had been most clear with him about her expectations, and he had failed her.

Mortification was not enough.

He had been stupid. Richard was loath to admit it, even to himself in the quiet of his mind, but he had been. What on earth had he been thinking?

All he had wanted was a distraction. Something to entertain. Something to make sitting endlessly in a chair worth the oxygen required to breathe.

In the end, it had almost led to something perfect.

Almost.

"You know, I have to congratulate you."

Richard bit down the sarcastic retort. "Oh, yes?"

Walden nodded thoughtfully as their horses slowed to a gentle walk. "Having never fallen in love myself, I have never much seen the use in it. Now that I have seen you in that state, I think I can firmly say that I have no wish to enter it."

Richard could not help but laugh. "And that is worth congratulating me?"

"You have taught me something that no one else has," said his friend with a grin. "And I consider myself a relatively worldly man. I am impressed."

Richard wasn't. It was the opposite of impressive, what he had managed to do: take a woman who had never harmed anyone in her life, and hurt her.

"So, you are a liar."

"No, not a liar, I—"

"You kept this a secret from me..."

"But perhaps you did not truly love her."

Attention snapping to his riding companion, Richard scowled. "You think so? You think the agony I am in does not meet your arbitrary idea of love?"

"Well, I'm just saying—"

"Evelyn is everything, you hear me? Everything." His lungs were too tight; he did not know how the words were coming out, and all Richard knew was that not defending Evelyn in this moment would be tantamount to a second betrayal. "She—the light she brings into a room! She doesn't create shadows; she merely beautifies a space, bringing a sort of... a golden..."

Richard swallowed. At some point, he had drawn his horse to a halt, the stallion stamping his feet and ready to be away, but he couldn't ride. He couldn't do anything except try to explain just how he felt about Evelyn.

"When I look at her, it's like... like all my perspective has altered. Like looking at a Canaletto. Everything else is still there, but it just doesn't matter. What matters is her. What anchors me to this ground is her." Conscious that he sounded like a complete fool, Richard did not cease. What was the point? He had lost everything of importance. Why not lose his dignity? "And her hair—like burnt umber. Her eyes, a mixture of cerulean and forest green, and her smile... When she smiles, I want to set the world alight because nothing will ever compare to her—nothing!"

He had shouted the last word. He had not needed to; Richard was almost certain that Walden, who was after all only a few feet from him, would have heard it if whispered.

He was panting. His hands had gripped the leather of his reins so tightly that his fingers were going numb.

Richard forced himself to slow his breathing, though the pounding of his pulse did not appear to be slowing.

"You really do love her, don't you?" said Walden quietly.

Heaving a dry laugh, Richard shook his head. "It's more than love. More than obsession, more than need. I don't have a word for it."

"And she's clearly had an impact on you, hasn't she?"

It was not a question, more a remark, and not one that Richard understood. "What do you mean?"

"'Cerulean'? 'Burnt umber'?" His friend shook his head ruefully. "I have never heard you speak of such things before. She has changed you, Sempill—I am not saying for the worse. It's pleasant to hear you speak so passionately. Unexpected, but pleasant. You have always held in check such emotions."

Richard swallowed.

Yes, he had. He had met a woman who defied Society and denied their expectations, clung on to her dream of being an artist and worked far harder than any gentleman, and she had changed him.

"I don't know what to do," he said, his voice broken.

Walden sighed. "You have to do something."

"I can't."

"You must, man!"

Richard's temper was rising to the surface again. "Well, what do you suggest? I cannot take back earlier words; I cannot change the past! No matter what I say or do now, I will always be a liar in Evelyn's eyes. She will always look at me and see a man she does not, cannot trust. How do you win back someone's faith?"

Walden looked helpless. "I do not know."

Richard did not know, either. No one did because there was no answer. There was no way back. He had burned the path he had walked on without even realizing, destroying any chance to be with her.

Sighing heavily, Richard dismounted and patted the side of his steed's neck. "I am sorry, old friend."

"Are you talking to me or the horse?"

Richard rolled his eyes. "I get more sense from the horse."

"Perhaps." Walden dismounted in turn, pulling two carrots from his saddlebag and handing one wordlessly to Richard.

The two men fed their horses and stood in silence.

There was a nervous energy within Richard that demanded he do something, but there was nothing to be done. Evelyn was not the sort of woman to be impressed by anything so pedestrian as a declaration of love or flowers or jewels.

Hell. He hadn't even prepared a promise ring. What was wrong with him?

"You have to do something."

Richard looked up. Walden was staring with a serious expression. "What do you mean?"

"I hate seeing you like this—it's worse than when you came back from France doing whatever it is you were doing out there, which I am sure was completely legitimate and not at all in the service of Her Majesty's government," said Walden with a slow and theatrical wink.

Richard rolled his eyes. "Yes, thank you for your discretion."

"My pleasure. But seriously—you have to win her back. This is killing you."

"There's nothing to be done," Richard said heavily, patting his horse once more. "I broke her trust, Walden. That isn't something you can just… just paint over."

For some reason, his friend shrugged. "Well, if you say so. Now I come to think about it, parts of France are much safer. What say you and I head over there and explore a few of the sights?"

An anger Richard had never known before burned. *Just go back to France?* Just return to where he had been grievously injured? Go back to the country where so many of his enemies lived, he had ceased attempting to keep track?

Give up on Evelyn?

"You must be out of your mind." Richard snarled, the rage coursing through him a welcome respite from the agony of heartbreak. "Is this your subtle way of revealing a death wish?"

"I don't know what you're getting so het up about," his friend said mildly. "You were the one who said that there was nothing to be done about Evelyn."

"*Lady Evelyn Chance* to you," snapped Richard, his anger not subsiding. "Just because I haven't thought of a way to win her back, that does not mean I am just going to give up! I can't just— the thought of leaving for France! I can't just leave her, I…"

Walden was grinning.

The hackles on Richard's neck started to dwindle. Only then did he notice that quite a few people in Green Park were watching him. Staring, in fact. Pointing.

Hell in a hamper.

"You're very clever, you know that?" he said dully.

Walden clapped him on the back. "I know that, have known that for years. The question is: are you clever enough to win back this woman of yours?"

Richard set his jaw as he inhaled slowly.

That was indeed the question. *Am I?*

Chapter Nineteen

June 17, 1840

S TOMPING REALLY WAS an excellent way to force one's head to stop thinking. Evelyn wondered briefly how she had never discovered it before, realized that meant thinking, and attempted to cease doing so immediately.

She was not going to think.

Thinking only led to pain. Why she had permitted herself to think that she and Richard—

No.

Evelyn swallowed hard as she waited at a crossroads for the trio of large carriages to pass by as Laurent spoke to her about some servant gossip or another. Evelyn had been sent out here on an errand for her father, and that was what she was going to do. No thinking. No wondering about the past and wishing for the future.

There was no future. At least, not in the way she had hoped. The future she had expected, had longed for once Richard had entered her life, was over.

Now all she could do was focus on her art. Which was what she wanted. Obviously.

Straightening her shoulders, Evelyn stepped out purposefully and—

"Do you have a death wish, child?" snapped a voice at her ear as something violent grabbed hold of her elbow.

Evelyn was quite ready to glare superiorly at whoever it was who had her arm in such a violent grip, perhaps even say something a tad condescending. Unfortunately, she was prevented from doing so by a rushing carriage that passed by so close, her hair flew up in the draft and a tingle rushed down her spine.

That had been close.

It was only when she turned to look at the person who was still tightly clenching their hand around her arm that Evelyn saw attempting a superior tone would be utterly out of the question.

It was Lady Romeril.

"You," said the older woman sternly, "should be more careful when crossing the road. Did your governess not teach you the basics, girl?"

Evelyn blanched. "Y-Yes."

Lady Romeril. One of the most respected, and most feared, women in Society. A good word from Lady Romeril could make or break a woman's reputation. A match made—or unmade—by Lady Romeril was considered finalized.

She was a domineering woman. A respected one. Even if she was imperious and self-righteous.

"You're one of those Chance girls, aren't you?" asked Lady Romeril slowly, peering down her nose at Evelyn.

"One of those Chance girls." Well, there are quite a few cousins. "Yes, Lady Romeril. I'm Evelyn, the Earl of Lindow's—"

"Ah, yes, Lindow," Lady Romeril said swiftly, preventing Evelyn from saying any more. "I suppose you're the artistic one."

"I suppose I am," said Evelyn helplessly, hoping to goodness that none of the passersby were listening in on their conversation. Laurent fidgeted behind her, standing beside a man and woman Evelyn assumed to be Lady Romeril's servants. It was hardly the done thing to be accosted by Lady Romeril on the street and interrogated about one's family.

Or perhaps it was. She wouldn't put anything past Lady Romeril.

"Hmmmm."

Evelyn braced, ready for the onslaught. It was unseemly for a woman of her standing to wish to be an artist. Perhaps the news had gotten out that Richard—that the Viscount Sempill had been sitting for her.

Doing far more than sitting for her.

Heat blanched her cheeks, but before Evelyn could say a word, Lady Romeril nodded curtly. "Good."

Evelyn blinked. "'Good'?"

Nothing felt good at the moment. Even ignoring the accosting—well, perhaps that was harsh, Lady Romeril had saved her from a dreadful carriage death—there was still the matter of her broken heart.

Though perhaps she would now make the best art of her life. Evelyn was no expert, and there was still a great amount of reading to be done on the subject, but had she not read once somewhere that artists had to be tortured to create their best work?

Twisting her arm, Evelyn discovered it was impossible to escape Lady Romeril's grip.

This was most definitely torture.

"Good," repeated Lady Romeril firmly, before—finally—releasing Evelyn's arm. "The world needs more art. More joy. More things to think about. Wonder about."

Evelyn's jaw dropped, despite her inner self shouting that she needed to hold herself in better control in front of a woman like Lady Romeril.

"More art"? "More joy"?

"I-I quite agree," she found herself saying, her voice not quite up to the task of speaking to a woman like Lady Romeril with complete equanimity. "I... I have always thought—"

"I can't chatter. I have a most important appointment with my modiste and if I am not careful, the Duchess of Axwick will steal her from me," said Lady Romeril vaguely with a wave of her hand. "Off you go then, young woman—and be careful when crossing the road! You, servant girl, watch your mistress better."

Evelyn winced, just ever so slightly, as Lady Romeril boomed her parting words for all to hear. *Honestly!* She hardly appreciated being spoken to like a child. Even if the warning was, admittedly, warranted.

"I am sorry, my lady," said Laurent.

Evelyn waved her off.

What had she been doing?

Oh, yes. Her father had asked her to go to the Dulwich Picture Gallery in Southwark and request some information about an upcoming exhibition. Why her father had asked her to do such a thing, Evelyn was not quite sure.

She pondered this as she—carefully—stepped across the road and turned left. The Earl of Lindow was not known for his interest in art. It had been all she could do to get him to consider her painting as hardly an affront to his name. So why did he want her to get this information?

It is probably naught but a ruse, Evelyn thought dully as she turned another corner and spotted the art gallery at the end of the street. Something to get her out of doors. Something to occupy her mind.

It had been kindly done, yes. But it was entirely impossible. She could not stop thinking of Richard.

"I love you!"

Evelyn halted, one foot on the step up into the art gallery, one still on the street.

The memory of Richard's words had hit her almost as hard as the carriage nearly did. Her body quivered, the impact felt despite its intangible form.

How was she ever supposed to go through life without thinking of him?

In half a mind just to return home, partly wondering if she should duck inside and have a good cry, Evelyn managed to force her feet to stumble onward.

She would get the dratted information for her father, and return straight home.

"Ah, Lady Evelyn," said a man who suddenly appeared to her left, bowing low. "We have been expecting you."

Evelyn blinked. "You have?" *Why on earth would anyone be expecting me?*

She glanced at Laurent, who simply shrugged.

"But of course," said the man, still bowing low. Was he not the owner of the art gallery? "And what an honor it is."

Perhaps this was all a dream. Perhaps she had not truly woken up that morning, but had instead continued to dream. That was surely the explanation for such a strange series of events.

Her father, taking an interest in art?

Lady Romeril, saving her from a terrible fate and then encouraging her art?

And now this—treating her like some sort of… of dignitary!

It was all too much.

Evelyn took an unsteady step back. "I don't quite understand."

"Everything is prepared," the owner said, finally straightening and looking at her with unabashed curiosity. "And may I be so bold as to say that it has been an honor."

"An… An 'honor'?" Evelyn repeated slowly.

Whatever the owner thought she had done, it apparently had been most impressive. He beamed, clearly delighted, and gestured toward the double doors that would take her into the art gallery.

Evelyn walked hesitantly toward it, Laurent on her heels. "But I needed to ask something," said Evelyn.

"All your questions will be answered inside, I think," the man said with a grin.

If it had been in any way suspect, Evelyn would have strode past him out of the door onto the street, her father's request be damned.

But it was a kind smile. One that suggested a secret was on the other side of these double doors… and Evelyn had never been the sort of person to ignore a secret.

Wondering what had gotten into everyone today, Evelyn stepped forward.

Her knees almost gave way.

Now she knew she was in a dream. No, this could not have been possible—she must have been dreaming, or hallucinating, or in some other way misunderstanding what her eyes were attempting to tell her.

There, hanging on the wall before her, was… was…

Was her Venice scene.

"It's not possible," Evelyn whispered, reaching out and touching the frame.

It was real. At least, her fingertips were agreeing with her eyes, and she had never had any cause to disbelieve either of them before. It was her painting, on the walls of the Dulwich Picture Gallery.

But… But…

"Beautiful," said Laurent, her mouth puckered as she stared at a painting on the wall.

"Oh, my word." Evelyn let out with a gasp as she turned and saw one of her studies of an apple tree hanging on the wall a few feet away in front of her lady's maid. On the other side of that, a study of a violet, pushing its way through the earth.

And on and on, it continued. There was no one else other than Laurent in the art gallery, something Evelyn could not think about now, not with her gaze falling on artwork after artwork that had come from her pencils, her paints, her fingers—her soul.

"My lady, do you know the artist?" Laurent asked.

But Evelyn didn't answer her. Pulse racing, eyes prickling with tears of astonishment or confusion or something else, she did not know, Evelyn felt her feet pace forward, her speed increasing until—

Until she came to a halt.

There it was. Or rather, there *he* was.

The Richard in the painting was not quite as handsome as the one Evelyn had studied… very closely. She still couldn't get his ears right, and there was something in the proportions that honestly, now that she could see the painting in a frame on a wall, was not quite right.

It still took her breath away.

Or at least, the painting did, its unexpected existence here. Evelyn placed a hand on her bosom, trying to calm her panic, but the movement did nothing to quiet her.

What was it doing here—what were *any* of her paintings doing here? How had they—had her father—

"…truly remarkable…"

"I have never seen such shading…"

"…see the landscape of Venice? My word, such an exquisite…"

And that was when Evelyn was almost certain that she was going to faint.

In her hurry to move from painting to painting, focused on nothing but seeing her art on the walls and uncomprehending of how they had gotten there, Evelyn had been wrong. There *were* people here.

In fact, there were several. None were people she recognized, and they moved past her without giving her a second glance. Instead, they spoke to each other, speaking of her art.

And what they said was good.

"This is probably my favorite," a lady wearing the most outrageously oversized hat said to her companion.

The gentleman nodded. "Oh, yes. I have never seen a use of the color blue in such a bold way."

Evelyn almost swallowed her tongue, but she managed to stay upright—which in the circumstances, she thought, was in fact to be applauded.

Here they were: all her studies, her practices, her paintings, all the things she'd thought had been not quite good enough, sketches she had worried about, paintings that had seemed not to hold any merit…

And people liked them.

Wait a moment. Evelyn shook her head, attempting to make her mind focus. People liked them because people could see them, and people could only see them because someone had placed them on the walls.

Who had done such a thing? What was going on?

"I've never seen this particular artist exhibit before," a dark-haired woman murmured as she and a woman who had to be her sister stepped gently behind Evelyn. "I hope he is featured again soon."

"She."

The singular answer was a whisper, and it was one that sent a shiver of anticipation down Evelyn's spine.

Turning, she caught sight of the astonished look on the woman's expression.

"No! A woman?"

Her sister, for that was who Evelyn presumed she was, nodded with shining eyes. "Isn't it wonderful?"

"Isn't it wonderful"?

Laurent stepped softly beside her. "My lady, are these works your own?"

"They are," Evelyn whispered, careful not to be overheard.

"They are remarkable," said Laurent. "Well done, my lady. Well done." Then her eyes darted over Evelyn's head, a small smile forming on her lips. "Excuse me. I shall have to examine them all."

Evelyn was too numb to do more than nod. A lump rose in her throat. It was more than she could have hoped for; more than she could have dreamed of. It was beyond all her expectations and it had happened in a way she still did not understand.

Her hopes swelled as she listened to the praise, gentle yet clearly honest, milling about her. None of the people here other than Laurent knew that the paintings, the sketches, the studies on the walls were hers. There was no reason for them to admire her work audibly, other than their genuine enjoyment of her art.

She'd done it. Somehow, inexplicably, beyond all sense... she was truly an artist.

"I hope you can see yourself now how I see you," said a quiet voice from just behind her.

Evelyn did not hurry to turn around. She knew the voice—would know it until her dying day. Seeing its face would remove all power of speech, she knew that, but it did not stop her gasp as she finally saw…

Richard.

He looked tired. Weary, even. There were lines around his eyes she had not seen before, and as someone who had carefully examined his face for hours—for the sake of her art, nothing else—Evelyn was fairly certain they were new.

His cravat was poorly tied. His waistcoat was inaccurately buttoned. And his face—

The lump had returned to Evelyn's throat. He looked exhausted. And happy. A weak smile broke through the grimness of his tired expression.

"I shouldn't have lied," Richard said hastily before Evelyn could even think to say a word. "It was foolish, idiotic of me to keep the truth from you. I wish there were an impressive explanation, but if I am quite honest… Well. It kept you out of the rest of my life. It kept you separate. I thought it would keep you safe."

And all the elation that had risen at the sight of him, the hope that it had been Richard who had put this plan into motion to make her see just how worthy her art was of being on walls…

It all disappeared.

Evelyn swallowed, hard, but could not dislodge the lump that had become a knot in her throat. He had wanted to keep her separate. Separate from his life.

He did not want to introduce her to his family, or his friends. He wished to keep her from his real life. From the reality of his existence.

She was just some secret he was ashamed of.

But—"'Safe'?"

"What I experienced in France was not pleasant, Evelyn, and I cannot promise that the danger will never touch these shores," he said in a rush. "I wanted to leave that part of my life behind and it was so easy, so terribly easy, to lose myself in the dreams of a future with you."

"I… I see." How Evelyn had managed to speak, she did not know. She had kept her voice low, hopeful that no one would overhear her.

They did not need to be burdened with her misery.

"No—no, I don't think you do," said Richard hastily. "Oh, damn, I practiced this, but speaking rationally in front of you is… It is difficult. You make me want to be a better person, Evelyn."

That is all very well, she thought, trying to dampen down the joy that had sparked when he had spoken her name. *But is he?*

"I thought by keeping you out of the rest of my life, my dull life, that you would be… be mine. Mine to treasure, not tainted with the nonsense of my past," Richard said quietly. "I'm not… I've not always made the best decisions, Evelyn."

"Yes, I know," she could not help but say.

Richard winced at the edge in her voice. "I just… I have never had anything as precious as you to worry about. And it was a… an artistic stretching of the truth. I never lied—"

"You never told me you were a—"

"I know, I know that," he said hastily, raising a hand as though that alone could placate her.

Only then did Evelyn notice that her hackles were raised. What was this? An apology, an explanation, or something in between? Was he instead merely attempting to justify himself?

Perhaps Richard could see her thoughts in her eyes. He sighed heavily. "I wouldn't trust me if I were you. I was wrong. I should have said something, should have been more honest."

"I thought I knew you," Evelyn could not help but whisper.

He flinched this time. Perhaps the softness, the longing in her voice, was more painful than the edge. "You knew the parts of me that mattered. My interests. My humor. My devotion to you."

"It wasn't enough," Evelyn breathed, unable to help herself, her heart thundering.

"I know," Richard said simply. "That is the trouble with love, I suppose. It happens all unexpectedly, not so much creeping up on you, but surprising you by its presence. It was there for so long without me noticing, I cannot tell you when it began. And now I have lost you."

It was not a question. He made the statement calmly, and Evelyn shivered to hear the despair in his voice.

"So then what is... is all this?" she asked, glancing about them.

Once again, her eyes were drawn to the painting of Richard with which she was still not happy. When her attention meandered slightly to the left, it fell on the real Richard, a man with whom she was still not happy.

But something inside her told her that she would never be happy without him.

"I wanted you to know how talented you were. How your art is ready for the world, even if you are not," Richard said with a wry smile. "I could not think of another way."

"You... You did all this, for me?" Evelyn whispered.

It did not seem possible, yet she could not refute the evidence before her eyes.

Here she was, standing in the Dulwich Picture Gallery, and it was her art on the walls, her art that people were looking at, her art people were praising. And she could not understand just how it had happened, and she was grateful, and angry, and she loved him so much.

That was the trouble, wasn't it? Despite everything, or perhaps *because* of everything—she was not quite sure—she loved him.

"I suppose I have an apology of my own to make," she said wryly, her gaze dropping to her hands for a moment before she took a moment to collect herself and then looked back up at Richard.

"'Apology'?" he said blankly. "Evelyn, you have nothing to

apologize for."

"I should not have reacted so strongly to the fact that you had already spoken to my father about… about us," Evelyn said in a rush that petered out at the end. "I… I should have trusted you. I should have trusted him."

"Yes, you should have," said an amused voice.

Evelyn groaned to see her father and mother step toward her, arm in arm. "I should have known you'd be involved in this!"

"And why not?" asked the Earl of Lindow, raising an eyebrow. "You think I was going to wait around for you to realize how talented you are?"

"We took bets," her mother added, her eyes twinkling. "I have rendered the bets forfeit, now that your father has intervened."

"And you're not upset? You're not worried, about me displaying my art in public? You always forbade it," asked Evelyn, her voice quavering.

Warmth. Comfort. A hand in hers.

Evelyn looked down. Richard had stepped to her side, just a few inches behind her so that she could continue talking to her parents—but it was his hand that had enclosed her own. It felt right. It *was* right.

"'Upset'?" Her father took in the pair of them and Evelyn flushed, heat burning her cheeks. "I am old, my dear."

"George!"

"Oh, Dodo, there's no harm in saying it! I'm not young anymore," the earl said with a dry laugh. "Times are changing. Sometimes they change far swifter than I can keep up with. Sometimes they change in ways I don't like, don't expect. And sometimes… sometimes they change for the better. Even an old codger like me can see that."

Evelyn's delight soared as her father reached out and cupped her cheek.

"Only do what you want, girl," he said seriously. "If you want to marry this bounder—"

"*George!*"

"—then you should do so," her father continued, ignoring his wife's exclamation. "But because you want to. Because you see in him something that only a wife's eye can see."

Evelyn swallowed. "And what is that?"

The Earl of Lindow glanced at his wife for a moment before smiling. "Potential. No one is perfect, Evelyn, and no partnership is. But it can become close to perfect. With practice."

Richard squeezed her hand and Evelyn turned to him, her thoughts all a muddle save one.

"And you still want to marry me?" she asked with a raised eyebrow. "After all this?"

Richard's smile was loving, and it was wistful, and it was one she had not seen before. The crinkle around the left eye, the way his chin tilted, almost with defiance. Yes, it was definitely new. She would have to sketch it.

"Yes," Richard said quietly. "Yes, I want to marry you. Rather badly, actually."

Joy flooded Evelyn and before she could think, before she could halt herself, she had thrown her free hand around Richard's neck and pulled him closer for a heart-stopping kiss.

It was magnificent. His arms were comforting around her and he smelled wonderful and his tongue trailed a dazzling delight across hers and she wanted to melt into him and be with him and—

"Put that man down!" Lady Romeril's eyes were wide...but so was her grin.

Evelyn and Richard broke apart with flushed cheeks and wild smiles.

"Ah," said Evelyn awkwardly. "People. Right."

"It's scandal, then, after all," Richard said ruefully. "I hope you don't mind?"

She could not help but laugh at that. "I don't see that we have any choice. Shall we get married, then?"

"Yes," he said softly, his smile adoring. "I suppose we should."

Chapter Twenty

June 30, 1840

THIS WAS PROBABLY a mistake, but Richard knew he had to make it.

He opened the door without knocking and almost ran into Cawthorne.

"My lord!"

"No time," Richard said hastily. "Where is she?"

The butler merely stared in absolute astonishment, as though he could not believe what he was seeing. "But—But my lord, you cannot be here!"

"I need to see her," Richard said calmly. At least, he *thought* he spoke calmly. His nerves were jangling and his lungs were tight and he had to see her.

Cawthorne blinked. "But my lord—"

"Where is Evelyn?" Richard persisted.

He should have done this days ago. Weeks ago. Why he had left it until today he did not know, but he was certain that he could not leave this unsaid.

Not on his wedding day.

A maid entered the hall and squealed as Richard strode toward her.

"Where is your mistress?"

"Th-The countess?" the maid spluttered, dropping the pile of linens she had been carrying.

Richard nodded. It would have made the most sense. Did not brides spend the mornings of their wedding day with their mothers, getting ready? Hair to be pinned and jewelry to select and… and that sort of thing?

Now he came to think, what *did* women do in preparation for weddings? He'd had a cigar and gotten dressed, a new valet named Dankworth hired especially to start by today. Surely, Evelyn did not smoke.

"Upstairs, of course," the maid said, eyes wide. "But—"

"No time," Richard shot over his shoulder as he took the stairs four at a time.

His pulse was pounding painfully, but not due to the exertion. It had been racing from the moment he had realized, about twenty minutes ago, that he had not told Evelyn enough. He had not been truly honest with her and if that were to come out…

He wanted to enter this marriage as he intended to continue it. With the truth between them and nothing else. He was not a liar, and he would make sure he never was.

He would just have to hope that she would not be angry with him.

Richard threw open a door but found an empty bedchamber. The next three were similarly devoid of his future bride. And—

"Richard!" Evelyn squealed as he burst into the bedchamber.

"My lord!" cried her mother.

"Oh, *mon dieu!*" Laurent said, stumbling backward and tripping over.

Richard halted, chest heaving, in the doorway.

Ah. Right. He should probably have knocked. It wasn't seemly to be bursting into lady's bedchambers, even if he was about to marry its inhabitant. Even if he had been upstairs here two nights ago, unbeknownst to the earl and countess, visiting his future bride and giving her further evidence of his potent affection for her…

His future mother-in-law stepped forward, eyebrow raised. "I suppose you have a good reason for your intrusion here?"

"It's bad luck for the groom to see his bride before they meet at the altar!" cried Laurent, who was being helped to her feet by a grinning...

Evelyn.

Richard's shoulders slumped, all tension disappearing from them as he beheld the woman he loved. Goodness, but she was beautiful. And stifling laughter, which boded well.

At least, for now.

"Nothing is wrong, I trust, my lord?" asked the countess quickly.

Richard opened his mouth, then closed it again.

His instinct had been to say that yes, there was something wrong. Very wrong. All the happiness that had filled him these last few weeks—it wasn't gone, exactly, but he was conscious that it could be gone at any moment.

If he didn't tell her, she would find out. He didn't know how, but she would. She'd spot one of those damned letters, perhaps, or overhear him giving instructions to Verwood to burn them. And then she would think—she would *know* that he had kept something else from her. Something important.

He met Evelyn's eye. She was curious, he could see that in the tilt of her head and the curving of her mouth. Curious, but growing concerned with every moment of silence that he did not speak.

Richard swallowed. *Speak, man!*

"I need to talk to my future wife," he said, his voice rasping.

Laurent disappeared through a door with a wink, but the Countess of Lindow did not move. "And should I be concerned, my lord?"

Richard did not look away from Evelyn as he spoke. "I am not certain yet."

The two women exchanged a glance, and he did not miss the murmur.

Lady Lindow clasped her hands together in front of her. "I can stay if you—"

"No. Please, Mama. Within a few hours, I will have to do this on my own."

His stomach curdled, though how, he did not know; he had only managed a mouthful of breakfast before starting off here.

"Do this on her own"? What was Evelyn talking about? Had they previously discussed him—oh, Christ, was this expected?

Richard managed to remain silent until the door closed behind his future mother-in-law, then he blurted out, "I should have told you this ages ago—"

"Do you mind if I sketch while you talk?" Evelyn asked breezily, turning from him and picking up a notebook. "It helps me think."

All his carefully prepared statements disappeared out of his mind as Richard stared. "I... I don't... What?"

"I always keep a pencil on me," said Evelyn happily, pulling said pencil from her bodice.

Richard swallowed. *Do not think about her bodice. Do not look at it. Do not admire the swell of her curves, the gentle rise and fall of her breasts as she breathes, don't think about—*

Damn. Now that was all he could think of.

"You have a most puzzling expression," said Evelyn softly as she lowered herself onto a chair and opened up her notebook. "I suppose we have the rest of our lives for me to attempt to capture your many facets, but I must say you are making it very difficult. So many, you see."

"Evelyn," Richard said, his voice half-strangled now.

Did she have any idea how disorienting it was, having her sit there? Knowing that he could pull the notebook aside and just kiss—

You came here for a reason.

The small voice at the back of his mind forced him to step forward. "Evelyn. I haven't told you everything."

"I don't suppose you have," she said, her voice vague now as her pencil started to move across the page.

Richard blinked. "You... You don't?"

Evelyn only glanced up for a moment before returning to her drawing. "Well, we've only known each other a few months. We have a lifetime to discover—"

"No, I have to tell you this now," he cut in, mouth dry.

Was she making this difficult on purpose? Or would it always have been thus?

He had never considered telling anyone this before. Even Walden only had a vague knowledge of what he had been up to on the Continent. It wasn't for them to know—there had never been any reason to make the knowledge public. He certainly didn't have the authority to tell the whole story.

But if she—*when* Evelyn found out, there would be hell to pay.

"I don't want to start this marriage off on the wrong foot," Richard said desperately, stepping forward and dropping onto the bed.

From here, he could see what she had been drawing. His nose. Did it really crinkle like that?

"You are most disobliging as a model, you know, moving before I am finished," Evelyn said with a snort, turning over a page and peering at him. "Though this is an interesting angle. Right. Don't move."

The instinct to obey was strong, born perhaps from the hours that Richard had already spent modeling for her. But he had to push past it. He had to tell her. He could not allow her to continue in ignorance.

"My maid is right, by the way. It is bad luck for a groom to see his bride before she enters the church," Evelyn added with a wry smile. "Not that I am that concerned. We were never going to be a conventional couple, were we?"

And her smile melted all the panic and fear iced around Richard's heart until he could feel the rush within him.

His Evelyn. The one person in the world with whom he wanted to be honest. He could tell her anything, almost certainly, and she would... Well, at the very least hear him.

Whether or not there would be a wedding in a few hours… that was quite a different matter.

Richard swallowed. *Now, how best to begin?* "I was a spy."

Oh, drat. He hadn't intended to say it that baldly.

Evelyn said nothing. She was continuing to sketch his profile, her hand moving in a strong, confident sweep across the paper.

And she said nothing.

Richard cleared his throat. Perhaps she had not quite taken in the import of his statement. Hell, he'd have to tell her everything.

Well. Not everything. That belonged to the Crown.

"I was a spy. For the Crown, for the government, not someone just out for hire," Richard added hastily. The last thing he wanted was for Evelyn to misunderstand him. "I was on the Continent for years, working there, attempting to serve my country. It's why you hadn't ever met me at a ball or Almack's or the like. It's why most of Society has never heard of me. Doesn't recognize me."

The lead swept across the paper, darting here and there to add details. Evelyn glanced up but seemingly only to ascertain a detail, for she swiftly returned her attention to her notebook.

Richard's pulse throbbed at his jaw. Did she not wish to look at him? Was she angry that he had kept this secret from her?

"It was dangerous, and as you have seen, there have been times when I have been… unpleasantly injured," he continued in a low voice, not sure why when they were the only two in the room. One could never be too careful, he supposed. "And I didn't want to put you in danger by telling you, which was my first instinct to keep this to myself, but I see now—I mean, I am hardly accustomed to telling people such a thing. And I realized this morning…"

Evelyn looked up and she was smiling. The adoration of her expression was golden sunlight onto his skin and Richard released the tension in his shoulder blades that he had not even realized had been there.

"I know this has come as a shock," said Richard awkwardly.

"Damn it, I'm not sure now whether I should have told you today, right before our wedding. I mean, you probably need to think about—"

"Richard," she said softly.

"—and I haven't given you any time. It's just, keeping secrets is so natural to me, it didn't occur to me to—"

"*Richard.*"

"—but I thought I could not wait until after we were married. I wanted to become your husband with no other secrets and—"

"Richard!"

Richard blinked. Evelyn was frowning, though somehow, it was a good natured one. "Yes?"

"I did know, you know," she said gently.

The words did not make sense to Richard's brain. "I beg your pardon?"

"I know. I knew, before," she said simply. Her attention—at least, her visible attention—had returned to her notebook. Her pencil moved confidently, the scraping of the lead on the paper the only sound filling the room until she said, "I'm sorry. Was it supposed to be a secret?"

It was a good thing Richard was sitting down. The words Evelyn had said had rocked him to the core, causing him to shake his head slightly, as though that could make her question make sense.

"I mean, it was a mite obvious," Evelyn continued, her eyes flicking up at him as she smiled. "Your injuries... I had never seen anything like it. And though accidents happen, and Lord knows there are plenty of people in London who have suffered a fire, you had been bound, hadn't you? And slashed with a knife, more than once."

Richard's lips parted. "I... I..."

"You see, artists notice things. We notice everything, even the details that others miss. Even if those details are the shape and character of your own skin," Evelyn said simply. "You've probably never seen the scars on your back, not properly, but I can tell you from a single glance that you had your hands tied behind your back when the fire happened. Men who gallivant about Europe for the art don't tend to be knifed in the back too often, either, though Percy might argue otherwise. So I didn't ask. I thought if you wanted to tell me, you would have."

She was extraordinary. How on earth had he never—but she was right, even with a looking glass, it was mightily difficult to properly see behind yourself. He had never seen the scars properly.

But Evelyn had.

"And… And that is what gave me away?" Richard asked in a croaking voice.

Evelyn nodded, brow furrowed now as she attempted something difficult on the page. "Yes. Yes, that and the fact that you mutter French in your sleep, and that you have been decidedly absent from England as far as I can tell, and I asked your nice friend Mr. Walden—"

"Walden?" Now Richard was sitting up straight. *What the devil was that blackguard doing with her?*

"Yes, I asked Mr. Walden whether or not you had been a spy, and he said, and I quote, 'Don't ask me. The idiot thinks he's being clever, but he's not been able to pull the wool over your eyes, I see,' and I said, 'No, not really,'" said Evelyn with an apologetic smile. "So you see, I did know. Sorry."

"Sorry"?

Richard tried to collect his myriad thoughts, but it was rather like attempting to outwit a fox that was already in the chicken coop.

She knew. She knew?

And that damned Walden hadn't done anything to help him.

When he blinked and Evelyn came back into view, it was to see her still smiling. "And… And you don't mind?" he asked.

"'Mind'? That you served your country and didn't want to claim all the glory by showing off and telling me?" Evelyn snorted, shaking her head. "No."

"I meant that I had not told you until now," Richard said, making a mental note never to underestimate this brilliant woman. "I know how you feel about lying."

A shadow flickered over her face. Oh, she had been hurt. Not just by him. That original injury had come from her brother, he knew. But he had added to the pain, and the scar would be visible for quite some time yet.

Perhaps everyone had scars, of one kind or another.

"It was not a lie, and I am glad you have told me now," Evelyn said slowly. "If—*how* this marriage will succeed is by being honest. I have my eye on you, though." She was grinning now. "No more spying, please."

"I think I can firmly say that I have left that life behind me," said Richard with a rush of relief.

Well, he'd done it. How he'd managed to do it, he wasn't sure. The fact that Evelyn still wanted to marry him—wait. She *did* still want to marry him, did she not?

"Besides," Evelyn added, "I have a few secrets of my own. In fact, I think I should probably tell you one of them now."

"Why not?" Richard said genially.

Whatever she wanted to tell him, he would gladly listen to. What would it be? Had she once stolen a tube of paint because she had not been able to afford it, her pin money all used up? Did she harbor some unpleasant thoughts about a rival artist? Could it be that—

"I am a spy too," Evelyn said solemnly.

Richard fell off the side of the bed. The floor broke his fall, though in a less comfortable and soft way than he would have preferred, and his head was reeling as he scrambled to his feet and stared, open-mouthed, at his future bride.

"You—You're…" His eyes must have been falling out of his head. "Really?"

Evelyn grinned. "Not in the slightest."

The sudden shock was more than enough to jolt his mind out of his skull, but at this juncture, all Richard could do was laugh.

The teasing look in her eye, the mischievous smile, the way she had utterly played him for a fool and enjoyed it immensely…

Oh, there was so much more to learn about this woman of his. So much to explore. So much to discover.

Here was a woman he could never get bored of.

"Now," said Evelyn, placing her notebook down and secreting her pencil down her bodice once more, causing a rush of heady need in Richard's loins, "shall we get married?"

It was all a blur. Richard knew that they took separate carriages; it would not do, the Earl of Lindow had said stiffly, for both groom and bride to emerge from the same carriage outside the church. People might talk.

They might talk more, Richard knew, if polite Society knew precisely what he and his bride had been getting up to almost every night from the moment they'd become engaged. What they'd been up to long before that. But perhaps that wasn't the best thing to think of as he stood here at the altar, waiting for his bride to meet him, Lucy and a Chance cousin having walked the aisle first.

When Evelyn stepped into the church, it was a struggle to catch his breath. Walden by his side said something—Richard did not catch the words—and there was a rush of admiring murmurs as she walked down the aisle, but he did not hear them.

All he could do was look at this beautiful, unpredictable woman, and thank his lucky stars that his own secretiveness had not driven her away.

"You know, the light and shadow in here is quite exquisite," murmured Evelyn as she reached him, her hand placed onto his own by her father, who appeared to be brushing away tears. "I shall have to bring my easel here one day."

"Do you ever stop thinking about art?" Richard muttered as the vicar started the marriage service.

Her bold gaze caught his and Richard's stomach lurched.

"Sometimes," Evelyn said quietly. "Whenever I'm with you, I'm thinking of art *and* you."

He could not help but chuckle at that. "I suppose I should be honored."

"Yes, you should," Evelyn whispered with a wry smile. "Don't you think of something else while thinking of me?" Her cheeks blossomed into pink as she saw his expression. *"Richard!"*

"I'm thinking about you," Richard shot back in an undertone, reveling in the way she responded to his mere thoughts. "And I'm thinking how fortunate I am, every moment that I'm with you. And I'm wondering how you're going to paint me next."

And as he placed a ring on her finger, he was almost sure Evelyn whispered, "In every way possible."

Epilogue

July 1, 1840

T HE SCREECH OF the birds, the salt, the blustering wind—
"Evelyn, are you listening to me?"

The way the sunlight poured down and scattered and shimmered—

"You're not listening to me, are you?"

And noise, noise everywhere, a cacophony of sound. How could one capture it with color—

"Evelyn!"

Evelyn blinked. The docks faded into the background after capturing her attention so fully, and she saw before her a man who was remarkably handsome and smiling with despair.

"Hello," she said genially.

"Hello," said her husband wryly. "Remember me?"

"You do look familiar, yes," she teased, her heart soaring. "Could I have seen you as the model in one of the great art galleries of London?"

"Perhaps you have done just that, yes," Richard said with a laugh. "But right now, I am having enough difficulty getting my wife to concentrate long enough to walk in a straight line. What on earth are you looking at?"

Evelyn could barely think for joy. *"My wife."*

It felt absolutely ridiculous, but there it was. She was a wife. Her husband was beside her, smiling and not censuring her, glorifying in the way she was rather than attempting to force her into a particular way of doing things.

It was wonderful. It was more than she could ever have imagined.

And so were these docks.

"You know, if I had guessed you would find the Dover docks so fascinating, I would have decided to have our honeymoon here instead," Richard said with a laugh. "Honestly, Evelyn, what are you looking at?"

"*Looking at*"? Evelyn had not been able to stop looking in amazement at the things around them ever since their carriage had halted at an inn right in the center of the town. Even there, there had been salt in the air. Evelyn had not been able to help it; as though dragged here by invisible spirits, she had found her way through the streets to the docks.

"Everything," she said simply.

Richard snorted. "Don't give me that. I mean it, Evelyn. What fascinates you so?"

"It's an adventure!" Evelyn said impulsively, stretching out her arms and gesturing at everything within a mile radius. "It's quite all right for you. You've traveled, you've been abroad—"

"I wouldn't call it much of a holiday," her husband muttered.

Evelyn grinned. "Perhaps not. But still, you have seen distant shores, eaten strange foods—"

"That, I have," said Richard, making a face. "Who eats snails? And frogs! Have the French never ventured more than a hundred yards from a pond?"

"Everywhere I look, there is something new I want to draw," Evelyn said enthusiastically.

It appeared her husband did not believe her. Raising a quizzical eyebrow under his top hat, Richard said, "'Everywhere'?"

It was a challenge, and Evelyn was always up for a challenge. At least, an artistic one.

"There," she said, grabbing her husband's hands and adoring the way that it felt so natural. As though he belonged there. As though they belonged together. "See that knot, over there?"

She watched Richard look over at a ship moored at the dock. There was a heavy length of rope pouring out from the stern of the boat, ending in a complicated knot, fraying and salt-encrusted, on the shore.

"Isn't it beautiful?" she said, enraptured.

When she finally managed to drag her eyes away from the complexity of the frayed strands of rope, it was to see Richard looking most unimpressed.

"It's rope," he said flatly. "It's a knot."

"Oh, look at it properly!" Evelyn said with just a dash of impatience in her voice. "Look at the curves, the spirals—the intricacy of the lines. Look at the dab of tar, there, and the burnt edge there. What a story it tells! What textures, what colors, what—"

"Fine, fine, you have convinced me. It is a very impressive knot," interrupted Richard with a laugh that made Evelyn's pulse skip a beat. "But you said that everywhere you look, there is something to draw!"

Evelyn jutted out her chin, reveling in the debate. There was only one man with whom she wanted to argue for the rest of his life, and here he was. "And I stand by that statement."

There was a glitter of mischief in Richard's eyes—as there so often was. "So you are telling me that while we wait for our ship—which, by the way, should be almost ready—I can point in any direction, any at all—"

"And there will be something there worth painting? Yes," said Evelyn emphatically.

Oh, this man. Sometimes she woke up in the night and wondered how on earth she had managed to be so fortunate. She would reach out, sure that she had dreamt him, and there he was. Just lying there. Richard Sempill. Her viscount. Her husband.

"So, if I point over there?" Richard said, pointing most unfairly at the sky.

But Evelyn had already guessed he would do something so

unsporting. "You mean the clouds, the shimmer of the sunlight, the arching of the birds?"

Richard laughed dryly as he lowered his hand. "Well, that's a remarkably good answer. What about... there?"

Glancing over her shoulder, Evelyn saw he was pointing at a metal post. "You mean the rust of that metal, gold and bronze and shimmering green?"

This time, Richard was shaking his head as he laughed. "You truly see beauty everywhere, don't you?"

And in that instant, Evelyn's confidence wavered.

It was perhaps a foolish part of her character—it was certainly not one many people shared. The more she saw of the world, the more beautiful and terrible it was. Full of elegance and charm, yes, but there was decay there and death and betrayal.

"I love that you can do that," Richard said softly, stepping to her and cupping her cheeks. "I love that you see the best in everything. I love that, Evelyn. Never change."

Evelyn's cheeks flushed as she smiled up at the man she loved. "I couldn't change, even if I wanted to."

"Good."

"And I don't."

"Even better." Richard laughed. "Though I admit I am not particularly surprised. Come on, then, it isn't long before we need to find our ship. Have you any further guesses for me?"

The game had started the instant they had been married, the day before. Richard had revealed that he had organized a honeymoon for them, not too long because he knew Evelyn would not wish to be away from her art supplies, but long enough to enjoy themselves.

Where, precisely, they would be going was something that he had, so far, kept a mystery.

"And you are certain it is not Berlin?" Evelyn asked, slipping her arm into the crook of Richard's arm as they sauntered slowly down the docks.

"Absolutely not," he replied firmly. "My German is terrible—

though do not let that make you think that everywhere in the Germanic states is off-limits."

"And I can't imagine that we would be going anywhere in France," Evelyn said softly, more to herself than as part of the conversation.

She had spoken too loudly. She felt the stiffening in Richard's arm, the tension that flashed through his body because she could not take back her words. His gait did not alter, but there was a tautness in his steps now.

Blast.

"I am sorry," Evelyn said softly.

"Don't be," came Richard's swift reply. "I cannot get through life without anyone ever mentioning France. If someone has to do it, I would rather it were you."

Her wonderful, brave husband. In a way, Evelyn could hardly believe what he had gone through, what he had done to serve his country, without any celebration or gratitude. Not, at least, in public. She would make sure, for the rest of their lives, that he would always know how proud she was of him.

Still. That did not help remove the memories that were so painful, or remove the scars.

"Given up guessing?"

Evelyn grinned as the docks curved around to the left. "How on earth can I guess if you do not tell me anything about the place we are going? It is hardly a fair guessing game."

Richard's eyes sparkled. "Oh? And here I was, thinking that we could make a fun habit of never telling each other everything."

Their laughter rang out and a few dockhands, loading up some of the floating ships, turned to look at them.

Oh, let them look, Evelyn thought joyfully. All they would see was a woman desperately in love with her husband, and a man devastatingly in love with his wife.

Despite all the confusion, all the secrets, all the lies of omission and the arguments... they had managed to make it here. To the beginning of the rest of their lives.

"I am still angry at you about it all, though," she said sternly, only half-joking.

Richard's expression immediately became more serious. "I know. It was a rotten thing to do to you—"

"And my extended family is still not completely convinced, I think," Evelyn admitted. "My parents and siblings understand the mien of an artist, but my Uncle William…"

Her husband halted in his tracks, searching out her expression with worried eyes. "And does that bother you?"

"Not… Not really, no," she said softly, pressing her hand on his arm. "Beyond the fact that I am so very different from my wider family… Well. They are not the ones who have married you. I am, and I love you, Richard. All of you. Even the bits that sometimes I don't like."

Richard's smile twisted. "I suppose that's a good thing."

"More than good!" Evelyn turned to face him, needing him to understand her as she spoke. "Richard, there is no perfect person. I did not expect to marry a man who was perfect—in truth, I did not think much about marriage. I know that the world forces us to make choices that are not ideal, and that there are flaws in every diamond. But I have an artist's eye."

He had to laugh at that. "I'm well aware, Evelyn."

"I mean, I see the beauty *in* the flaws, not *despite* them," she said softly, lifting a hand to cup his cheek. "You think I would give up on a painting merely because I could not get every single inch perfect?"

There was mischief in Richard's expression. "I mean, you have been known to be reasonable in that regard."

Evelyn nudged him as she laughed. "You know what I mean! I am hardly perfect, and you love me, don't you?"

It was not a question, but her husband instantly responded. "Of course I do, Evelyn. I defy anyone not to know you and love you."

"Well, there you are, then," she said firmly, as though she had irrevocably proven her point. "If you can love a—an artwork in progress, then so can I."

For a moment, Richard just looked at her. The blazing look in his eyes was one of possession and devotion, and Evelyn could not help but love that she was the one who'd sparked it. Who had made him look like that.

He pulled her into his arms for an embrace—an almost chaste one, at first, but one that swiftly grew in heat as Richard placed his lips on hers.

Evelyn responded passionately, not caring that they were in public, not caring that they were standing on the Dover docks, which was not, strictly speaking, an appropriate place for a daughter of an earl and a viscountess to be standing.

None of that mattered. The instant Richard began kissing her, the two of them were the only people in the world. The way his mouth possessed hers, the tingling ache building between her legs, the way his hands grasped her waist, his tongue teasing pleasure from every inch of her mouth...

When they finally parted, Evelyn was not surprised to see that they were both a little breathless.

"I could do that all day," panted Richard in a low voice.

"Don't tempt me," she replied in a whisper.

Oh, it had been so long since they had lost themselves in each other. What, an hour? How long had it been since they'd exited the carriage?

"I wish I could lie down here and—"

"Party of Sempill?"

Giggling, Evelyn stepped out of her husband's arms and looked up into the honest and flushing face of a man dressed like a seafarer.

"Yes," said Richard with a nod of his head. "And you are the captain?"

"I am that," said the man. "Ship's just this way. Luggage?"

"Our trunks are in the carriage at the end of the docks," said Evelyn. "I'm afraid I've brought quite a lot—not knowing where I was going, packing was an absolute nightmare."

She cast a glare at her husband, but Richard only grinned. "All the more fun, I suppose! We'll be with you shortly, Captain."

The man nodded, still staring a little curiously at them before turning back to his ship.

"We really shouldn't be kissing in public," Evelyn murmured.

"Oh, poppycock," Richard said bracingly. "Come on. Let's collect our trunks from Dankworth. Laurent doesn't get seasick, does she?"

"I have no idea. Though she's crossed the Channel before." That was something she had not thought about. "In truth, I do not know if *I* get seasick. What fun we'll have, finding out. I had hoped to use the voyage to finish off a few sketches."

Richard laughed as they walked slowly along the docks, hand in hand. "I thought you said that you had finished all your projects?"

"All my paintings, yes," Evelyn said happily, attention wandering over a set of three barrels, placed in a beautiful trio that would have made an excellent charcoal drawing. "Completing the one of Leopold with his bow and arrow was a particular triumph, though I say so myself."

"It looked marvelous," her husband very obligingly agreed. "But... Well. I thought you did not like people looking at your paintings. After creating such a masterpiece—"

Evelyn scoffed. "*Richard!*"

"Such a masterpiece," he repeated with a relentless grin, "you have to expect that your cousin will wish to display it. By the time we return to London, you may find that you and your talents are even more famous."

It was a heady thought, and not one she wished to give much time to. "I suppose so."

Richard clasped a hand around her shoulders as they neared the carriage. "I'm proud of you. The world doesn't deserve you and your art, but I am inclined to think it needs it. Sharing your talent with the world truly is very brave."

A rush of relief poured through Evelyn at his words. That was it—she was brave. She did not have to like it, but there it was.

"I've spent so much of my life hiding my art away," she said quietly. "I… I suppose it is time for me to truly test myself."

"And it was with that in mind," Richard said, halting suddenly, "that I organized our honeymoon."

Evelyn stopped beside him, her heart skipping a beat. With what in mind? Her art—her bravery? Testing herself?

What on earth had Richard done?

"You did?" she said nervously.

Richard grinned. "I did. We are going on a tour of Italy—Rome, Venice, Sienna, Morena—all the best places."

Evelyn's mouth fell open. "We're not."

"And at every stop, we shall be halting for a few days," Richard continued, pure delight radiating from his face. "A day to relax, a day for you to meet one of the great local artists and receive instruction, and a day to enjoy amorous congress. Sometimes all in the same day."

Face burning with the hope that no one had heard that, Evelyn lowered her voice, hardly daring to believe it—believe *him*. "We are?"

"Your art means everything to you, and you mean everything to me." Richard took her hands in his, his face serious once more. "And I am going to spend the rest of my life making sure that you are happy, Evelyn. You have an eye for art, I do not deny it, but I have an eye for the chance. This Chance."

Evelyn gave a laugh, hardly daring to believe it. Italy! Rome, Venice—all the places she had longed to go!

"I'm a Sempill now, actually," she teased, stepping closer and pressing a kiss upon his cheek. "You might not have heard."

"Oh, I heard," Richard said in a low voice, pulling her into his arms as Dankworth and Laurent started to take the trunks out of the carriage, ready for the adventure across the water. "And I can't believe how fortunate I am, Evelyn. I just can't believe it."

And as he lowered his lips to Evelyn's waiting ones, and she lost herself in his fiery kisses… neither could she.

A Short Letter From the Author

Hello! Thank you so much for reading *An Eye for the Chance*, the seventh novel in my The Chances series. I truly hoped you enjoyed it and fell in love with Richard and Evelyn just as much as I did.

If you've read the first six books of this series (which I strongly recommend!), then you'll have seen the four uncles fall in love, and two of the cousins. I had always wanted to write a series of brothers, but I could never 'meet' the characters who were quite right. After waiting years to meet them myself, I have had a lot of fun writing the four Chance brothers—and now we're diving into their children. Make sure you go back and read them!

If you're desperate to read the happily ever afters of Evelyn's siblings, then you'll want to look out for Book 13, *Give Him a Chance* (Lucy's story), and Book 16, *Jump at the Chance* (Percy's story). Our next Chance adventure is going to jump to a different branch of the Chance family, and you'll meet Leopold's happily ever after...

Being an author can be a lonely business, but knowing that there are readers from all over the world who are going to adore my stories makes it all worthwhile. Thank you for support, and I hope you love reading more of my books!

Happy reading,
Emily

About Emily E K Murdoch

If you love falling in love, then you've come to the right place.

I am a historian and writer and have a varied career to date: from examining medieval manuscripts to designing museum exhibitions, to working as a researcher for the BBC to working for the National Trust.

My books range from England 1050 to Texas 1848, and I can't wait for you to fall in love with my heroes and heroines!

Follow me on twitter and instagram @emilyekmurdoch, find me on facebook at facebook.com/theemilyekmurdoch, and read my blog at www.emilyekmurdoch.com.